DODGING BULLETS

OFFBEAT OMEGAS

BOOK TWO

GRACE McGINTY

FOREWORD

This book contains references to a fictional cult. While the religion in this book is a complete work of fiction, religious trauma is real. As always, please take care of yourself first and foremost.

A full list of warnings can be found on my website.

Stand Alone Novels and Novellas:

Bright Lights From A Hurricane/The Last Note/ Inside The Maelstrom/Pay-Per-Heart/8 Seconds to Fly/Make My Heart Race/The Daymakers/Hunting Isla

Hell's Redemption Series:

The Redeemable/The Unrepentant/The Fallen

Damnation MC Duet:

Serendipity/Providence

The Azar Nazemi Trilogy :

Smoke and Smolder/Burn and Blaze/Rage and Ruin

Dark River Days Series:

Newly Undead In Dark River/Happily Undead In Dark River/Pleasantly Undead in Dark River

Eden Academy Series:

The Lost and the Hunted (Prequel)/Heart of the Hounded (Prequel)/ Rebels and Runaways (Book 1)/Sweethearts and Savages (Book 2)

Shadow Bred Series:

Manix/Frenzy/Feral/Crave

Penalty Box Players:

Sticks and Stone/Break My Bones

Omega Lottery:

Tryst In The Dark

Hanging By A Thread Duet:

Tangled Threads Of Fate/A Single Thread of Hope

Offbeat Omegas

Ruffled Feathers/Dodging Bullets

For all the readers who use books to find a connection in this chaotic world.

And for Maddie B., whose joy reminded me why I get up every morning and stare at my computer screen.
Thank you.

ONE

PALOMA

"Paloma, where are you?"

Sister Roberta's voice sounded exasperated, but when wasn't she at her wit's end with me? Sometimes I felt like I'd crawled out of the womb as a disappointment.

I quickly pushed the magazine I was reading back into the secret pocket sewn into one of my traditional ceremonial skirts that hung in the closet. Luckily, the skirt was long and heavy, so the magazine didn't even weigh it down. I rarely got the opportunity to wear the skirt, because if there was a ceremony going on, I was normally kept in my room, in case I embarrassed Leader Malakai. I didn't mind. I didn't like the ceremonies anyway.

Hurrying from the closet, I took a moment to ensure all the clothes hanging in there were perfectly inconspicuous before stepping in front of the small chest that held my everyday clothing. I quickly dragged on the long black skirt I'd draped over it, and when Sister Roberta appeared in my doorway, she just saw a vain child fussing with her clothes.

Despite the fact I was twenty and no longer a child. On the Homestead, we were all children until we were married.

Sucking her teeth in irritation, Sister Roberta grabbed the long veil of black lace from the stand in the corner. "The guests are arriving, yet you are nowhere to be found." She didn't say I was an embarrassment out loud, but she really didn't need to. "And you are not even properly prepared."

I still didn't understand why I had to attend this ceremony, when normally, I was confined to my room. Or why I wasn't in the same ceremonial skirt as Sister Roberta. Instead, I was in a plain black skirt, long and voluminous, with a long-sleeved lace shirt that clung uncomfortably to my upper body and itched at my armpits. I looked like a curtain.

"Sorry, Sister Roberta. I couldn't get my skirt to sit right."

A lie. Leader Malakai had spoken to me about my lies, but I couldn't help it. I wanted to fit in. I wanted to be right. I didn't want to steal the small box of forbidden magazines I'd found in Leader Malakai's office. But sometimes, the little voice in the back of my head that had bad ideas took control.

Sister Roberta looked at me for a long time, her eyes

appraising, until I was squirming in my skin. It was her superpower; I was sure. Something flashed in her gaze, but it was gone before I could analyze it.

"Never mind that," she snapped as she threw the lace veil over my face. It hung down to my wrists, making me completely unrecognizable beneath it.

The veil was the only part of this outfit that was familiar to me. Omegas were given the veil when our designation came in. It was another reason why I was a disappointment to the Homestead. I'd been born an Omega—the Betrayers, that was what our teachings told us. When our god, Izuny, rose from beneath the earth, he created the perfect environment for his love, the goddess Melize. However, when he returned below the earth, he found that Melize had betrayed him with his brother, Basric. Enraged, Izuny cast out Melize, cursing her and all her progeny to be base, animalistic creatures who couldn't control their own urges. Omegas.

That was how the designations were born. Alphas were made in the image of Izuny, and were the supreme leaders in all things. All of our Leaders were Alphas, but Alphas were dying out. We hadn't had an Alpha designated in decades. Betas became Brothers and Sisters. Some community members didn't designate at all, and they were just Homesteaders—below the Brothers and Sisters, but still above the Omegas with the taint. If one of the community designated with the taint of Melize— an Omega—they were forced to wear the veil of mourning, so their temptation couldn't sway any more brothers to betrayal.

Sister Roberta was pushing me towards the door. "Hurry now, Paloma. They're waiting."

I frowned back at the elderly Sister, but she was staring purposefully ahead, a determined tilt to her chin. Still, I couldn't stop myself from asking, "Who's waiting?"

Huffing at me, she didn't answer, just shoved me down the hall toward the main meeting room. There were people loitering around in the halls, and when I saw Nim, I tried to ask her with our own hand language what was going on, but she just shrugged, her eyes wide and concerned. Nim was a good, obedient Beta, but was somehow still my friend.

Despite my non-ceremonial dress, we ended up in the ceremony room. Leader Malakai was sitting at the head of a long table, a pleasant smile on his face, though I was an expert at reading the tightness around his eyes now. He was annoyed at being kept waiting, and I'd pay for it later on.

The other Leaders were there. Leader Victor, Leader Yahn, Leader Thomas. It was odd to see them all in one room together, unless it was a large gathering. But the Leaders were the only people in this room, except Sister Roberta, a couple of the other Brothers and Sisters, myself, and three men I didn't know.

It was the men I didn't know that gave me pause. It was odd. I knew everyone.

We'd learned in our lessons that we were the last people left after Izuny destroyed the world for our sins. It was why we had to be good. Had to be obedient to the Leaders' teachings. Had to do... other things. Because we were the last of the humans, and it was our god-given mission to heal the world. It was why I was so addicted to those magazines—they were time capsules of the creatures and civilizations that existed before the Great Smiting.

We lived behind high walls that kept out monsters, in four separate houses, run by four separate leaders who made decisions that would keep us safe. It was the way it had to be.

It was why the appearance of three unknown faces was a shock to me.

Leader Malakai waved a hand. "Ah, here she is. Please, come closer."

Fear tingled down my spine, though I wasn't sure why. Something about the men in front of me had me on high alert. Still, Leader Malakai had always stood between us and the monsters outside, and if he wanted me to come closer, that was what I should do.

Stepping closer to the table and the strangers, I clasped my hands in front of me, the perfect show of obedience. I allowed my eyes to watch Leader Malakai, and happiness flushed through me at his approving look.

"Lift your veil, Paloma. Show these men your face."

Shock had me freezing on the spot. Lift my veil?

Show these men my face? That went against everything I'd been taught. Everything we'd *all* been taught.

"Leader?" I questioned, and the approving look on his face disappeared in an instant, to be replaced with one I knew intimately. Abject disappointment.

Growling, he leaned forward, like he wanted to leap to his feet and punish me as usual. Yet, he held himself back. "Do as you are *told!*" he yelled, the sound echoing around the room. Shock at his anger had me quickly lifting my veil, letting it fall back until it caught around my shoulders.

Their eyes lingered on my head, which was completely shaven, as was the custom here for unmatched females. Your hair was for your Alpha only, when you were officially mated.

In this case, I was waiting for my mating with Leader Malakai, even though he was sixty and the thought of lying with him made my stomach feel queasy. But I'd like to have hair again, even if that was vain.

The large man on the right side of the table gave a hum of approval, his eyes lighting up with another expression I couldn't understand, his dark eyes holding secrets that scared me. "Are you sure we can't convince you to skip the brand thing? It significantly lowers the value of the merchandise." He had a cadence to his voice I hadn't ever heard before, and something about his words made me shiver.

Leader Malakai shook his head. He lowered his voice until I doubted the Brothers and Sisters behind me could hear. "Unfortunately, I have to insist. For the optics, you understand."

I couldn't hold my tongue any longer. "What is going on?" I asked again dumbly. "Leader?"

But Leader Malakai isn't listening to me. He waved a hand. "Sister Roberta, if you would?"

Whirling on my feet, I looked at the woman who'd all but raised me. I didn't have a mother, per se, though I knew enough to know that one of the women in the community had physically birthed me. However, everyone was raised by the village, all children being progeny of the community and not a single person. Sister Roberta had been the maternal figure in the House of Malakai for as long as I could remember, and so I looked at her like a mother.

Which made her betrayal as she grabbed me and shoved me down into a chair all the worse. She was holding a long piece of metal, with a thick red handle and a long black cord. The end of the metal was glowing orange, and suddenly, the word *brand* made a lot more sense.

I struggled, but more Brothers and Sisters came forward to hold me. Only the elder ones, though, dutiful members of our community.

"Be still, child. It will all be okay," Sister Roberta murmured, but the guilt in her eyes betrayed her. A hysterical whine burst from my lips as she stepped closer.

"Hold still," Brother Ned grumbled, holding my chin so tightly that my jaw ached, yanking my head to the side and baring my neck. I screamed as I felt the hot press of the brand against the base of my throat. The scent of burning flesh fogged around me, my nerve endings lighting up with unimaginable pain.

"Izuny be damned," Sister Roberta cussed, shocking me. "Hold her tighter so she doesn't burn herself all the way to the muscle."

And then there were more hands holding me too tightly, the sizzle of skin becoming louder. Finally, the long rod pulled away, and the hands released me quickly, stepping away like my fate might be contagious.

Desperate fingers pulled at the lace veil, and I dragged it up over my head, but the sensation of the scratchy lace on my abused skin made me want to scream again.

Leader Malakai stood, as did the three men with him. The guy on the left had a winning smile, with perfectly straight teeth that gleamed white under the oil-lantern chandelier. At any other time, I'd have even considered him handsome. "Thank you. If you have any further merchandise you'd like to dispose of, give us a call."

The guy next to him was like a cornered animal, looking this way and that, like he was expecting an attack from the shadows in the room. The last guy, the one on the right, looked at me with hot eyes that burned against my skin, right along with the brand. They made me want to run away screaming.

I felt nothing now. Except maybe cold. Another part of my brain was aware of the excruciating pain at the base of my throat.

Leader Malakai stopped in front of me. "Please, Leader. I..." I didn't understand. Even now, I could almost smell the stench of my fear and the negative emotions of the others over the burnt flesh scent.

Leader Malakai held up a hand, and like a well-trained dog, I stopped completely, the words shuddering to a halt in my throat. "Children marked by Melize are no longer welcome in the safety of our walls. You will go with these men, Paloma, and your actions will appease the torment of Izuny, and put us back into his favor." He shoved me toward the dark-eyed man, who held me tightly in his arms like I might run.

He was right to believe that, because I struggled against his hold. Because the men weren't just strangers, they were Alphas. Strange Alphas were holding me.

"Please, Leader!" I screamed as the dark-eyed man picked me up, throwing me over his shoulder, like the potatoes I'd hauled up from the storage sheds today.

All the Leaders turned their back on me, and that was it. I no longer existed to them.

I looked up, straining. "Sister!" I yelled at Sister Roberta, and again, guilt flashed across her face, before she dropped her eyes to the ground, unable to look at me.

Taking a door I'd never even seen before, the men carried me down a long, dark hallway.

"Help!" I screamed, until the handsome man who'd thanked Leader Malakai grabbed my ear and pulled me up so I was forced to look at him.

"*Quiet!*" I felt his words wash over me like an oily

coating, and no matter how loud I screamed, no sound passed my lips.

We reached a large metal object, which I'd only seen in one of Leader Malakai's magazines. A vehicle. They were all meant to be relics of the past, but this shiny black machine didn't look like a relic.

My breaths felt like they were too big to leave my lungs, and I was panting. I couldn't breathe. I was going to die.

Stuffing me into the back of the car, the dark-eyed guy stopped in front of me, his hands almost gentle on my cheeks. *"Calm."*

It was a command; that much I could tell, but I didn't understand why my body went lax like I was floating in one of the communal baths. Maneuvering my body, the Alpha strapped me in carefully. Just like that, my heart rate slowed, my muscles untensed, and my eyes got heavy. Something about this Alpha even began to feel safe.

"Sleep," he whispered, and no matter how hard I fought against the command, no matter how horrifying I thought being unconscious around these people was, I slipped into darkness.

I was being betrayed by my own body now.

Two

Rio

"Come here, Pretty-Pretty, so I can wring that scrawny neck."

Not that long ago, I could have sat on my couch with a beer and not been threatened by a psychotic chicken. Those days were long gone. We'd been bamboozled by the Omega who ran an animal rescue, but I had to admit, he made my Beta Max really happy. Maybe a foul-mouthed parrot from a crackhouse was what our Pack had needed.

I looked over at the gray bird that sat on a large perch in the corner of the room. "RUFIOOOOO," he screamed at an ear-piercing level, and I sighed.

Maybe not. *Fucking Rufio.*

Max walked in, wearing dark cargos and a black tshirt. He had his contacts in, and his hair was slicked back by his fingers. Walking over to the African Gray, he cooed, "You're the cleverest boy, Rufio."

"Where's my money, cocksucker?" the bird replied in an ominously low voice.

Max just scratched the bird's head affectionately. "Step on. You have to go back to bed while we're out."

The damn bird climbed onto Max's arm, like a well-trained dog. We had a giant cage in what had once been a mudroom, but was now filled with more enrichment toys than a toddler's bedroom. While the bird and I were still feeling each other out, Rufio had decided he was devoted to my Beta Packmate, and Max seemed happier than he had in a long time. Caring for something else had really made a difference.

I had to give it to Otillie-James—she was good. I guess if you were an animal rescuer, you were always on the lookout for good homes. She hadn't seemed too worried that we had more blood on our collective hands than some armies.

Jealousy surged up in my chest. Not because I wanted Otillie-James, but because my buddy Lance had everything I'd ever wanted but couldn't have. Not in good conscience, anyway. An Omega. A functioning Pack.

Max came back into the living room, his face serious once more. "Ready?"

Uncurling from the couch, I nodded. Maybe Lance was right. Maybe doing this mission would help us get some good karma, blot out some of the red stains that still spotted our hands after all this time, and fate might find us worthy of matching with an Omega.

When Lance had come to us about a rescue mission to shut down an animal cruelty case, we'd been quick to agree. Some douchebag was farming out rescue animals to illegal fighting rings as bait animals—and probably worse—and I had no hesitation shutting this fucker down permanently. Even better would be to bury him in a shallow grave in a ravine somewhere, where no one would ever find his body.

But Lance had said he'd ensure that the guy would get his legal comeuppance, and that was good enough, I guess.

Walking to Max's SUV, I climbed in, pushing down the anxiety of being in a car. It had taken me a long time to be able to sit in a vehicle again, but we were working through it. And by we, I meant me and my VA-appointed fucking therapist.

My therapist, August, was tough as nails, because no matter how uncooperative I was, he'd just kept gently nudging at the edges of my wounds until they were healing over, and I hadn't even noticed. Unfortunately for him, I was riddled with wounds, so not even decades of therapy could fix me. There was no me left. There was just a shadow of who I was.

"We're meeting Lance at a bar on the outskirts of the city. I'll get us the information we need and we'll take it from there." It was rough as far as plans went, but if anyone could get us information, it was Max.

I looked at my Packmate. Our bond had been shut down for years now. I'd closed it as soon as I'd been taken

—I shut the door on that memory before it crippled me. But I wasn't mad that our bond was broken; I'd do anything to keep this darkness that festered inside me from him. The other option was something I already struggled to live with.

Not for the first time, I considered setting Max free the only way I knew how.

Not tonight, though. Tonight, the animals needed me.

We pulled around the back of a bar that looked like it needed to be shut down by the health inspectors, and probably thoroughly hosed down. Maybe burned to the ground. The paint was peeling, the sign was barely hanging on by one rusted bolt, and as I climbed from the SUV, the scent of old piss burned my nose. *Fucking disgusting.*

Max's eyes bounced around, looking for threats, gathering information. "I hope you're up to date on your tetanus boosters," he muttered. He scrunched his nose, then wiped the expression from his face, giving me a crooked grin instead. His goofball expression. Somehow, it took him from a near-twenty-six-year-old veteran to an awkward teen whose balls had barely dropped, in the space of fifteen seconds.

It was why he'd been such a good intelligence agent. A spy.

There was no security at the door, so we just wandered in. I could see Lance in the back corner, and we stepped over broken glass and old food to get to him. Lance lifted his chin at me and fist-bumped Max.

Max smiled down at him. A real smile this time. "Love looks good on you, my friend." He was right; Lance looked better than I'd ever seen him. I slid into the booth with my back to the wall, Max moving in beside me.

Lance handed us each a beer bottle. "Don't drink anything on tap unless you want to get salmonella," he murmured quietly. I had no intention of drinking anything, the beer was a prop. "The fuckwad arrived about ten minutes ago. He's up there at the bar, downing tequila."

Snorting, Max rubbed a finger through the condensation rings on the scarred Formica table top. "And I thought this might be a challenge," he said softly. Louder, he announced, "I'm going to get some shots. You boys want one?" He sounded like a jovial college Chad, and didn't seem even a little perturbed when we both shook our heads. He bounded up to the bar, like he had no troubles in the world. I knew it wasn't true; you didn't do the things he'd done without some darkness, but you wouldn't see it on his face.

We let Max work while I held my beer as if I was going to put this pisswater to my lips. For a little while, Lance and I talked about the nothing things: guys from the VA, the weather, baseball. Then we talked about his Omega, and that fucking bird, all the while drinking as little of the beer in my hand as I could.

Out of the corner of my eye, I watched the front door, and Max. He'd sidled right up to Joseph Powell, the shitstain who was working with some reality TV host to peddle animals for fucked-up reasons. I couldn't imagine the balls it took to have your face flashed all over some TV show, rescuing the very creatures you were sending out to be tortured.

I fucking hated people.

What felt like hours later, Joseph Powell was stumbling down the hall towards the men's bathrooms, and Max gave me the signal. *Go time.*

"I'll go around the back," I told Lance, who nodded.

"I'll get the car."

I followed him out the front door, then took a sharp left down the piss alleyway. I didn't have to wait long for Max to push Joseph Powell out the door. The guy was drunk as fuck, but not so drunk that one look at me didn't make him want to add to the layer of piss already coating the concrete.

"Who the fuck are you guys?"

Lance arrived with the car, slowing just enough that Max could wrench open the door and I could shove the asshole in. Max hopped in the front next to Lance, as I climbed in after Shitstain McGee.

"Where are you taking me? You're going to regret this! Do you know who my boss is? I'll have you *arrested*," he shouted. I tuned him out, trying to pick up what Max was saying up front. I couldn't hear jack shit over the sound of Joseph Powell's whiny voice, though.

"Seriously, man, just pull over and let me out, and we'll forget this ever happened. Or my Pack will hear about this. They're rich. They're connected. I can make your life *miserable*."

I knew that Joseph Powell didn't have a Pack, let alone a powerful one. He wasn't done, though, and went about immediately contradicting himself.

"I don't have any money, and no one will pay a ransom. You guys have the wrong guy."

Fuck, I hated *stupid* people.

"Do we?" I asked in a low voice, the one that promised violence and probably death.

"I mean it—I won't say anything..."

Oh, for fuck's sake. This guy was so tedious.

Without warning, I wrapped my arm around his throat, putting him in a sleeper hold as he slapped against my forearm. He stood no chance of shaking me off, and soon enough, he was quiet and still. I pushed his unconscious body from mine, his head smacking the window a little harder than I intended.

Lance raised an eyebrow in the rearview mirror, and Max huffed. Crossing my arms over my chest, I frowned. "What? He was annoying."

Max pinched the bridge of his nose, but didn't disagree. Lance lifted his chin at an intersection in front of us. "Doesn't matter. We're almost there."

Fucking finally.

THREE
PALOMA

Sound was muffled down here. There was no warmth. No sunlight. Just a small room with a bed and a table. I hid beneath my veil, like a child would hide under its blankets. Like the intricate fabric walls hid me from the horror of the fact I was trapped down here.

The brand at the base of my throat was red and crusted, and I thought it might be infected, but I had no poultice to put on it and no voice to ask for it, even if I would. I'd woken up down here what seemed like forever ago, and other than another strange, weaselly-looking guy —who said his name was Joseph—coming to give me food once a day, I hadn't seen anyone. The stubble on my head was starting to grow in, so it had to have been at least a week, maybe even two.

I could hear the sounds of animals faintly, and I often wondered if I was inside a zoo. Just another creature in an enclosure. I'd never seen a zoo, but I'd read about them. They were from the before.

I was beginning to wonder if there even *was* a before, or whether my whole life had been a lie. I'd seen the vehicle. Been inside it. They weren't meant to exist anymore. I'd been taken by *strangers*. They weren't meant to exist either.

They were almost like a dream now, or maybe a nightmare. I hadn't seen any of those Alphas since they'd taken me. Perhaps they'd never existed, and it was just Joseph. Somehow, I found that reassuring. Joseph was undesignated, I thought. He couldn't compel me to do things.

The sounds of the animals increased, and I frowned. They were especially loud today. Howls echoed around the space; I wondered if they were wolves. I pulled the veil closer to my body and curled up on the bed. It was cold tonight, and wherever I was, I was below ground, because the walls were solid and the cold damp came up from the ground. The only time I could be warm was if I rolled myself up in my blanket and lay in the middle of the mattress.

I missed my home. My sisters and brothers. I missed knowing who I was, my place in my world. If I could leave, I might even go home, beg Leader Malakai to take me back. I would be a better Omega. I'd be so good; he'd never have to punish me again.

Anything was better than this.

A steady thump pounded through the ceiling above

me, and I looked up. Was it time for Joseph to come again? I looked over at the half-eaten rations on the table. Normally, I rationed out the food so I wasn't hungry. The hunger in my belly was the only way I could partially judge the time, so I didn't think it had been that long.

Fear rushed up to gag me. Unusual was not good. An optimistic part of my brain wondered if they were going to let me go, but every other part of me immediately shut it down. They hadn't taken me from my home to keep me as a pet. Something worse was about to happen.

The hatch in the ceiling opened, and I curled up tighter in the bed, hearing the ladder squeak as someone climbed down.

"Fucking hell," a voice growled, and I twitched. That wasn't Joseph. I moved my hands from my eyes and lowered the blankets a fraction.

The man who stood in the room with me wasn't one of the people who'd taken me from the Homestead. He was tall, taller than any man I'd ever met, and almost gangly. Like his arms and legs had grown out of control. His jaw was strong and smooth, and his eyes were dark, or maybe the shadows cast by the small battery-powered lights just made them look that way. He smelled like the slightly spicy Christmas cookies we used to make as kids.

"Omega?" he called softly, his voice now far more gentle than when he'd first jumped down. "I'm not going to hurt you. My name is Max, and I'm here to rescue you."

Would he take me back to the Homestead? Despite

my thoughts a moment ago, something inside me rebelled at going back to the place that had discarded me so easily.

As he took another step toward me, I curled tighter into a ball. This was my chance to leave this hole. But what if this man took me somewhere else? Did something worse?

He squatted down, so he wasn't looming over me. "I promise you're safe now. Do you have a name?"

I still couldn't speak. Not since that smiling Alpha had told me to be quiet. So I said nothing.

The guy, Max, lifted the blankets a little. "We have to go. I'm not going to make you do anything you don't want to do, but you can't stay down here."

I sucked in a shaking breath. I had to be brave. He was right, this unfamiliar Beta. I couldn't stay here, so I had to take a chance on him. I sat up on the bed, and the Beta shuffled back a little, his hands still out in front of him. As I pushed the blankets from my legs, his eyes ran over me. Not in the way that the Leader's eyes had sometimes looked at me, but the way you might appraise an injured animal.

"Are you hurt anywhere?" I shook my head. "Can you walk?" I nodded.

He gave me a wide smile, and something stuttered in my chest. It was a nice smile. It made me feel... warm. Safe even, which was ridiculous, considering where I was.

"That's so good, Omega. Now, we're going to climb

out of this hole, and I promise, no one will ever trap you again. Let's go."

I stood, making sure my veil was over my head, preventing him from seeing my face. I needed this curtain between me and this world I didn't understand. He stood back up to almost his full height, his shoulders curling in a little, like he didn't want to scare me by being tall. He could be five feet tall, and I'd still be terrified.

I moved toward the ladder on wobbling knees. A few weeks of poor meals and no space to move around had made my muscles weak. Climbing one step at a time, I felt Max move to stand at the bottom of the ladder.

"I'm here. I'll catch you if you fall, I promise."

It was oddly reassuring from a complete stranger. But I put one foot in front of the other, the soft, silky slippers on my feet providing very little grip on the rungs, and my long skirt getting caught on every step. When I slipped close to the top, large hands were on my waist, steadying me.

"Almost there," he murmured, removing his hands as soon as I was secure.

Finally, I climbed over the top edge and into what looked like Leader Malakai's office back at the Homestead. Big walnut desk. Spinning chair. A couch along one wall. Knotted rug that was rolled back to show a trapdoor.

Max was up over the edge behind me in seconds, stooping down to help me to my feet, but my legs felt weak. "Would it be okay if I carried you? If you need to get down, for whatever reason, just tap my shoulder twice and I'll give you space."

I didn't want to be manhandled again, but worse than that would be staying here longer than necessary. Nodding, I raised my arms, and he grabbed a blanket from the back of the couch and wrapped it around my shoulders. I hated that it smelled of Alpha, but I liked that it was one more thing to hide beneath. He slipped his arms behind my knees and under my back, then I was hefted into the air like I weighed nothing. He shouldered his way out the door, moving at incredible speed toward wherever we were going.

I could smell the fear and terror in the room we strode through, along with the burnt scent of anger. I turned my face into Max's chest and breathed in his Christmas cookie scent instead, like my life depended on him.

I almost cried when I felt the cool breeze on my face a moment later, though the darkness remained. It was night time, that was obvious, and there was a cacophony of noise coming from a large box vehicle on my left.

"What the actual fuck is *that?*" someone growled, and my whole body went stiff with fear.

Alpha. Another Alpha.

I whimpered dand tightened my grip on Max. I needed to run. But I couldn't outrun an Alpha. Max had said he would protect me, but so had Leader Malakai. What if he was just here to hand me over to another Alpha? The burning citrus in this Alpha's scent made me want to lose the miniscule amount of food I had in my stomach.

I screamed silently at the injustice of everything.

Max tightened his hold on me. "Watch your fucking tone—you're scaring her," he snapped back in a whisper-yell. "Seems Anthony Small wasn't just peddling animals. He'd moved onto Omegas too."

The burning smell surrounded me in a thick cloud, until I thought I might choke. "I'm going to *kill* him," the Alpha snarled so fiercely that I trembled harder. I listened to his footsteps as he stomped back into the building, but then Max was moving toward a vehicle. A car. That's what they were. Cars. I'd read about them.

"Don't worry about him, Omega. He's mad that you've been treated so poorly. His anger is not for you." He poured reassurance into his words, and I found myself believing him. "Let's get out of here." Opening the door to the car, he placed me gently into the back. As he slid the restraint thing across my chest, I tried not to shake too hard. "I'm going to sit up front so you don't feel crowded."

His eyes snapped to the front window as a huge man strode out of the building. Without even scenting him, I knew this was the Alpha from a moment ago. Even as I watched from behind the veil, he stopped outside the driver's door and took a large breath, his barrel chest expanding, before his shoulders curled a little.

When he opened the door, his scent was less on fire —though still singed at the edges—and more citrus. Like barbequed lemons. His eyes met mine, though he couldn't see me behind the veil. "Let's go. We'll get her back to Otillie-James, and they can take care of her."

Max looked at me over his shoulder, and I couldn't read his expression. "Okay. Hold tight, Omega. It's almost over now."

I didn't know who Otillie-James was, or where they were taking me, but my gut said it had to be better than where I'd been.

Turns out, Otillie-James was an Omega. She was short, had wild blonde hair that stood up everywhere, and kind eyes. She also looked at me like I'd just spawned in front of her like Izuny crawling from the ground, somewhere between shock and horror.

"Human cattle? That's what he said?" she hissed like a feral cat, and unlike the Alpha's rage, I knew her anger was definitely on my behalf. She was hugging me tightly, and I kind of liked it.

The Omegas weren't allowed to live in the same houses back at the Homestead, and I'd been the only one left after Omega Patricia had died three years ago. Plus, the Homestead discouraged displays of affection, though sometimes Nim and I had hugged in the closet while we read the magazines.

Maybe Nim wasn't such an obedient Beta after all. I missed her so much.

Otillie-James—she'd said to call her OJ if I liked—

looked at the big, scarred Beta who had kissed her like she was his only reason for living. "You burned it down, right?" she asked with such venom, I almost smiled.

Since we arrived, I'd been tucked into the corner of a sofa that felt too soft, and despite OJ trying to get conversation out of me, I couldn't give her anything. Another Omega—a male Omega, could you imagine?—had also tried, but in the end, frustration got the better of me and I hid my face in the couch cushion. Now they were talking around me, and I was okay with that.

I didn't understand anything. Nothing in this home made sense to me. Not the big black window on the wall. Not the white thing that was moving around the floor by itself, making a loud noise. Not the little rectangles they all looked down at occasionally, or had conversations into like the person was there. Or like the rectangles could talk back? Nothing made *sense*.

I jerked as a weird little dog jumped onto the couch beside me. Looking down at it out of the corner of my eye, I realized it only had three legs. Had these people taken its fourth leg? It didn't seem scared of them, or me. It climbed onto my lap, its two front paws on my shoulders, and started licking my face on the other side of my veil.

I lifted my hand to push it off, but instead, I buried my fingers in its wiry fur. It was both coarse and soft. I scratched at its skin, and the dog wriggled its tiny butt happily. It seemed to... like me? So I scratched some more until it flopped over, putting three legs in the air and exposing its belly.

"That's Doodles," OJ said softly. "He likes belly rubs."

Doodles? What a weird name. But still, I stroked the belly of the little dog. His fur there felt far softer than that on his back, and he lay there with his mouth open, his tongue falling out the side and his eyes closed. It was fortunate that I could feel the steady thump of his tiny heart against my fingers; otherwise, I'd wonder if he was dead.

The action was comforting, giving this small creature happiness and giving me something else to focus on. I wasn't sure how long I stroked him for, but suddenly, OJ was in front of me.

"Hey there, would you like to shower? Maybe I could lend you some clothes?"

I felt disgusting. My hair was itching stubble, and my body odor was... not great. I looked down at the dog, realizing my hand was curled in his fur. I didn't want to leave him.

OJ seemed to sense my reluctance. "Doodles can come. In fact, I think he'd insist on it. He really likes you." She held out a hand, and I took it, allowing her to pull me to my feet. As she predicted, Doodles the dog leapt to his feet, fell over, then got back to his feet again. He hopped down the hall behind us as OJ led me to a room that smelled a little like her, but not like Alpha.

I couldn't work out why the scent of another Omega

was making me uncomfortable, but I wanted to escape already.

"There's a bathroom through there. I'll find you some clothes and leave them just outside the door. Do you have any injuries?" she asked quietly, and it was hard to miss the empathy in her voice.

Taking a shuddering breath, I slid my veil from my head. Her eyes widened when she saw my head, but I assumed that was because she already had her Alphas and therefore could grow her hair out without tempting others. I pointed to the base of my throat, and she let out a hissed curse. I watched her swallow her anger, before she nodded.

"I'll bring you some antibiotic cream to put on it. It looks quite infected. Is that a brand?"

I nodded. That had been what they called it.

"Is that the reason you can't speak?"

I shook my head, and OJ chewed her lip. "If I got you a piece of paper and a pen, could you write out your responses?"

I nodded vigorously, and she smiled widely at me, moving to a bedside table and pulling out a pad of paper and a pen, which she handed to me.

She let out a hopeful breath. "Firstly, do you have a name?"

I wrote my answer on the paper. *Paloma.*

"Paloma. That's a real pretty name. Other than the wound on your throat, do you have any other injuries? Is there something I can do to help you speak, perhaps?"

I hesitated. I knew one of the Alphas could command me to speak, but I didn't want that oily feeling over my body again, didn't want someone else to be in control of me. But I didn't want to be mute forever either. I wanted my voice back.

So I wrote it all down. The commands. What had happened. OJ didn't ask questions, didn't interrupt.

At the end, I wrote *Is there an Alpha I can trust?*

Nodding, OJ's big, watery eyes met mine. "Okay, Paloma. How about you shower first, and we'll work out everything else later, okay?"

Putting off my problems until they caught up to me later was definitely something I could do.

FOUR
MAX

This was a giant clusterfuck. I'd sent off Joseph's audio confession from an anonymous email address to every reporter, social media influencer, and animal activist I could Google, and then to the cops. There was no way that this would be buried.

I had, however, gone over the audio once more, just to ensure there were no references to the Omega in there. I didn't want her to be dragged into this, especially considering how traumatized she already was. I wasn't an Alpha, but even I could scent the bruised smell of an Omega in distress. I'd been extensively trained in body language, but I could have been blind and still know that she had shut down from the trauma.

It didn't help that her appearance was causing the other two Omegas in the house distress also. Their soured scents were riling the Alphas, and this whole thing was now a powder keg of hormones.

I was going to blame that for what happened next. When the topic of the Omega and what should happen with her came up, I felt the words leaving my mouth, despite my better judgement. Despite the problems that might arise from it.

Despite Llew.

"She can come home with us. We have the space." My voice sounded more sure than I actually felt, and I could feel Rio's eyes on the side of my face. He probably thought I'd lost my mind.

Lance grunted. "I'm not sending her home with two unknown Alphas. She stays here."

I was a little pissed he didn't think I was as much of a threat as the two Alphas in our house, but he was probably right. Rio was shrouded in darkness and a healthy dose of PTSD. And Llew...

I'd forgotten that we'd told Lance about our other Alpha, Llewellyn, after a particularly hard group session at the VA. Llew had been our Packmate since we were kids. Three best friends who'd been through so much together. Our Packbond had been the kind that most people could only dream of, until the dream became a nightmare.

Rio growled. "What are you insinuating?"

Lance had the good grace to look a little guilty. Honestly, if we were talking about strangers and not my Pack, I'd probably have agreed with him. But something deep in my chest felt compelled to care for the Omega. Even now, I was fighting the urge to get up and leave the room, to make sure she was okay.

Rio was arguing softly with Lance about how there was no one better to protect her than our Pack—which I agreed with—when the girl reappeared, and my heart stopped. She was dressed in an oversized sweatshirt that hung to her thighs, and a pair of loose sweats that hugged her hips, but billowed down her legs.

Her face stole my words. Her features had mostly been obscured behind the veil, so all I'd seen was a small button nose, with eyes that were big and dark. Now, she'd lost the veil, though I could see it clutched tightly in her hands. On her head was a small knitted cap, but it didn't hide the fact she had no hair.

Was she sick? Did she have alopecia? Her lack of hair did nothing to detract from her beauty, though; or the urge that burned in my limbs to stand up and scoop her into my arms. To hold her in my lap and tell her everything would be okay.

I noticed Truett, Lance's Alpha Packmate, appear in the hall behind them, but he was already quickly moving back to his other Omega, Strat.

Clearing her throat, Otillie-James speared us all with a disapproving expression. "How about we let Paloma decide for herself? I think she's probably had enough of Alphas telling her what to do to last her a lifetime."

Paloma. Her name was Paloma. She met my eyes, and I tried to convey promises I had every intention of keeping, without looking like an overwhelming stalker.

Paloma and Otillie-James whispered to each other, and I couldn't quite pick up their words. Otillie-James kept a careful amount of space between them, though, and she was doing a lot of validating nods. Finally, she gave the Omega a quick squeeze on her forearm and turned back to us.

"She insinuated that her Omega doesn't like being around two other Omegas, and she wishes to go home with Max and Rio." Paloma leaned close to whisper to her once more, while I tried to get my heart to restart in my chest. "Also, she'd like it if Doodles could come too," Otillie-James added.

I was nodding before she'd even finished. "Of course." I'd bring home the entire animal hoard if it made her more comfortable. A three-legged dog that looked more like a wire brush was an easy thing to give her, if it put her at ease.

Every Alpha in that room stared at Rio and I. While they had nowhere near enough training or Alpha strength to stop us from leaving with the girl, I found I didn't want to fight. I would protect Paloma from violence at all costs, if I could. But if they prevented us from executing her wishes, I would do what was necessary to ensure our exit. I didn't look too hard into why I was suddenly willing to throw down for a girl I'd only just met—probably some biological impulse because she felt so wounded. We were all wired to protect Omegas, even us Betas.

Which was quickly confirmed by Lance, the only

Beta who might be able to stand between an Alpha and something he wanted. "She's treated with the utmost respect. Her wishes are final. Or I will fuck you both up; I don't care how well trained you are."

I knew a little bit about Lance, and his time in the military. He could probably fuck me up, but he wouldn't stand a chance against Rio. Not that we'd ever test that theory. If we ever disrespected Paloma, or any Omega, I'd happily lie down and let him kick the shit out of me.

Rio must've agreed, because he gave a short nod of assent.

After that, everything happened so fast. We borrowed a car from the Pack, and put Paloma in the back with the dog on her lap. She seemed... stressed to be in the vehicle. Her scent turned acrid as soon as I shut the door, and I couldn't tell why. I wanted to sit in the back with her, but I didn't want to crowd her, or make her feel like she had a prison guard.

I hadn't thought this through at all, but we'd do the best we could.

"Paloma," I said softly, tasting her name on my tongue. "Are you hungry? Is there something you'd like to eat?"

She frowned at me. "An apple?" she whispered so softly, I had to strain to hear.

An apple? "Sure, we have those at home. What about something more substantial? Chinese food, maybe?"

She looked at me, a small crease between her brows, but shook her head eventually. Rio hit the brakes hard as someone pulled into the intersection without looking, and the scent of Omega stress went through the roof.

I looked back at her. "Are you okay? Do you not like driving?" Had she been stolen from a car? Had she been in an accident?

"This is only my third time in a vehicle." Her voice was trembling. How could anyone have only been in a car three times in their entire life?

Shooting a quick look at Rio, whose knuckles were blanched around the steering wheel like he was physically restraining himself from losing control, I sucked my teeth. "Would you feel better if one of us was in the back with you?"

She looked up at me, and I realized her eyes were a deep, almost impossible emerald green. "You?" she said softly, and I looked at Rio for signs that he needed to comfort the Omega so he didn't lose his shit.

He was already pulling over onto the shoulder of the road, then tilted his head at the passenger door. "Go sit with her."

I was so out of my depth right now. I could infiltrate a terrorist bunker, or a guerilla militia, or a cyber-terrorism cell, but consoling a frightened Omega seemed outside my abilities. But I'd try, just to ease the stench of her fear in the cab of the SUV.

Opening the door slowly, I gave her plenty of time to tell me to stop. To escape. To give me any sign that she might find my presence abhorrent. However, she just watched me with those gemstone-green eyes. I slid into the back seat, and wariness was all her body language was projecting.

Buckling myself back in, I placed a hand on the seat between us. Doodles the dog reached out and licked it, between all my fingers, like he was giving me a tongue bath. It was gross. I chuckled softly as Rio pulled back into traffic, wiping the dog slobber on my pants and putting my hand back out.

"I made a promise, and I don't break my promises," I told Paloma softly. "I've got you now. You're safe."

Her lip trembled, but despite her fear, she put her hand in mine. I threaded our fingers together, giving hers a gentle squeeze. A reassurance, even though she barely knew us and had no reason to trust my word. I couldn't imagine the choice she'd had to make in that bathroom. Go with the strangers you knew, or stay with the strangers that were like you, but being near them made instincts inside you go haywire.

Nothing like being betrayed by your own designation.

I needed to tell her about Llew. Or at least warn her not to go to his end of the house, without it sounding like we were holding him captive.

"I need to tell you that there's another Alpha at the house. He stays in his room almost all the time, but if you see him in the hall, he would rather stab himself through the heart than harm you. His name is Llew. I'll try and introduce you, if he's up to it." If Llew was in the right headspace. If he was here with us, in the present.

Her eyes slid toward me. "Is he sick?"

Fuck, what did I even say to that? "No, not physically." I met Rio's eyes in the rearview mirror. How did I even start to explain Llew to someone who wasn't in a Pack? "He went through something traumatic, and he's still finding his way back from the darkness."

We all were, but Llew... He'd had it the worst.

FIVE
PALOMA

A picture on the wall was moving. I'd seen these in my magazines. A television. I thought they'd all been destroyed during the apocalypse.

The big Alpha, Rio, stood beside me, but a careful distance away. Now my initial panic had subsided a little, I could almost examine my emotions without shying away from the pain. The other Alphas—the ones who belonged to OJ—had made me feel like I needed to find somewhere dark and small, and hide. It wasn't a sensation I was used to; I'd always loved being outside with the sun on my face, unless I was hiding in my closet reading my pilfered magazines.

Thoughts of Leader Malakai made my heart race with fear. Would he know I was gone? Would he send those men back out to fetch me and take me back, or worse, to bring me home?

There was a low rumble, and I noticed the Alpha Rio

had moved closer to me, a growl deep in his chest. "Calm, Omega. You're safe." He didn't have Max's softness, his response blunt and almost cold, but I believed him. I knew deep down in my chest that this Alpha would hurt anyone who came to take me back.

I nodded once, and that seemed enough for the Alpha. I lifted my finger to point at the television. "How does it work?"

Frowning, he turned to face me fully. "You don't know how a television works?"

"I thought they were all destroyed during the Great Smiting." Maybe this one had been saved. Or maybe my whole life had been a lie.

The look on the Alpha's face suggested it was the latter. "The Great Smiting?"

I shook my head. I didn't want to talk about it. Didn't want to talk about my family, or the Homestead.

But the Alpha wasn't ready to let it go. "It's important, Paloma." His tone was softer than I'd heard it so far, and I looked at him out of the corner of my eye.

"The apocalypse. I'm beginning to wonder if it was all a lie. You have vehicles and televisions, and there's so many more *people.*" My whispers felt like sandpaper as they left my throat. "We were supposed to be the last people left. The Devoted Children of Izuny." I felt at once stupid and untethered, like I had nothing left to cling to.

There was another low rumble, and the Alpha

stepped closer. "You know you're an Omega?" he asked softly.

I wanted to scoff, but given how little I knew, was it really unrealistic that I wouldn't know my designation? So I just nodded, not trusting that if I opened my mouth, a sob wouldn't come out.

"And you know I'm an Alpha?"

Another nod.

"That's good. I have to tell you that the scent of your distress is making my Alpha... agitated. I would like to console you, if I could. But it's completely your decision. From this point on, you are the one in control." He cleared his throat. "But Omegas, uh, from my experience and reading, enjoy the tactile nature of being held by an Alpha. It soothes them." He swallowed hard. "If that's something you'd like to try."

The only Alphas I'd ever met before I was taken were the Leaders, and the idea of them giving me anything but that crawling skin feeling seemed preposterous. However, right now, Rio was closer than any other Alpha had been in a week, and my body was leaning towards him like a flower toward the sun.

Did I want to try being held? Yes. Desperately. But I couldn't. The echoes of the barked commands that had rendered me immobile were still there, too close, and I couldn't put myself in that position again.

"I, uh... No, thank you?" It was hard to hide the longing in my voice, but Rio, true to his word, didn't push it.

"That's okay, Omega. The television works using data signals. I don't know the exact science, but I can find out for you. Out of interest, what year do you think it is?"

I turned my head to look at him. "2125, of course."

His shocked face told me everything I needed to know. It was just one more lie I'd been told. It was too much. A tear rolled down my cheek, and I blinked furiously, trying to hold the rest back.

The edge of Rio's hand brushed mine, like he couldn't help himself. When I didn't pull away, he linked our pinky fingers. We stood there in silence, staring at the television that showed people throwing around a ball, and I realized I knew nothing at all.

I was worse than helpless. I was helpless and alone.

Max had prepared a room for me, and it was three times as large as my room back at the Homestead. It was unlike any room I'd ever seen. It had its own bathroom, which Max had said was just for me, a bed that was bigger than my room back home, and then a third room off it.

This other room made something in my chest lurch with longing, in a way I didn't understand. It was small; Max would have to duck if he wanted to go in there. It was dark, with little lights that made the room look like it was illuminated by lanterns, but had no fire. There were oversized pillows on the floor, like the whole room was one big bed. It was layered with soft blankets, and I just wanted to curl up in it and never leave.

Max looked down at me in the room, his eyes soft. "You don't have to come out until you want to. This is your nest. Did your previous home have a nest?"

I shook my head. Birds had nests. Wasps had nests. Not Betrayers. "No," I said softly, rubbing the weave of a throw blanket between my fingertips. It was impossibly soft.

He looked like he wanted to say more, but instead, he just shook his head. "This is your place, Paloma. No one can come into this space, or any of the others, without your permission. There's a lock on the bedroom door; don't be afraid to use it." He chewed the corner of his bottom lip. "Tomorrow, we'll take you out to get you some more clothes and anything else you need."

A scratching noise on the floor announced the fact that Doodles was coming down the hall at breakneck speed, after Rio had taken him out to the bathroom. Not waiting for permission, the little dog launched himself into the nest with me, burrowing under the blankets, his tongue hanging out the side between toothless gums.

I loved Doodles. Was this what love at first sight was meant to feel like? I curled my body around his tiny one, burrowing beneath one of the many blankets until my eyes blinked slowly shut.

. . .

My eyes snapped open, and in the darkness, I wondered if it was all a dream. My rescue. Not being in that hole anymore. Max and Rio. Had it all been just a delusion, a hopeful fantasy?

But there was a putrid smell wafting over my face, accompanied by a soft snore, and when I looked over, Doodles was asleep on the pillow next to me, snoring like an old man, his dog breath unpleasant.

Doodles was here. I was okay. It wasn't a dream.

I shifted quietly from beneath the blankets, desperate to go to the bathroom. I shouldn't have worried about waking up the dog, though, because he didn't even flutter an eyelid as I crawled from the nest. In fact, if he wasn't snoring, I'd wonder if he was dead.

Quickly moving through my toilet routine, I eyed the big glass cube in the middle. OJ had introduced me to showers last night. She'd talked me through how to use the digital temperature settings, and even turned it on for me. Nothing in her demeanour said she pitied me, having obviously never used a shower before. At the Homestead, we'd always had bathtubs that most of us hauled water from the well for if we needed to bathe, but there didn't seem to be a tub in here. I'd have to ask, I guess. Or I could just use the shower. It couldn't be too different, right?

Suddenly, the idea of being clean again was an overwhelming compulsion. Stripping off my clothes, I folded them and left them on the sink. This shower had a control pad, like OJ's, and when I pressed what I assumed were the right buttons, water fell from the large head fixed in the roof.

I grinned as I stepped into the perfectly warm water. I stood beneath the stream, washing away my worries and fears, even if it was just for a moment.

Maybe it could be even warmer. Turning to the control pad, I pressed a few more buttons, but nothing happened. Maybe she'd pressed that button too—

Water poured from every single direction, straight at me. My face, back, legs, belly were all suddenly pummeled with jets of water. Screeching, I mashed at the digital pad, but somehow, it just made the water colder.

"Argh!" I needed to get out. I felt like I was drowning.

The door to the shower was wrenched open, and big arms were lifting me out, someone else pressing the buttons that controlled the shower, shutting it off. A large hand ran over my face, wiping away the water from my eyes, and I stared up at Rio. Max appeared beside him, a large fluffy towel in his hands, and I realized I was naked.

The Alpha was holding me naked.

We appeared to realize it at the same time, and he dropped me to my feet, Max quickly wrapping me up in the towel. Though, calling it a towel seemed almost offensive. It was so large, I could've wrapped it around myself twice.

Rio was staring down at me with dark brown eyes, like he was assessing me for damage. "Are you okay?"

All I wanted to do was climb back into his arms again. It made no sense, but I wanted to drag him into my nest and push him back against the pillows and lie on his chest. Once again, my body and my mind were at war.

As if sensing my turmoil, Max gently nudged me toward the bedroom. "We'll be in the kitchen. I've made breakfast, if you'd like to join us?" It was a suggestion, not an order. I knew if I said no, they'd still feed me.

I nodded jerkily, and Max shoved at Rio's shoulder until they were both out of the bedroom and I could hear the soft sounds of them padding down the hallway. Sucking in a deep breath, I moved to the bag of clothing OJ had lent me last night and pulled out some more loose pants and an oversized sweater. They ballooned around my body, and smelled a little like the other Omega, which made my skin itch.

Why did the scent of other Omegas make me feel wrong? Was it just being out in the world, surrounded by other Omegas and Alphas, that was making my senses go haywire?

I let out a silent scream. There was so much I didn't know, decades of knowledge to learn. I hated this *so much*. I wanted to climb back into my nest and never come out.

That's what Leader Malakai would have wanted. For me to give up. I wasn't going to give him the satisfaction.

Because now I knew he was a liar. He hadn't been there to protect us, protect me. He'd been the evil force keeping us down, and that knowledge caused another sensation I didn't get to feel often.

It made me incandescent with rage.

Six

Paloma

When I emerged from my room, I nearly ran into Rio coming back down the hall. He had a tray of food in his hands, including a big travel mug of what smelled like coffee. He gave me a quick smile. "Go on down the hall. I'm just dropping off breakfast to Llew."

Llew. The unknown second Alpha in their group. The one who was sick, but they were hesitant with the details. Maybe it was Alpha prerogative to be liars. Betas too.

Rio waited until I was headed down the hall before he continued on. Just before I turned the corner, I couldn't help but look back over my shoulder. Curiosity had always been my biggest sin, according to Sister Roberta, and she was probably right. Hers had been self-righteousness.

Through the now-open door, I could see the shadow

of Rio and another, almost impossibly large silhouette in front of the window. I felt the moment the eyes of the other Alpha saw me, like a caress on my skin. Felt it down to the very atoms of my core.

Scared, I disappeared around the corner, almost running until I made it to the kitchen. Max was there, smiling as he flipped pancakes onto a serving platter. A designated man cooking made my brain fizzle. The Leaders didn't cook. They didn't even serve themselves. Not even the Brothers and Sisters cooked; that was the role of the undesignated. But here was Max—who wasn't an Alpha, granted, but was still a powerful Beta—in a short, frilly apron with what looked like a pair of sequined underwear embroidered on the front. I stared at the apron for longer than was probably polite.

Looking down, he flushed red. "Oh. It was a gift from my sister. She has a weird sense of humor. Come and sit down. Would you like coffee? Juice?"

I looked at the table, then back at Max. "Shouldn't I... Don't you want me to serve you?"

Max's eyes widened in shock, but he quickly chased away the expression. "No, we share all our chores pretty equally here, and you don't ever have to serve us. You aren't hired help. We're big and ugly enough to get our own food. Especially Rio," he teased with a wink.

"Brat."

I startled. I hadn't heard Rio re-enter the room. It was like my whole body was in tune with his every move-ment. It turned with him as he stalked to the kitchen, making up a plate of food with a little bit of everything. When it was piled unbelievably high, he ushered me gently to a chair.

"Sit." It was a command, but not a bark. I wasn't physically compelled to sit, but I still did as I was told. He placed the plate in front of me, and I looked up at him, my brow creasing again as I was at a loss. "You don't ever serve us, Omega. In this house, Omegas are to be nurtured and cared for. Your needs are paramount. If you want something, you just have to ask."

I was already shaking my head. It didn't make sense. "I don't understand." I felt like that was the only sentence I could string together anymore.

Sitting down across from me, Max placed a consoling hand on my arm. "I know you don't, Paloma, but I promise, we can help." He looked at Rio. "Maybe we should rip it off, like a bandaid."

Rip what off?

"Paloma, you were a member of an isolationist cult. The year is only 2025, not 2125. I believe your leaders altered things to keep their followers disconnected from society and the world around them. Eventually, when you're feeling more settled, we'd like your help finding where you came from, so we can stop what happened to you from happening to any other Omegas in your former community."

They were all words that I understood. Except the word cult. The word sounded wrong, foreign. "Cult?"

Rio looked helplessly at Max, and I got the impression that he was the brains to Rio's brawn. "A cult is like a religion, I guess, or a system of beliefs, even, but they kind of operate in secrecy and seclusion, and they try to ostracise their members from the outside world."

Confusion and betrayal flooded my system until a soft whine was bursting from my lips, echoed by Rio's rumbling growl. Standing, he strode from the room without a word, and I watched him go, pain throbbing through my chest. Was he angry with me? Disgusted?

Max was still watching me. "It's not you, Omega. He's struggling to respect your boundaries, especially when you're in such obvious emotional pain." He seemed to be chewing over his next words, his eyes dipping down to where my arms were banded tightly around myself. I hadn't even noticed. "Would you like me to hold you? I'm a Beta—I can't compel you to do anything, can't alter anything with my pheromones. But I can console you, if you'll let me."

Last night, when OJ had been bustling around, keeping me distracted as her Alpha lifted the compulsion on me, she'd talked about her Omega like it was a separate entity to herself. Her Omega didn't like these sweats, so I could have them. Her Omega loved the feeling of this fabric or scent or whatever. hadn't understood why she was talking about it like it was someone else.

Right now, though, I kind of got it. My head thought crawling into the lap of a stranger for comfort was ridiculous, but that urge, the one that sat deep down in my chest, already had me moving toward Max. Had me climbing into his lap, which should've been uncoordinated, but was almost instinctual. Much like burying my nose beneath his chin and breathing him in, until the world stopped closing in around me.

Max stroked up and down my back. "I know this is difficult, Paloma. I know you feel like you're floating around untethered in the world. But I'm—*we're* here. Anything you want to do from this point on is entirely up to you. We'll support you, and so will OJ's Pack. You have a place here with us for as long as you want it. Until you find your feet, we'll prop you up."

The feel of his arms around me, bracketing me in on all sides, settled my nerves more than anything had in so long. I wasn't sure I would ever move again.

Sighing heavily, Max continued. "But we'll have to go over what happened, whenever you're ready. We need to assess what you know, and what you need to know, so you aren't... taken advantage of in the real world." The real world. Not the fantasy world I was born and raised in. "I'd like it if you met with a therapist. Do you know what that is?"

He was talking to me like I was a child, and I hated it, but also I understood, because I hadn't known how a television worked or what a cult was, or probably a million other things.

So I nodded. "I read about the advancements of brain health in a magazine."

I could feel his shock as he tried to piece together the dichotomy of what I was saying. "You had magazines?"

Nodding, I pressed my face into his chest until my voice was muffled. "From before the apocalypse. Leader Malakai had them in his office. *National Geographic.* I used to... steal them." My confession sat between us heavily. Now they knew I was stupid *and* a thief. Maybe they'd throw me away.

Instead, Max squeezed me, letting out a happy hum. "That's wonderful, Paloma. So good. You'll have a foundation to build on. August can help you with the rest. And us too, of course. We can help too."

"August?"

"He's a therapist down at the VA. That's Veterans Affairs—Rio and I are former military."

From what little I knew about the military, it made sense. They held themselves with the kind of self-assurance that could only be gained through knowing how to kill another person in under a minute.

"When you come back from war, they like for you to talk about what happened, so you can start to heal. I think you'd also benefit from that. Plus, August is an Omega, and he could probably answer your Omega questions better than I could." There was a slight pink tinge to Max's cheekbones, and I wasn't sure if it was embarrassment because he didn't know something about Omegas, or if it was the thought of this other Omega, August, that was making him flush.

I frowned, pulling back. "Is he your Omega?"

Max spluttered, shaking his head. "Uh, no. He isn't. He's just a friend."

Something about Max's scent sharpened, but I didn't know what. Sighing, I let myself relax deeper into his chest. He was right; this contact was comforting. "Okay, I'll meet with your friend." I hesitated, but made my request anyway. I wasn't going to be punished for asking for things here. "Could he come here? I'm not ready to…" I trailed off, because there were so many things I wasn't ready for. To go back outside. To face how much I didn't know. To be bombarded with more people.

"WHERE'S MY FUCKING MONEY?!"

The sudden shout made me jerk in Max's arms, almost leaping off his lap. His arms tightened around me, and he let out a sound that was half put-upon sigh and half chuckle.

"I guess it's time to introduce you to the loudest member of the family." Shifting me gently to my feet, he kept hold of my hand and led me to a small room off the living room. Judging by the shelves, it would have been a storage room once upon a time. Now, it housed a giant cage and the biggest bird I'd ever seen in my life. "Paloma, this is—"

"RUFIOOOOOOO!"

Another sigh. "Yep. This is Rufio." Max moved over to the bird, calmly putting his hand out like he wasn't going to get torn to shreds by the sharp-tipped beak. "Rufio was one of OJ's rescue animals. He's… well, he's not harmless, and I wouldn't suggest you handle him until you have more experience with parrots, but he's an—"

"African Gray Parrot," I breathed, stepping closer. I'd read about these birds, about their intelligence and their ability to interact and solve problems. They were highly intelligent. I'd thought they were extinct, much like everything else that wasn't readily visible inside the walls of the Homestead. "I saw them in a magazine," I added, as Max watched me closely. The parrot was also watching me, with eyes more intelligent than any creature should be.

Max stroked his head softly. "Rufio, this is Paloma." Max met my eye and smiled fondly down at the bird. "I'm not sure he'll be able to master the name Paloma, but he manages curse words like a pro. He was rescued from a crackhouse." He saw the confusion on my face. "Uh, a place where people sell and take drugs. It means he has a very colorful vocabulary."

The bird had moved to the end of Max's arm while he was talking, his whole body leaning toward me. I watched him closely, fascinated and a little scared.

Max lifted him higher. "I think he wants you to scratch his head, but don't feel like you have to. We can take it very slowly."

No, I wanted to overcome my fears, and this bird seemed like a safe first step. Reaching up, I mimicked the way Max scratched his head, and all of Rufio's feathers stood up as he tilted his head closer to my fingers.

Chuckling softly, Max held him closer. "Rufio, you charmer. You like the scratches from the pretty Omega, don't you?"

The bird jumped suddenly from Max's arm to mine with a small flap of his large wings. I froze, my eyes going to Max. He didn't try to get him back, but I could tell he was watching the whole interaction closely. The bird climbed up toward my elbow, where he was definitely close enough to attack my face if he wanted.

"Hey, pretty bird wanna scratch?" the parrot whispered in my direction, but his voice was deep and came out kinda scary. His feathers were all fluffed up, and he looked at me kind of adoringly. "Scratch scratch?" he crooned at me.

Lifting my free hand, I did as he asked, and he turned his head this way and that, until I was getting all the good spots. I stared down at this wonder of nature on my arm.

Max was watching us closely. "He really likes you. He hasn't taken to anyone so quickly. It took me a week to get him to sit on my arm. He still kind of hates Rio. I think his previous owners were Alpha males and kept him in a small cage."

I looked down at the bird's intelligent gray eyes. "We have that in common."

SEVEN
AUGUST

It was quieter than usual at group therapy today, but it was bound to seem smaller without the large presences of Lance, Rio, and Max. I didn't know where they were, but my Omega senses were tingling when those three went AWOL together.

I might have even worried, if I hadn't gotten a message from Max during my clinic lunch break, asking if I could do an after-hours consultation. I didn't even ask what for; I assumed it was for their Pack Leader, Llewellyn. Llewellyn Barrie had been the lead Alpha in the Barrie Pack at the time of Rio's enlistment, and had been listed as the next of kin in his paperwork.

Somewhere during Rio's tour of the Middle East, Llewellyn had lost his hold on his sanity and his Alpha. I had my professional opinion on why it had happened, and I knew the guys did too, but none of them were ready to face the hard facts so that they could truly begin to heal. They weren't ready to poke at the wounds, if it meant that they could lose Llew forever. Instead, they were living this kind of half-life, particularly Llew.

I'd talked about it in one-on-one sessions with Rio, but he shut down at any mention of the Alpha. I never pushed—a sacrifice to maintain the connection we had established.

Sighing, I tried to turn my attention to the Beta who was currently speaking, but my mind kept wandering back to the Barrie Pack. I never pushed, because I didn't want to lose my chance to see them once a week. I needed to hand off their case to one of the other psychologists, because I was more than a little in lust with two of the three Barrie Pack boys.

The Beta finished speaking, and I pulled my head back into group therapy. These vets deserved my full attention. I could daydream about the Pack that couldn't be mine later.

By the end of the day, I was exhausted. I squeezed the arm of Trish, an Alpha female who'd lost her leg in an IED explosion a year ago, giving her a smile of support. "You've come so far already, but sometimes it's hard to see that, when you're slogging through every day. Lean on your support network—you would be there for them in times of need, so allow them to be there for you." I said the words gently, because with these military types, any suggestion of weakness at the wrong moment could set them back months of recovery.

I smiled at Trish's Omega and the other Alpha in her

Pack as they came to collect her from the session. Giving them a quick wave, I hurried back into the poky little room that doubled as our meeting place. I packed up quickly, wanting time to run home and shower before heading over to the Barrie Packhouse. Max had offered to come and collect me, but while I trusted them implicitly, part of being a solo Omega meant that I needed to have my own means of transport whenever I went anywhere new.

I stacked the chairs and washed out the coffee pot, then it was finally time to head home. I was the only unmated Omega in our apartment block, but there were three Beta couples, a few single Unshown, and two completed Packs in the complex. I was as safe as I could be, and when my heats were due, I tended to either take myself to a Heat Clinic or tough it out at the cabin I had out near Lake Norman.

Looking at the dark shadows of the VA parking lot, I wondered if I shouldn't have taken Max up on his offer of a ride, but I pushed the feeling down. I wasn't helpless. I wasn't unsafe here. But still, I hurried to the car as fast as I could, my keys already in my hand. When I made it there, I locked the doors immediately.

Life as an unmated male Omega wasn't dangerous, but I was coveted, I guess would be the right word. Omegas were respected, but not everyone gave a shit about the law, or ethics, or polite society. If we were attacked, it always came back to our biology, like we were some kind of honey trap for Alphas who just couldn't help themselves.

Bullshit. I could manage to be surrounded by Alphas every day and not whine and try to climb onto their knots. Alphas could do the same, if it wasn't so damn socially accepted that they were little more than animals.

I let out a frustrated noise at the injustice of it all and wove my way home. I had forty-five minutes to shower and get across town, so I had to hurry. It had me waving hello but not stopping when my neighbors shouted hello. I was in my apartment, already undressing in the hallway.

After having the world's quickest shower, I wasted precious time deciding what to wear. I went with well-loved jeans that I knew hugged my ass and an equally well-loved, long-sleeved navy sweater. It was so soft that it appealed to my Omega nature.

Being an Omega pigeon-holed me into almost a feminine role, and I'd hated that when I was a teen. Now, at the grand old age of twenty-five, I knew that being in touch with my emotions was a blessing and not a curse, especially when I'd decided to move into therapy.

And I was willing to top any Alpha who needed me to show them that just because I was an Omega, it didn't mean I was submissive. Still, I liked all those Omega trappings: soft fabrics, a nest, pleasant scents, all those sensory pleasures.

Touch. I was touch-starved. I was an Omega without a Pack, with neither a family Pack close by, nor a romantic one. Sometimes, I'd find myself reaching out, not to appease traumatized soldiers, but to just get a little physical input.

I needed to find a lover. Maybe a nice Beta who'd let me tell them how good they'd been.

Why did my mind go straight to Max?

Climbing into my car, I made sure I had my tablet in my briefcase. I wanted to have all the resources right there for them, for their Pack Alpha. Plugging their address into my GPS, I followed it across town. My 1999 Honda had a check-engine light permanently on, and the upholstery in the back seat was so threadbare that you basically sat on the springs. Being a therapist was emotionally rewarding, but it wasn't particularly financially beneficial.

When Max had given me his address, I'd kind of expected the place to be a single-story bachelor pad. I knew there was a good side and a bad side to this suburb, and I'd just assumed they lived on the bad side. Being a returned vet didn't pay particularly well either, and I wasn't sure what either Rio or Max did now they'd been discharged.

But when my GPS led me to the nice side of the neighborhood, I began to wonder if I knew these guys at all. The houses weren't mansions, by any stretch, but they were mostly two-story places with green front lawns and manicured gardens. The type of places that said there was money to waste on landscaping.

The house I stopped in front of was average-looking,

but little details spoke softly of wealth. Stacked stone sidings. Fancy wrought-iron trim. A freshly painted picket fence. Obviously, they weren't hurting for cash, and somehow, that made me feel inadequate.

Growling at myself, I parked in the driveway. I was here in a professional capacity. They weren't courting me, and in fact, if they *were* to court me, it would be extremely unprofessional on my behalf.

Pushing that thought to the forefront of my mind, I stepped out of the car and walked up to the door. Knocking lightly, I looked around the garden for the night-blooming jasmine that I could scent. It had always been my favorite, despite the strength of it sometimes. It reminded me of my grandmother's house.

The door swung open, and Rio was there, his stern face softening a little as he saw me. I pushed my Omega down as he rose up to meet the strong Alpha in front of us.

"August. You came."

Not yet, but I'd like to. I kept the words firmly inside.

"Of course. Max sounded like it was urgent." Rio didn't disagree, and my stress level ratched up a notch. "Is everything okay?"

That was when I realized that the soft scent of jasmine wasn't coming from outside, but from in here. *They have an Omega?*

I didn't realize I'd said the words out loud until Rio stepped to the side, ushering me into the house. "No, not really. I mean... kind of, right now. It's hard to explain. Come in, and we'll fill you in. I'll grab you a drink."

Stepping into the room in a daze, I tried to push down the whine my Omega was urging me to release. *Not my Alphas. Not my Pack.* I had to get that into my thick skull damn fast.

I followed Rio through to the living room, the Omega scent getting stronger and stronger until right there, sitting beside Max, was a girl. She had no hair and was dressed in an oversized sweatshirt, with wide green doe eyes and a frown on her face.

My heart thumped in my chest with something like finality. *Ba... bump.* She was beautiful. *So* beautiful. In her eyes was a pain that I didn't even know how to verbalise.

And at the base of her throat was a giant, infected burn.

My eyes shifted to the men that moments ago I'd lusted after, respected, and something soured in my stomach. "You better start explaining why you have such an obviously traumatized Omega on your couch before I call the damn cops," I hissed at them, moving toward the Omega to... what? Protect her from the military-trained soldiers?

I knew in my heart I'd try.

The girl just looked up at me with eyes that were fearful. Fuck, she was so young. She couldn't have been more than nineteen or twenty. I sent out every wave of reassuring Omega pheromones I could conjure, watching her relax gently into Max's side.

As I eyed him, he raised his hands. "It's okay, August. None of this was us. Sit, please, and we can explain."

Rio sighed. "I can see how this would look... bad. This is Paloma. She was rescued from a human trafficking situation two days ago. She was sold to them by the cult she grew up in."

I was often praised by my coworkers for my poise and my professionalism. For being able to hear the most fucked-up things and keep a neutral, caring face. But right now, I felt my jaw unhinge, and I was worried it would hit the floor.

I looked at Rio. "I think I'll take that drink now."

EIGHT

PALOMA

The man in front of me was a male Omega. Before yesterday, I hadn't known male Omegas even existed until I met Strat, the male Omega in OJ's Pack. But here in front of me was the most beautiful man I'd ever seen, and he was an Omega.

Unlike OJ and Strat, the man in front of me didn't put me on edge, like I was in someone else's territory. No, this Omega felt like *mine,* which was insane, because I'd only just met him and he hadn't said a single word to me.

He had stepped up to protect me, though, and that made that little voice inside my head coo happily.

As he sat down on the coffee table opposite me, the Omega's eyes ran over my face like he could see into my soul. He would soon find I was split open and rotten at the core, like spoiled fruit. That's what Sister Aurelia had always said to me anyway. Broken and rotten.

He gave me a soft smile. "Hello, Paloma. I don't

know if these guys have told you, but my name is August." His expression was so honest and open and warm. Had anyone ever looked at me like that before?

"Hello." I wished my voice was stronger, not so beaten-down.

I saw Rio twitch, and August's eyes flicked toward him before coming back to me. "You have my word that I will leave anytime you want. We can talk about as much or as little as you want. I'll answer any questions you might have. Would you like a drink?"

I lifted the water bottle Max had given me earlier. "No, I'm okay."

Another warm smile that made my heart race. "That's great. Not to state the obvious, Paloma, but you have no hair. Is there anything medically relevant we should know to help you?"

I lifted my hand to rub over the stubble of my hair regrowth. He thought I was sick? "No. The Leaders believed that an Omega's hair was only for her Alpha mates, and was a source of temptation to others, so all unmated Omegas had to have their heads shaved and wear the lace."

"The lace?"

I chewed my lip. "Uh, a veil?"

"Ah, I see. Wearing a head covering is very popular in modern religions. Did you do it for religious reasons or just cultural ones?"

I didn't know how to answer that. Our religion *was* our culture. They were one and the same. "Uh, I guess, cultural ones. The Sisters and Brothers didn't have to wear them to honor Izuny. Just the Omegas. A kind of divine penance for our betrayal."

"Izuny? Was that your Prophet?" Something about August's light tone put me at ease, or maybe it was Max's big body pressed close to mine, keeping me safe.

So I shook my head. "No, Izuny is our god. The supreme Alpha. We worship him and live how he wishes."

"Were the Omegas worshiped too?"

This time, I laughed out loud, but it wasn't a joyous sound. "No. Uh, what's the opposite of worshiped?" I asked August, and he tilted his head as if pondering my question.

"Reviled would be the right word, I think."

That sounded correct. "Yes, that. Omegas were reviled. We were marked by the Betrayer goddess, Melize, the first Omega."

He was being very good at keeping his own thoughts to himself, but I could see the recoil in his expression. "That's quite unlike our society as a whole, but very interesting. What about Betas?"

I licked my dry lips. "Betas are the children of Basric, Izuny's brother. While not punished by Izuny for being led astray by Melize, Basric's children showed they were unwilling to put the good of their people above being led into temptation by Melize, so they could never become Leaders. They became Brothers and Sisters, keepers of the faith, and they worked to keep the Homestead going."

"The Homestead? That's where you lived?" Max asked, and I turned to look at him, his intense eyes boring into my own.

The scent of rich melted chocolate swept over me, and I knew it was August. It made me feel languid and chased away the anxiety that lived in my chest like a monster. "That's what we called it. It was a big community, with a fence around the perimeter to stop the bad things from coming in. But I'm beginning to think that maybe it was to keep us from getting out?"

Panic was crawling up my throat, and Max pulled me onto his lap again. I turned my cheek to the firm muscle. Strong. Safe. I could just stay here forever.

"We thought that we'd been through the apocalypse. That we were the last people left. I was born on the Homestead. I thought I'd die there too."

"What about your parents? Did they live there too?"

I shrugged. "We didn't have parents. All the children were raised by the households." I couldn't even be sure who my mother was, despite my guesses.

As if he sensed my discomfort, Doodles appeared. I'd left him in my nest an hour ago in his favorite position, which looked a lot like a dead cockroach. He launched himself at the couch, missed because he only had one back leg, and landed on the floorboards. He was quickly back up, though, panting and happy, as he scrambled onto the couch and pushed his way into the warm space between me and Max.

August looked down at the decidedly ugly dog. "And who is this?"

"Doodles," I said softly, looking down at the little dog with glaucoma and missing teeth. How could anything so ugly be so full of love?

Reaching out slowly so Doodles could sniff his hand, August scratched behind his ear, the knuckles of his hand incidentally touching my hip. I felt each brush like he was electrified. "He's kind of ugly-cute. He seems to adore you."

Rio chuckled. "Lance's new Omega is an animal rescuer. We've somehow adopted a dog and a psychotic bird since they became a Pack."

And an Omega. But no one said that bit out loud.

August raised an eyebrow at Rio, his scent swirling around me. "I didn't realize Lance had an Omega?"

Shrugging, Rio's eyes drifted from August to me and back again. "It's a new thing, but he's really happy. She's perfect for him."

I hadn't known Lance before last night, but the devoted way he looked at OJ had me agreeing that they were perfect together. A moment in their presence made it undeniable. Would anyone ever love me like that, or was I too damaged? Did I even want to be loved like that?

The instant yearning in my chest at the thought told me yes, I did.

Smiling softly at the thought of Lance getting his

happy ending, August turned his attention back to me. "Do you want to tell me how you ended up here? I'm sure you don't need me to vouch for these guys by now, but I can personally guarantee that you will be safe and protected here. However, if you'd rather some other kind of lodgings, there are refuges and help for abused Omegas."

Abused Omegas. Was that what I was? I didn't feel abused—at least I hadn't, until Leader Malakai so easily handed me over to Alphas I didn't know, throwing me into a world I didn't understand. Those Alphas hadn't really hurt me either, though I had no doubt that eventually I would have been.

I didn't realize I was shaking and whipping my head back and forth until Rio was beside Max, lifting me off his lap and placing me in his own arms. A low vibration emanated from his chest, making my body feel lax and calm. *Woah.*

"What are you doing?" I slurred, and when Rio stopped, I clawed at his chest to make him continue. "No, don't stop." I felt settled in a way I wasn't sure I'd ever felt.

It was August who answered me. "He's purring for you, Paloma. It's a way that Alphas can calm and aid in the physiological regulation of panicking Omegas. Your heart rate should be slowing. Your breathing should regulate. Do you feel that?" August's voice was working its own magic.

"Yes. I'm okay," I murmured softly, wondering how I

would ever drag myself away from this feeling. "I want to stay here with Max and Rio. They make me feel safe."

Rio's purr got louder, like he was happy. Like a cat.

"And Llewellyn?" August asked lightly, but his eyes had gone to Max and Rio, and their bodies had stiffened beneath mine.

The silence in the room was so loud that I could almost feel it against my skin. If I closed my eyes, I could still feel the weight of the other Alpha's eyes when he'd seen me this morning.

Rio felt tense beneath me, and I rubbed my face on his chest and neck. I didn't know why, except... it just felt *right*. I was rewarded by more vigorous rumbling in his chest.

August smiled a little. "Your Omega is almost all instinct. Trust her, and she won't lead you astray. What she's doing right now is scent marking Rio, which can settle Alphas in the same way purring settles Omegas." He looked at Max. "Paloma cannot live here if she hasn't met all the Alphas. You can't know if they'll have an adverse reaction to each other. Has Llewellyn even been in the presence of an Omega since..." He trailed off, and the guys shifted uncomfortably. "I didn't think so," August sighed.

"He wouldn't hurt her. Or any Omega," Rio argued, holding me tighter. August placed his hand on Rio's knee, and I looked at the connection between their bodies. I almost felt that creature inside me tilt its head, like it was trying to decide if it liked another Omega touching the Alpha holding her. It was mere seconds, but she decided. She liked the Omega in front of her.

I liked August too. I wanted him to hold me the way Rio was. Actually, maybe I'd like Rio and Max to hold us both.

I let out a small whine, which immediately had every set of eyes on me. Flushing pink, I shook the thoughts away.

Standing, August looked down the long hall. "Only one way to find out his reaction to an Omega." He strode down the hallway as Max shot off the couch and followed him.

"August, get back here," Rio snapped, but then he was placing me gently on the couch and heading after them.

Well. I wasn't about to be left behind, was I? Curiosity had always been my greatest weakness.

NINE

LLEWELLYN

Lieutenant Rio Barrie, United States Marine Corp. Lieutenant Rio Barrie, United States Marine Corp. Lieutenant Rio Barrie, United States Marine Corp.

Screaming. Always so much screaming. I could do it. I could do it. They promised me someone would be getting him soon. I only have to hold on a little longer.

A knock startled me out of my waking nightmare. Or my reality. Waking reality?

"Llew?"

Max. My Max.

I turned, giving him a smile that felt a little loose on my face, like it could slip right off. He smelled nice. He told me they'd brought home an Omega, like they were telling me they'd brought home a case of fireworks. Waiting for me to lose it. Always waiting for me to lose it.

"Max," I said softly, and watched his shoulders relax.

Poor Maxie, always the strong one. I wanted to hold him, but it made him sad. I could smell it, and it made the wild surge up.

"I've brought a visitor, Llew." Still so hesitant.

I lifted my nose. *Omega.* But not the one whose scent had been permeating the air for the last two days, whose bruised scent made my Alpha feel rage. And protectiveness. Feral.

Her pain made me feel raw. But luckily, that sour scent had disappeared as my Pack took care of her. I knew they would. My Maxie would lay down his life for them. And Rio...

Rio.

Shaking my head, I scented the air. No, this wasn't that Omega. This one smelled of decadent chocolate and sweetness. Deep and potent. Not the same Omega, but still delicious. My Alpha shook himself from the confines I kept him in, and I held on tight to my control.

I wouldn't hurt an Omega. I'd die first.

"Max..." I almost whined, but he knew.

"It'll be okay, Llew. I trust you, so trust yourself." Stepping aside, he ushered someone inside my room. The master suite had always been the biggest room, with a walk-in robe, its own bathroom, and large sliding doors onto a balcony. It made an excellent cell. I guess it was time for visitation. "This is August. He's a therapist down at the VA." Max cleared his throat. "He wanted to come and say hello."

There was something they weren't telling me, but I

didn't blame them. I didn't have a firm grip on reality most days. Today, though, I felt good. I turned, hoping I didn't look like a serial killer, but wouldn't bet on it. Not a lot of need to groom if you never left your room.

Heh. That rhymed.

A tall, slight man entered my room, his scent pouring in after him. It flooded all the nooks and crannies, and I knew it would linger for days after he left. My mouth watered. He had a shock of dark brown curls, and full lips. His skin was a soft gold, his jaw so sharp I might cut myself on the edges. His energy was like a Xanny straight to the veins, and I wondered if that was why he'd become a therapist.

He was completely confident as he walked toward me, his hand out in front. "Llewellyn, it's a pleasure to finally meet you. The guys speak highly of you."

I snorted. Maybe they spoke highly of the man I used to be. Now, I was a shadow.

Chains and rope. Burn. Burn. Burn.

Pushing the madness down, I reached out and gripped the Omega's hand, shaking it gently. I was so big. Big hands. Big body. Big madness.

"Call me Llew. Only my mother and the DMV call me Llewellyn."

August chuckled softly, a sound that was like a balm over my exposed wounds. "Llew it is." He looked around the room, and I wondered what he saw? The expensive furnishings? The light divots in the wall that were the remnants of gouges and holes made by fists?

Swallowing hard, I indicated the small table and chairs over by the windows. "Have a seat. We'll sit and visit like proper Southerners."

"You're a South Carolina native?"

I held out the remaining seat to Max. He was my Maxie. My Pack. He got everything he deserved, and he deserved the whole world. He was a stubborn brat, though, and when he shook his head, I insisted with my eyes. Not through the bond. Our bond was broken. Irreparable.

Sighing heavily and rolling his eyes, Max sat down opposite August. I saw the way my Beta's eyes took in the other man, like he was eating him up with his gaze before he ate him for dessert.

Interesting.

Finally, I looked back at the Omega to see he was watching our interaction with intensity. "We moved here from Wales when I was a kid and settled in Charleston. We moved up here, because Max was based out of Charlotte."

"I moved here for work too," August said, settling easily in his chair. So comfortable in a strange place in front of a feral Alpha. I knew what my aura was like. I knew that my Alpha pheromones were wild and felt like sandpaper on the skin of outsiders. But this man, this Omega, sat opposite me without a care in the world.

Maybe he was really an Alpha masquerading as an Omega, because he had some serious brass balls.

The silence stretched between us, and August

steepled his fingers. "I'm going to be straight with you, Llew. I'm kind of a test dummy to see how you react to Omegas, but you seem in control."

I snorted out a mirthless sound. "You got me on a good day, Omega. But I swear, no matter how... out of touch I get, the urge to protect is still overwhelming. I would never hurt you, or anyone who wasn't a direct threat to my Pack."

If someone threatened Max or Rio, I would put them in the ground and enjoy it. I didn't say that to the Omega in front of me, though.

"Might be a good time to introduce you to the Omega who will be living in your house then?" August asked lightly, and I had no doubt that it was entirely up to me. My Alpha surged to the surface, desperate to see with his own eyes that the Omega with the bruised scent was really okay. However, getting crazy Alpha eyes wasn't going to convince anyone I was safe.

I looked at Max, then at the door where I knew Rio was standing. My Rio. "I feel good," I told him. Them. "It'll be fine."

Rio spent a few more seconds probing at my Alpha with his own, and I missed the bond. Missed the time when he would've known in an instant how I was feeling, and I'd have known how he was too. It was in the past, but I couldn't help but mourn the connection.

Finally, Rio turned and looked over his shoulder. Saying something softly, he stepped to the side, and the most beautiful creature I'd ever seen appeared in the doorway. She felt too big to be in such a tiny body, her features small and cute and elfin, and every protective instinct I had surged to the surface.

Looking at me with big eyes, she lifted her face to the air, like she was scenting me. She sucked in a deep breath, her nose screwed up, and her eyes went wild. I watched the pupils blow out, and honestly, I couldn't have stopped what happened next even if I knew it was coming.

No one could have.

The Omega raced around Rio, hurdling the low couch and slamming into my body with the force of a train. Well, maybe the force of a toy train.

"*Mine!*" she hissed, and then she struck. Her teeth were in my throat, bonding me. Claiming me. The intention flowed down the connection that was created between us immediately, and I was frozen in fear.

"Fuck!" someone swore, but when hands tried to pry her off me, I growled. The Alpha surged to the surface, any chance of holding him back gone the minute her teeth broke the skin of my throat. I gripped the back of her skull, the stubble of her hair both rough and soft against my palm. Beautiful perfection.

My chainsaw purr echoed around the room, and she finally dislodged her teeth from my neck. She lapped at it, and I could almost feel the moment her Omega ceded control back to the more human side.

She wiggled, and I knew I should let her go, but my arms were locked. I wanted to bite her back. It took everything in me to not, and perhaps it was Rio's hands on my head that prevented me from lunging.

Max's eyes were wild. "Uh…" He looked between me and Rio, like he was waiting for one of his Alphas to take control of this shitshow. But I could only feel this soft little Omega in my arms, her body bowing toward me.

I realized she was crying. *Fuck.* Was I hurting her?

I let her go, but she wrapped her arms around my neck, her nose buried in my throat just above her mark. I looked over at Rio, at the new Omega, August. What was happening?

August came over. "Paloma? Sweet girl, are you okay? You have to let go of Llew."

She shook her head against my throat. "So much pain."

Was she hurt? *Oh shit.* Had I squeezed too hard? Was my blood toxic?

"Are you injured?" August asked softly.

She lifted her face, and I could feel the tears dropping from her cheeks onto my skin. "Not me. Him. Llew. So much pain." Then she sobbed into my neck, like her heart was breaking. Breaking for me.

Her tears healed me and then broke me again, right along with her. Rio got into my face, and I growled softly. I didn't like the way he was looking at me right now. He sucked in a deep, calming breath. "You have to shut off the bond." He sounded as panicked as I felt at the sound of her tears.

It was Max who pushed between us. "He can't.

Unless he bonds her back, the bond is pouring one way, and there's no shut-off valve."

Rio stumbled back. "Fuck."

Yeah. Either I bonded the Omega back—the obviously traumatized, helpless Omega—and be the biggest piece of shit ever, or I kept the bond open for her to absorb all my demons.

"Fuck," I echoed.

TEN
PALOMA

I didn't need to be an expert at reading people to know that I'd fucked up. I couldn't have helped it if I'd tried. That Omega, that little beast who lived inside me, saw that big Alpha, sensed his pain, and it was like I no longer had control of my limbs or my thoughts. She wanted, and she took.

His pain was like a burn beneath my skin, his trauma beating against my brain over and over. *Pain. Fear. Anger. Pain. Fear. Anger.* Then briefly, he'd look at me, and it would be adoration. *Wonder. Joy.* Then he'd look at the guys again, and it would be back to pain.

I didn't understand what was happening right now, though I knew I'd bonded him. They'd said as much. I'd tied us together for life without his permission, and guilt ate at my gut.

Picking at the skin of my forearms, I listened as they discussed what had to happen. I'd bonded him, and he needed to bond me back to turn off the battering waves of his emotions.

Fear. Pain. Anger.

I whined and crawled back into his lap. I felt so guilty. Leader Malakai had been right; I was a curse on society. I was a selfish, *selfish* child who took what she wanted, without thought of anyone else.

Llew didn't kick me off, didn't throw me away like trash, didn't scowl at me in disgust. No, this Alpha that I'd just attacked and trapped, wrapped me back up in his arms and walked me to the bed in his room, curling his huge body around mine and purring softly.

He growled when Max stepped forward to take me back. "She's fine," Llew grumbled, and as I snuggled further into the cocoon of his warmth, I had to agree. I was fine. Perfect.

Wonder. Joy. Fear. Pain. Anger.

"How do we break the bond?" Rio asked softly, and my Omega whined and cried harder.

I didn't want to break the bond. He was mine. *Mine.*

"She claimed him before she bit him. We have to consider that perhaps they're... that they might be..." Rio trailed off.

I just wanted to scream, *What?! We're what?*

As if he could see the question on my face, August squatted down in front of me. "Fated mates. There's an idea that they once existed, but it doesn't happen much anymore. However, given that Llew's Alpha is so close to the surface, and your Omega has been constrained for so long, perhaps it was a perfect storm."

My Omega hummed at that, or maybe it was Llew's purr. It was nice—different to Rio's, rougher and maybe not as soothing, but still, it made me feel secure. Safe. Everything was okay.

"He should bond me back." My voice sounded more sure than I felt.

They all looked at me like I was an alien. "I don't think you're in a position, within yourself, to know what that would mean. Not just for now, but forever. There's no undoing a completed bond, Paloma." August's voice was soft and sure, not judging, just informing.

I frowned. "Bonding him was the first thing I ever did for myself." Even if I hadn't understood why at the time, I still didn't regret it. "I might be oblivious to the world around me, but my instincts are just fine. I know what I feel from him, and it feels right." I didn't mention the negative emotions. Rolling over, I looked at Llew. "Unless... you want to break the bond?" I hated how fragile my voice sounded at that moment.

His eyes ran across my face. They were large and hazel, like they hadn't been able to decide on a color and settled on both, and I could see his brain turning over. More than that, I could feel it through the bond in my chest. His yearning to keep the bond. The guilt that I'd be saddled with him. The selfish urge to bond me back. The feeling of responsibility was like a heavy weight on his shoulders.

I didn't understand anything about the world, but I understood this. I understood *him.*

Hesitantly, he shook his head. "I don't want to break the bond. I don't think the Alpha would allow me to, even if I could."

Something relaxed in my chest. He wanted me back. In a move that was almost entirely instinctual, I tilted my head to the side, exposing my throat to the Alpha behind me.

Rio stepped forward, and I held out an arm to stop him. I wanted this.

I felt a bearded cheek scrape along my skin, up over the nape of my neck. He inhaled deeply, and it made something deep in my gut clench with need. Lips brushed my skin, and I held so still, waiting.

"Are you sure about this, Paloma?" His voice was barely a whisper against my ear, but my lips curled. I was sure. Surer about this than anything since I'd been dragged away from the only home I'd known.

"Yes. I'm sure."

"This will hurt a little. I'm sorry." Then he bit me. And he wasn't wrong; it did hurt. More than a little, it hurt a *lot,* making me scream.

Everyone lurched toward me, but then my scream turned into a moan as the bond settled between us. The bad emotions were gone in an instant. No more fear. No more pain. No more anger. There was only joy and pleasure.

I moaned, and the energy in the room changed

dramatically. August let out a small sound between his teeth that could have been a whine. Then he looked at my big beast of an Alpha and stuck a finger in his face.

"You do nothing without her express, informed permission. I want you to talk through every little decision, until she's so sick of talking about it she takes matters into her own hands. She does *nothing* she could regret. Otherwise, I'll make you share her regret every single day of the rest of your life."

He didn't say how he'd achieve that as an Omega, but he was so vehement, I didn't doubt him for a second. Neither did Llew, I guess, because he rumbled his agreement.

Something like completeness washed over me, and for the first time in days, weeks, maybe even years, I fell into the deep, contented sleep of someone who knew that they would be safe forever.

I woke in the living room, but still pressed tightly to Llew's chest. "You're awake," he said softly, the warmth of his breath clouding over the top of my head. My cheek was directly over his heart, its steady rhythm soothing in a way I didn't understand yet.

A lot had happened in a short amount of time, and it was all catching up to me. I just wanted to bury myself in Llew and the security that he blanketed me with, wishing that the first twenty years of my life had been just a bad dream.

There was a light waft of a cocoa scent, and I looked around for August. He was sitting across from us, and the clock on the wall told me it was late, nearly midnight. Why was he still here?

"Hello, Omega. Are you feeling okay? Any ill effects of your... bonding?" I wasn't sure why he hesitated over the word.

I wanted to feel bad about it. Honestly, I wasn't sure if I could have controlled the impulse. It was a poor excuse, however. I'd tied the man beneath me to me for life.

I looked up at Llew, whose eyes were as warm and reassuring as his presence. I smiled back at him and felt the pulse of contentment down the bond between us. There were more emotions there, but they felt like they were hidden beneath a thick blanket, only giving me the good and vague awareness of the bad.

"No. I feel... right? Like, inside myself, I feel almost happy?"

Llew rumbled, holding me closer. "Almost is not good enough. I know this isn't what you planned for your life, but I promise I will make you so happy, you won't have any regrets." I could feel his conviction down the bond.

"Considering that my future held either becoming a wife to Leader Malakai, or being sent to be some kind of Omega slave to unknown Alphas, this might be exactly the life I wanted."

As his body stiffened beneath mine, a low growl

pulsed from Llew, a subtle shift in his scent making him smell wild. Scary. Angry and sad, and no longer all the warm feelings that I was previously basking in.

A whine passed my lips, and I crawled up his body until we were cheek to cheek, before wrapping my body around his. I wanted to chase that scent away from him, wanted to bare my teeth at the thing that was causing him to feel this way. But I couldn't find a threat.

I had ceded control to the Omega again, and August's words about Omegas soothing their Alphas by scent marking played back through my head. I felt lost, because I instinctively knew how to help, but it made me feel out of control of the only thing that was mine. My body.

Llew let out a deep breath. "Apologies, my Omega. I'm okay now."

His words were a crooning promise, and the way he said *my Omega* made a thrill pulse through me. I was his. He was mine. I'd chosen this man in front of me—kind of.

"I just don't like the idea that there's someone out there who wanted to hurt you. Who wanted you to be anything but the very center of their world." He looked over my head at the other men in the room. "Does anyone want to fill me in?" His voice dropped low. "I'm in control, Rio. I swear. Having her is like a gift I didn't expect, or even deserve. I'll protect her with my life." He rubbed his rough beard on my own cheek, and I hummed a happy noise.

How could this be anything but right?

Eleven
Rio

What a shitshow. Lance was going to murder me, but honestly, I didn't even care. Because Llew was back, right there in front of me, a clarity in his eyes that I hadn't seen since the day I'd deployed overseas.

There was still darkness in their depths, an edge of mania that sat just below the surface, but for the first time, this man who stared down at the Omega in his lap with empathy and compassion was the same one I'd created a Pack with over a decade ago. Whatever bonding with an Omega had done, it had healed something inside him.

And for that alone, I would lay down my life for Paloma.

I explained about Lance, about the mission we'd carried out to rescue a bunch of animals and instead found an Omega. About Paloma's cult. I kept waiting for

Llew to lose it, for his Alpha to take over and start destroying things in a rage he couldn't contain, and my body stayed prepared to grab Paloma and protect her.

The feral rage never came. Oh, Llew was angry all right, but it was the anger of a man in control. The anger of any reasonable human being, who knew that the woman in his arms had been abused for so long and had come terrifyingly close to ending up trafficked for sex, or god knows what. That only a random Omega with a love of animals had led to us saving the one in front of us.

Finally, silence fell across the room as we all tried to make sense of everything that had happened. It was well past midnight, and Paloma had fallen asleep once more. I wanted to take her from Llew, not because I was worried, but because I wanted to feel her soft body draping over my own.

Shaking the thought from my head, I looked at the other Omega in the room. August yawned, his soft scent swirling around us. Max had always laughed that I had a crush on the VA therapist, and he was probably right. But more than that, I respected August. He was good at his job, and I knew that I had many VA buddies this side of the Pearly Gates *because* he was so good. He was both strong and soft at the same time, and incredibly smart. What was not desirable about that?

It could never go any further, however. August was a professional, and now...

I looked at Paloma. Now, our Pack already had an Omega, and it was common knowledge that Omegas were territorial at best. They couldn't share a Pack, their space, with other Omegas. At least, not normally—there were a few exceptions, like Lance's Pack. Paloma had known barely nothing about her Omega, but her instincts wouldn't let her stay in the same house as Lance's Omegas.

Regret swelled in my chest, warring with the happiness that we had Paloma. She was Llew's fated mate. That was an almost unheard-of anomaly these days. We should be content.

I stood and stretched. "I'll drive you home, August."

He waved a hand. "I can drive myself home, Rio." I raised a single eyebrow, and he sighed. "You aren't going to let it go, are you?"

I mean, he was an unbonded Omega who lived on the bad side of town, and it was the middle of the night. "Not unless you want to stay here tonight?"

August's eyes flicked to Paloma and Llew, then back to me. "I shouldn't. I have to be at work for an early appointment tomorrow." Standing, he stretched, and a sliver of his golden stomach peeked out. Lust hit me in the chest, but I pushed it down. It was inappropriate, at the very least.

Pulling my boots on, I waited by the door as August gave Max a quick hug, then shook Llew's hand once more. Paloma was sound asleep, and he just gazed down at her sleeping face, her bottom lip caught softly between her teeth. He didn't wake her, though.

Finally, we stepped out the front door, and I walked

with him down the front steps to the driveway. His car had seen better days. Hell, it had probably seen better decades.

August chuckled as he stood beside it. "If you could see your face right now." He held up the keys. "Do you want to drive, or are you good with being the passenger princess?"

I growled at him, making him laugh harder. I grabbed the keys off him and held open his door. "One of us has driven in a warzone, Omega. I'll drive; you be the passenger princess."

He gave me a cocky smirk, and I felt like I'd just done exactly what he wanted me to, but I didn't have it in me to care. He folded himself easily into the car, looking up at me with a smile that promised mischief. "Yeah, but one of us has driven this shitbox all the way to California, though I'll let you drive if it makes you feel better." He was teasing me, but I was still relieved. Being in control of things helped keep my demons at bay, and August was an expert on my demons. I'd definitely played right into his hand.

The car took two turnovers to fire, and I slid my eyes to August. He just shrugged. "This is going to blow your mind, but the VA doesn't have a lot of money to pay its therapists. This old girl still gets me where I need to go."

Barely, I thought, but didn't say anything else as I pulled away from the house. We were quiet for a moment until I got on the freeway, and I wasn't happy with how shaky this hunk of metal felt as soon as you went over fifty miles per hour.

Finally, I cleared my throat. "I can't thank you enough for coming out today. I know it kind of went sideways there, but we're kind of out of our element with Paloma. There's so much trauma there that I feel like I'm walking along a goat track with landmines either side. We don't want to inadvertently cause her more damage."

August nodded softly. "Anytime. I mean it. I would like to come and visit her more often, perhaps help her get acclimatized to the world she now lives in." He let out a sigh, the sound loud enough to be heard over the loud whistle of his car engine.

How did this thing even run? I wondered if he'd let me take it to my mechanic to get it looked at.

He continued. "Can you imagine living life thinking that the rest of civilization had perished in an apocalypse, only to discover it wasn't true?"

I shook my head, because the very idea made me both disbelieving and full of rage. "If I ever get my hands on her supposed 'Leader,' I'm going to tear his head from his body. He abused her. Did you see that brand? That is the *least* of the physical markings on her body, let alone the emotional scars. He kept them locked away, convinced her she was worthless."

For a moment, I wondered if I'd gone too far in my vehemence. August just stared out the windscreen, lost in his own thoughts. Eventually, he turned back to me. "Let me know if you need an alibi. I have no sympathy for people who abuse Omegas."

I'd forgotten that August worked with people who'd seen the worst of humanity from both sides of the political lines. Scary Alphas didn't faze him. In another world, he would have been a great addition to the Pack.

Smirking, I watched the road. "Good to know."

August opened and closed his mouth a few times, like he was trying to find the words for what he wanted to say next, which was odd for the normally self-assured therapist. "You should also know that I think she's only a few weeks from her heat. And if I had to guess, I'd say she's been on heat suppressants for a while. She should have had her first heat years ago, but she seems completely unaware of anything to do with her Omega nature. She's been here for a few days now, and before that, in whatever hellhole you found her in, so I would bet my medical license that she didn't even know what she was taking before. She wouldn't even think to ask for them now."

I clenched my back teeth. "Should I find her a supply elsewhere?" Suppressants weren't exactly legal; Paloma wouldn't be able to walk into a doctor's clinic and request them. But I could find someone, if August thought that was what was best for her. I needed another Omega's opinion on this, because I didn't know shit about Omega biology and the effects of delaying a heat.

"You should ask her, of course," August said simply.

I pulled at the collar of my shirt at just the idea of

that conversation. Was it hot in here? "Maybe you should have the birds and the bees talk with Paloma. It would be better coming from you." Or maybe even Otillie-James. Lance would bring her around if I asked.

"Alpha soldiers never cease to amuse me. You just told me you drove a vehicle through a warzone, but the idea of talking to an Omega about her heat sends you into a tailspin?" He chuckled softly, a sound that soothed my frayed nerves. "She's unaware of the world, Rio, but she isn't stupid. Explain it to her in layman's terms; she might surprise you." I opened my mouth to argue again, and he raised a hand. "But if you think she'd be more receptive to hearing the facts from another Omega, I'm happy to address it with her."

Relief coursed through me. Not that I didn't think I —well, probably Max—could've had that conversation with Paloma, but we all had a vested interest in how her heat would progress. August was an impartial expert on the matter.

We were silent again, both lost in our own thoughts, until he directed me through the scummy part of town to his apartment. It stood tall and dark beneath a broken streetlight, and I felt my molars grinding. "This is where you live?"

August shrugged as he pointed to a designated carpark out the back of the apartment block. "Yep."

"Is it safe?" I was on edge, the shadows in the parking lot making me feel jumpy. "Stay." I nearly barked, just pulling back from commanding him. Fuck, that was bad, but I hated that he was about to walk across an area with bad lighting and too many hiding places. I walked to his car door, watching the shadows for threats. Opening it slowly, I looked at his tense face and hung my head. "Sorry. I didn't mean to compel you to stay. Old habits."

August stared up at me, his eyes seeing far too much. Finally, he gave me a short nod and stood. "I understand. But if you try to bark at me, I'll stab you in the kidney."

A laugh burst out of me, ricocheting around the empty area and bouncing off the darkened buildings. "Fair. Let me walk you to your door. Please?"

Shaking his head softly, he grabbed his briefcase from the footwell and followed me to the security door. He scanned a keycard, the door popping open. "I'm really quite safe from here," he told me softly. "The area is sketchy, but the other tenants in this building are good people."

I chewed my lip, trying to work out how I could insist on seeing him to his door without sounding like a creep.

He shook his head. "But please, walk me to my door."

I gave him a guilty, lopsided grin as he muttered about Alphas, and followed him up the stairs. There was an elevator, but it had a giant *Out of Order* sign on it. Given how it was curling at the edges, the sign had been there a while. There was also graffiti throughout the stairwell, and despite August's reassuring words, I didn't like that he lived here alone. At least, I thought he was alone.

"Do you have a Pack, August? I just realized I don't know very much about you. Is someone going to want to break my nose for walking you up?"

If he said yes, maybe I'd break that Alpha's nose first for not taking proper care of his Omega. Who let their Omega walk into some other Pack's home without accompanying them? And who let their Omega walk through a dark parking lot alone, or didn't check on them once if they were late home?

We went up another flight of steps, and I tried not to stare at his ass. "Nope, no Pack," he told me. "I'm committed to my work, and it doesn't leave a lot of time for other things."

Things like love and Packs.

"Married to the job. Apparently, it's not just limited to us grunts," I said lightly.

One more flight of stairs, then August scanned his way through another security door, moving quickly down the hall. Okay, so the security was all right, but it was still far too easy for someone to follow him through these slow-closing doors. Too easy for someone to take him in the stairwell and hurt him. I hated it.

He stopped outside a plain door with the number thirty-seven on it. "Well, this is me. Thank you for seeing me home."

"It's the least we could do. Thank you for having our backs tonight. We owe you one."

August shook his head. "You don't owe me anything. I'll see you soon, Rio." Then he was in his apartment, the door closed softly behind him, while I stood there and stared at it like an idiot.

Why did it feel like I should have kissed him?

Shaking my head, I left back down the stairs and out into the darkness. I'd walk a bit before I got a rideshare home. I needed to clear my head, obviously, and if I got lucky and someone tried to jump me, maybe I could get rid of a bit of pent-up energy too.

TWELVE
PALOMA

I had an anchor in the world, and my attachment to an almost perfect stranger might've been cause for concern, but it just felt right. Max had insisted that I sleep in my own room, that I needed time and space to process what had happened today, but he didn't know what it had been like to be floating through this alone, and now have this barrier of safety surrounding me.

I felt *free*. I felt like I could explore myself. It helped that I had a direct line to Llew's feelings. Sure, it wasn't all sunshine inside his head, but when he looked at me, the joy he felt took my breath away.

Despite all that, I still missed my home. I missed my friends, and the Brothers and Sisters who'd raised me. I missed the barn cat. It might have been all lies, but it was the only life I'd ever known.

All these jumbled thoughts swirling around in my brain was why I found myself creeping into the master suite as the sun just touched the horizon. I hadn't slept, and my body was so tired that it was almost buzzing. I needed... Well, I guess I needed my Alpha.

The room smelled like Llew, like something wild and masculine. Earthy, yet somehow sweet. Llew was asleep, shifting restlessly in the bed. I hadn't had time to look around his space yesterday, and I could see pictures of their Pack on the walls. Rio, Max, and Llew were in various poses, back when they were much younger. They must have grown up together, given that there was a picture of Rio with more than a little acne, his arm around Max. Llew was huge, even as a kid, and his grin was wide and carefree.

Who were these boys, and how had they become the damaged men who haunted this house now?

Creeping further into the room, I noted that the bathroom light was on, and the curtains were drawn tightly shut.

"No," Llew whimpered, and my startled heart jumped in my chest. Looking at the bed, I knew immediately he was having a nightmare. His brow was sweaty, his eyes scrunched tight. The burned smell of his normal ocean scent told me it was bad.

I poked at the new bond in my chest where all Llew's feelings sat, and I could feel his terror. I whined softly, climbing onto the bed, and I tried to gently push back his wild hair from his sticky forehead.

Suddenly, I was flipped onto my back, a hand around my throat. I went completely still, the panic in

Llew's eyes not directed at me, but some ghost. I couldn't see the threats he saw, even as panic lit up my own body and I clutched at the wrist around my throat. He was so big, so strong. He wasn't pressing too hard, but with enough force that my breathing was labored.

"Llew, wake up!" I squeaked, my Omega pheromones billowing around us. Llew's hand flexed and let go, but he still didn't wake. Instead, he dropped heavily onto my chest and buried his face into my neck. He sucked in deep breaths, a rumbling groan thrumming through his chest.

Something about the noise made my own body go lax, moving from terror to something else so fast, it made my head spin. When his hand slipped from my throat to wrap around the back of my head, his hips pushed forward, and I realized my thighs were around his waist and his cock was hard at their apex.

I'd touched myself before, even though it was frowned upon by the community, and if any of the Sisters had found out, I would have gotten a beating. Pleasure was not for Omegas on the Homestead. It was for married Alphas and procreating Brothers and Sisters. Never for Omegas.

But those fumbling touches had nothing on the feeling of Llew's huge body between my thighs, or the way he ground down into me. The pleasure that coursed through my body made me understand how Melize could have tempted Bazric into falling. I knew I should wake Llew up, but instead, I took my pleasure from his sleeping form.

It was wrong.

But it felt so good.

His heavy weight on my chest was making it hard to breathe, though, which made it easier to do the right thing.

I poked him in the eyeball.

His eyes snapped open, and I could see the dawning horror as he realized where he was and what he was doing. "Omega! I'm so—" He shifted off me. "What are you *doing* in here? Are you okay?"

I decided not to tell him about the fact that he'd almost choked me. I didn't think any good could come from that, and really, it was my fault for sneaking into his room like a creep. So I let him run to the other side of the bed. "I couldn't sleep. I thought I might sleep better with you."

His face softened, and he moved closer. But he still didn't touch me. The feelings coming down the bond were fear, and some kind of fondness. "Sweet Omega. I'm always here for anything you need, but it's not safe when I'm asleep. I don't have complete control. I'm..."— he paused, as if saying the next words hurt—"damaged. I could be dangerous to you."

Yeah, I'd found that one out the hard way. Instead of saying those words, I reached across the space between us. "Is it bad that I liked it?"

Llew groaned, burying his face in his hands and

breathing deeply. "Not bad at all, Sweet Thing. Anything that makes you feel good, that brings you happiness, can't be bad. Tell me what you need, and I'll provide it for you. On my honor as your Alpha." He hesitated. "But I'm not sure you're ready for what you're actually asking for."

"I'm well past the age of maturity." I wanted to pout. My body felt wired, like it was desperate for something that was sitting just out of reach. "I know what I want. I want to feel good. I want *you* to make me feel good." I wasn't sure where my boldness was coming from right now; I would have never made these demands of an Alpha before. Something about the feel of Llew between my thighs sparked this urge in my body that made me desperate. "Please, Alpha."

He shuddered, shifting closer. "Are you sure, Paloma? This is all very new, and I don't want you to rush into anything you'd regret." I nodded furiously, and I could see his jaw work. "Sweet Thing, you make it hard for an Alpha to keep his head. How about this? *I'm* not ready for us to take this all the way, not ready to slide inside that delicious body and pull you down onto my knot—" He let out a choked noise. "But I can make you feel good, and help you find release. What do you think?"

I launched myself at his body, done with this distance between us. "Yes, Alpha. *Please.*"

His huge hands caught me easily, and he pulled me tightly to his body, his hands remaining gentle. "Have you ever done anything like this before? The guys told me that your old home was pretty, uh, strict."

I shook my head, hoping that I wasn't too inexperienced for him. I didn't want him to change his mind now, especially not when my body was humming at the very idea of what he was offering. "No, but I'm a quick learner."

He laughed and rolled onto his back, dragging me up until I was chest to chest with him. "I bet you are. First, if it's okay with you, I'm going to kiss you."

I sucked in a deep, shuddering breath and held it. I held it even as his lips came towards mine. Held it as they brushed softly against my own. Let my lungs burn as his tongue dipped out and ran along the fullness of my bottom lip.

"Breathe, Paloma," he whispered against me, and the breath whooshed out of me loudly.

"That was really nice. Everything I'd imagined," I whispered, and he looked at me seriously.

"Was that your first kiss?" His eyes were burning with intensity, and my stomach felt like it was filled with butterflies. I nodded, making him groan. "I'm the luckiest bastard on the whole planet. But I can do better than nice."

Shifting his head to the side, he plundered my mouth, his tongue licking against the seam of my lips until I opened for him. I did what felt natural, even if it was kind of awkward. Soon enough, I was too lost in his lips, in the soft noises he made, the scratch of his beard, the roaming of his palms to worry about the fact that I was awkward and that this probably felt terrible for him. Like there was too much saliva. Or my tongue wasn't doing what it was supposed to. I mean, what was a tongue even meant to do?

I was selfish, because I didn't care. I took and took and took from him until I was moaning softly into his mouth. He had somehow removed my underwear, and I only had one of Rio's oversized shirts on. His fingers skimmed between my legs, and he sucked in my oxygen along with my tongue.

He moved his head away, breathing deeply. "Baby, you're going to undo me, especially the way you're grinding on my stomach." I realized I was riding his abs, and my cheeks flushed. "I love it, Omega. But now I'm going to want you to do that to my face."

I blinked down at him. "Your face?"

"My face. I'll use my tongue to make you feel so good that you'll be screaming my name." He kissed me again, his tongue spearing between my lips like he was showing me what he was about to do to my... female parts.

I looked at my thighs spread around his torso. "Will you be able to breathe?"

He grinned, his straight white teeth flashing in the morning sun. "Not if I'm doing it properly." He gripped my thighs and pulled me up his chest, and even that little bit of friction had me letting out a mewling sound. "Don't worry, Sweet Thing. I'm going to enjoy every millisecond of this. Hold onto the headboard if you need to, and if you need to stop, just say the word, Paloma. This goes at your pace."

Lifting me easily, he placed me on his face, and my eyes widened. His face was in the most private part of my body, and the idea almost made me recoil. Maybe I should tell him to stop? But then he leaned up and sucked something, and I felt like my body had been electrocuted.

"Oh my goddess," I breathed as he eased off, but not for long. Soon, his tongue was sliding inside me, the sensation wholly foreign. He held me to his mouth, and for lack of a better term, fucked me with it. He moved me until his nose was hitting the sensitive little bud at the top of my folds. Something was *just* there. Something big, something momentous, something that would change my life if I could just grab it.

Then I gripped the headboard as he sucked me hard, and that feeling was like falling into a vat of pure bliss. My whole body shuddered and convulsed, and the sound I made didn't even appear to be human.

"Holy freaking heck," I panted, my body feeling heavy and full.

Then I realized I was still on Llew's face, probably suffocating him. I scrambled back until I was sitting back on his chest. He was grinning, his face shiny with my juices.

I blinked at him, wide-eyed. "That was..." My voice cracked, and he let out a deep, rumbling laugh filled with happiness.

"Yes, it was, Omega. You taste like paradise. I'd ask if you enjoyed it, but I can feel your release coating my face."

My cheeks flushed. "I'm sorry."

He pulled my face to his. "I'm not. In fact, I'd like to do that again, whenever you're ready."

"Now?" I said with a soft voice. I was addicted. I felt real pleasure, and I wanted to chase that feeling over and over again. "Or do you need to rest?"

He purred low and flipped me onto my back. "What my Omega wants, she gets," he growled, then moved down my body, shifting up my shirt so he could suck one nipple, then the other. When he moved further down my body and hooked my legs over his shoulders, he stared up at me, his eyes sparkling with pure delight.

I would never forget that sight, not for as long as I lived.

THIRTEEN
MAX

I was rock hard. My morning wood was more like a concrete pillar at this point, especially when I woke to the sweet sound of an Omega coming. And coming. And coming again.

At the first moans, I'd been up and moving before I was fully even awake, getting all the way to Llew's door in a panic before my brain registered they weren't sounds of pain, but of pleasure. And a lot of it, judging by the sounds.

I stood there for a long time, well into her second orgasm, to be sure that Llew had a hold on his Alpha. On his madness. The way he was talking her through it told me that he was not only in full possession of his faculties, but he might have actually been in heaven.

"That's it, Omega. Come for me again. Give me one more—you taste so good..." he breathed, and I bit my knuckles to hold back a moan. I needed to move away. I was an uninvited participant in this.

I headed straight to the shower, glad that Rio's room was on the other side of the house, so he'd be oblivious to what was going on in Llew's room. Turning the water to frigid, I jerked off to the pretty Omega, who I had no business desiring the way I did, especially after everything she'd been through. I tried not to think about her big doe eyes or the way her lips pillowed when she frowned. I didn't imagine her whispering my name as she came, or how she'd taste, or having her between me and the men I loved more than my own life.

My jizz created an impressionist painting on the shower tiles. "I'll call it 'Blue Balls,'" I muttered before rinsing it with the showerhead. I'd go make breakfast, make sure my Pack was fed. Because she was Pack now. The bond between me, Llew, and Rio was broken, but we'd chosen each other long ago, and I wouldn't abandon them now.

I made quick work of cooking Rio's favorite breakfast—because I was fairly sure Llew was already eating his favorite breakfast, if what I'd heard was correct—dicing up the vegetables I'd need for a shakshuka. I didn't make it too spicy, because I didn't know what Paloma's heat tolerance was, but found myself excited to introduce her to the world, including its food.

I put some rolls in the oven too, then pulled out my phone to check my emails. I'd put out some feelers for the cult that had sold Paloma while Rio had been driving

August home last night, both through official channels and... less official channels. I'd put in as much information as I could without outing that we had her, in case someone wanted their "merchandise" back. It might've stopped with Anthony Smalls, the guy who'd been selling rescue animals for baiting and testing, but you could never know how deep it ran, and I wouldn't put Paloma in harm's way.

There was a message from a hacker named simply J3wel, and I raised an eyebrow in surprise. She was part of a larger group that was all about global social justice, but she normally stayed out of the small stuff. A small-time cult wasn't usually her thing.

On it.

That two-word response made me smile, because she was good. Well, I assumed she was a she, but you never knew on the dark web. It was the great equalizer. But if J3wel was on it, then I'd have answers. She was a much better hacker than I could ever be.

Nothing had turned up from my official databases, but that didn't surprise me. They weren't a terrorist cell, so they wouldn't come up there unless they were considered extremists. From what I could tell from Paloma's descriptions, they were just regular Alpha dirtbags. They might still be in an FBI database somewhere—at least, I hoped so. I'd called in a few favors, so hopefully someone could come up with something soon.

"Want a little rub and tickle, good boy?" Rufio crooned from the other room, and I went to let him out of his cage. He'd been locked away for a day, and that usually made him kinda mean. I'd let him out and put him back when Paloma woke.

"You're a bit of a pervert, Rufio—you know that?"

"RUFIOOOOO," he screamed and flew around the room, stretching out his wings. Doodles lay on his bed in the corner, his three legs in the air, and I walked over to poke at him. He kind of looked dead, but he looked that way even as he walked around.

I nudged him, and nothing happened. I nudged him again, and his body was completely lax. *Oh fuck.* I poked him harder, and his body just rolled with the movement. "Hey there, bud. Wake up now. Doodles!" I picked up his floppy body, and it just hung there.

Oh crap, he was dead already. More than one Omega was going to murder me if this ancient, decrepit dog was deceased. Otillie-James would be devastated, and Paloma... Paloma was using this dog as a security blanket, and he was dead.

I looked down at him. Where the fuck did I find a replacement zombie dog before breakfast? Laying him gently back down, I stepped away, and the fucking thing yawned and blinked slowly.

Relief washed over me. "You little asshole, I thought you were dead. Jesus," I breathed, scratching him behind the ears.

"Fucking cocksucker," Rufio added, and I had to agree.

"That was a dick move, Doodles." I grabbed a

handful of veggies from the container in the fridge for the parrot and a cup of kibble for the zombie dog.

I swear, he'd just shaved a year off my life. The idea of causing Paloma any more heartache soured my gut.

Rio was in the kitchen when I emerged, and he was looking down the hall at Llew's room. It was silent now, thank god, but the scent of satisfied Omega permeated the hall like someone had sprayed it with Fuckbreze.

His eyes were filled with heat, but he turned away and pulled a bottle of juice from the fridge, downing half of it in one go, as if it could cool his blood. *Good luck, buddy.* I was hard again already.

"What the fuck happened down there?" he groaned, standing in front of me at the breakfast bar, his eyes constantly drifting to the hall.

I gave him a shit-eating grin. "Well, when an Alpha bonds an Omega, sometimes they fu—"

"I know *that,*" he grumbled. "I know that he wouldn't hurt her, but..."

I nodded. The Alpha we'd known, who'd been the head of our Pack, would never have hurt a woman—Alpha, Beta, Omega, or Unshown. But that man had been broken by a war he never even signed up to, and we were all still learning who he was now.

"When I went to... check, he was talking her through every step, and she was enthusiastically onboard. She might be naive about the world, but she seems to know what she wants." And from the sound of it, what she'd wanted was for Llew to feast on her for breakfast.

Rio nodded solemnly. "August thinks she'll go into heat soon."

My whole body locked up. My horny-ass brain supplied images of Paloma riding me as I satiated her heat. Images of her lips wrapped around my cock as I fed her my cum. I swallowed hard and bit back a groan. "We'll have to talk to her about what to expect."

"August said he'd do it."

Thank goodness for that.

Rio had that look on his face that he always got when he talked about his VA therapist. He wanted him—had wanted him for a while actually—but didn't think he deserved an Omega. Rio was fucked up; that was obvious. We all were, after what had happened. But if anyone could have handled his demons, it was August.

Now we had Paloma, and I knew Rio wanted her too. There wasn't a choice anymore, and part of me lamented the loss of the possibility. The other part of me was excited that we had an Omega, even if she wasn't exactly ours yet. I didn't want to pin fixing our fucked-up bonds on her yet, but maybe one day, she could act as the nexus to our Pack, instead of Llew. Maybe one day, we could be whole once more.

We sat in silence until eventually, the door to Llew's room opened and Paloma slipped out. She seemed to freeze when she spotted us down the end of the hall, caught like a deer in the headlights, until Llew came up behind her, scooping her up into his arms and cuddling her like she was his own personal teddy bear.

His grin was wide, his eyes sparkling with the satisfaction of an Alpha who'd bathed in the release of his Omega. I kind of hated him a little at that moment.

Rio cleared his throat. "Morning."

Turning Paloma until she was wrapped around his body, Llew carried her down to the kitchen and set her on the bench beside Rio, his face alight with mischief. She smelled like heaven, and I watched Rio's pupils dilate.

I frowned at Llew. "That's mean."

He shrugged. "Sharing is caring, and she smells delicious."

Paloma's cheeks flushed so red, I considered getting her an ice pack, but instead, I served her up a hearty helping of shakshuka. "This is a Middle Eastern dish. I thought you might like to try some different cuisines?"

She blinked up at me with those wide eyes. I scooped up some of the breakfast stew with a crusty bread roll, still warm from the oven, and held it to her lips. Something visceral flexed in my chest as she took a bite of the food I'd made. That I'd provided.

I wanted to feed her as I fucked her with my tongue.

Rio cleared his throat, giving me a hard look, and I blinked away the dirty thoughts. "What do you think?"

"This is amazing!" She went back for a second bite, and I wondered if I could convince her to only eat from my fingers from now on. "It's so... flavorful? Nothing like we had at the Homestead."

Rage washed over me, like it did every time I thought

of where she came from, but unlike the Alphas in the room, I was better at hiding it. "Oh, what would you eat in the mornings there?"

"Only Leaders ate breakfast. We had a midday meal and an evening meal. Overfeeding was the first failing of hedonism."

She was skin and bones, even now. She didn't look like she'd ever been overfed, and Omegas were naturally more curvy than other designations.

"I see. Don't worry, we believe breakfast is the most important meal of the day. In fact, there are no restrictions on food. If you're hungry, you're welcome to anything we own." *Our food. Our home. Our hearts.* "On that note, I thought if you felt up to it, we might take you to the mall to get some things you need."

She chewed her lip, and Rio pulled the soft flesh from between her teeth. "If you aren't ready, that's okay too. Max or I will go and get the basics. This is just a small step in discovering who you are, Paloma."

I gave her another bite of her breakfast as she thought about it, chewing slowly. *God, how is that so hot?*

She looked up at Llew like he could save her, and I pushed down the jealousy that she didn't look at me like that. Yet. One day, I would earn her trust and her bite.

"Can Llew come too?"

We all froze, her big Alpha included. Llew hadn't been outside in over two years. No further than the backyard, at least. But just like with the Omega, I knew he was ready. Pushing him wouldn't help, but maybe soon, he could manage it, holding her hand.

He reached out and stroked her cheek. "Not this time, sweetheart. I'm not ready, but you're braver than me. And our Pack will be there every step of the way."

Our Pack. It had been so long since we'd been a Pack. Fuck, I was going to cry if we didn't move this along.

I squeezed her knee. "Every step of the way. And if it gets too much, we can turn around and come home."

She looked at me, trust I wasn't sure I'd earned in those big green eyes. "Okay. I'll go and change." She ran a hand over her head, and panic at the stubble crossed her face once more. "I need…"

Rio nodded reassuringly. "Whatever you need is yours. Go change; we'll wait for you. Take as long as you want."

FOURTEEN

PALOMA

The anger I felt at my former life was a molten rage by the time we walked through the department store at the mall. They'd manipulated me; they'd manipulated *all* of us, and for what? To be gods of their own domain? For power over us lesser folk?

A steady thrum of strength pulsed down my bond with Llew, and I took a deep breath. The mall was... a lot. Filled with people, from screaming toddlers to whole groups of teens—staring at what I now knew was some kind of telephone—to people as old as Brother Whitt from the Homestead. There were so many people here that it seemed almost unbelievable. I gripped Rio's hand tightly, his strong body like a pillar I could tie myself to. A safe harbor. It helped that his scowl made everyone else get out of the way, so no one got too close.

Max seemed to be the master of making lists, and he

had a list of everything that I would need. There were things on that list I didn't even know, let alone understand the necessity for.

I had a big woolen hat pulled down over my head, even though it was late spring, so not cold enough to warrant it. I didn't care. I didn't want to wear the lace veil, but I also didn't want to go out with my head exposed in public.

"Okay, nesting materials," Max said lightly. "Just touch anything and see what you like."

I frowned. "Like, for what?"

"For your nest," Rio murmured. "That little nook in your bedroom is a nest, and you can fill it full of anything that makes you happy. Like this pillow." He pulled a fluffy blue square pillow from the pile and handed it to me. "Do you like how this feels?"

I stroked my fingers through the fabric. It was so soft, so fluffy, I imagined it was what clouds felt like. Nodding, I rubbed my cheek against it, and Max smiled, taking it from me and putting it in the already overflowing cart.

"Perfect. What about this one?" He picked up another pillow, and while it looked soft, it was ribbed and rough. I hated it viscerally. Shaking my head, I quickly passed it back to him.

Rio chuckled low. "Trust those instincts. Anything that makes you happy like the first pillow, even if you just like the color, or the way it looks, you put it in the cart. That goes with clothes, lights, blankets—anything you want." He leaned down and rubbed his cheek on mine, like he couldn't help himself. When I didn't push him away, Max leaned down and did the other cheek, and I flushed pink. I just wanted to purr and curl up in their arms.

Max kissed my cheek softly. "I'm just going to get some other supplies. I'll leave you in Rio's capable hands." Smiling goofily, he wandered away, and I watched his butt as he left. It was a nice butt. Firm and hugged tightly by the casual pants he wore. Could I be envious of a piece of clothing?

Grabbing the cart with one hand, Rio twined his fingers in mine and gently tugged me along. "Are you checking out my Beta, Omega?" he teased.

"Checking out?" I wasn't sure what that meant.

Tugging me closer, he let me sink into his warmth. "Appreciating the way his body looks with your eyes. I understand, though; Max has always been the most attractive of our Pack, both inside and out."

I frowned, because while I couldn't argue that Max was indeed handsome, they were all appealing in their own way, to both the woman and the Omega in me. I didn't know how to express that to Rio without admitting I was indeed "checking out" Max, or sounding like I wanted to betray my new Alpha already. So I said nothing, just snuggled into Rio's side as he dragged me around the soft furnishings aisles, putting anything I even lingered for a second on into the cart.

Finally, we walked over to a large counter, where a

girl with a bright, smiling face and long golden hair greeted us. "Get everything you need?" she purred at Rio, dismissing me completely.

The barely suppressed rage I'd been holding onto all day rose up inside me, and I gritted my teeth. I wanted to lash out, but instead, I swallowed it down. Aggression was punished; subservience was rewarded. No one wanted an aggressive wife. An aggressive Omega.

Missing my veil, I stared down at my feet, so the people in front of me couldn't see the crazy rising up inside me. Damaged. Broken. Useless.

"Paloma?" I looked up at Rio, and whatever he saw in my expression had him frowning. "Are you okay?"

Nodding, I forced a smile onto my face. "Yes. I'm fine." Almost unwillingly, my eyes flicked to the girl behind the counter, who looked as if she was feasting on Rio's good looks. This was a prime example of "checking out."

But Rio was *mine*.

A soft snarl reached my ears, and my cheeks darkened to red when I realized it was me. I was growling.

Leader Malakai would be horrified right now.

Rio turned his back on the girl, an eyebrow raised. "You don't seem fine, Omega."

How did I explain to him that I wanted to claw out the eyes of a perfect stranger, then stomp on them so she could never look at him again?

"I don't know..." My eyes slipped back to the girl,

who was now staring, and I ripped my gaze away, embarrassment making me hot.

Rio leaned forward, brushing his lips across mine. It was a soft caress, but I could feel the claiming in them. He was declaring that he was mine in front of this beautiful girl, who would look amazing beside him. Who wasn't stunted emotionally and socially. Who wasn't damaged inside and out.

Like he could sense my thoughts, he deepened the kiss. He wasn't just marking himself as mine, he was claiming me as his. A soft noise that I didn't understand bubbled up in my throat and into his mouth.

Rio pulled back and smiled down at me. That expression was like... It made my chest feel too big, too full. Rio's smiles were like the first sunny day after a long winter. "Are you purring for me, Omega?" I flushed again, and he wrapped me up in his arms. He finished paying for our stuff and walked out of the shop, not saying anything to the attendant who'd served us.

"Where are we going?" I asked as he hustled me through the mall.

"To find Max so I can tell him how beautifully you purr."

"Rio," I gasped, and he laughed.

We got to a large, open cavity in the mall, and my feet stilled as I looked up. "Oh my..." I breathed, and Rio stilled beside me.

In the empty mall cavity were hanging shards of shiny mirror. Or maybe it was metal or glass; I wasn't sure. But it swayed gently in some artificial air, twisting like bright stars in the sky and adjusting colours, depending on which way the mirrored pieces spun.

"It reminds me of these extinct creatures I read about once, shifting colors like that," I breathed to Rio as I watched it in rapt attention. "They'd adjust the coloring on their scales, depending on their environment."

Rio frowned. "Do you mean a chameleon?"

"Yes. Reading the *National Geographics* in Leader Malakai's office was my bad habit. I'd sneak in there and read about all these old animals and technologies..." But they *weren't* old. They were modern. The disconnect was still embedded in my brain.

Watching my face, Rio pulled me back to his chest. "Chameleons still exist. You can keep them as pets."

I chewed my lip, holding back the tears. "How can I function in this world when everything I know as true is a lie?" My voice broke, and he tucked me tightly against him.

"We will help you every step of the way. Llew, Max, and me. August. Otillie-James and Lance and their Pack. You have a network for anything you want to do from now on. I swear to you, I'll tell you nothing but the truth. No lies between us."

"Do you promise?" It wouldn't be that easy. I didn't think I could accept anyone's word ever again. But with Llewellyn and his Pack—my Pack now, I guess—surely I could center myself in their truth?

"I swear on my life, Paloma. No matter what, no

matter how painful I think you'll find the truth, I won't ever lie to you."

And just like that, he'd given me a foundation to stand on. When the world felt like quicksand, Rio would be there, giving me solid ground.

I felt exhausted, the day sucking the very energy from my core. Licking my dry lips, I pulled away from him and looked up at the mesmerizing piece of engineering. I would learn. I might be floundering now, but I would learn. I could read. I wasn't stupid, and I could work hard.

I looked up at Rio. "Where can I get books? I want to know everything."

He gave me a solemn look, but kissed the top of my head. "We'll stop at the public library on the way home. It's just around the corner from our house, and you can get as many books as you can hold. And then I'll show you the internet."

"The World Wide Web still exists?"

His low chuckle washed over me. "Yeah, it does, and I promise you, it's a scary, wonderful place. Let's go home."

Home. Home was with Llew. With Rio and Max.

And I laid another foundation stone to my life.

FIFTEEN
AUGUST

It had been a week since I'd seen the Barrie Pack, and the guys hadn't been to group therapy at the VA either. I was finding more and more that I missed them. I was getting attached, and that was bad news for me. Cutting off my professional and personal ties would be best, but even the thought made my Omega whine deep in my chest.

Still, when Max messaged to invite me to dinner and to have the birds and bees talk with Paloma, I answered yes so quickly, I was fairly sure it was an out-of-body experience.

Now, I was fussing over what I was wearing, like it would make any difference. Rio had insisted on picking me up again, and I knew he was just being a normal, worried Alpha. I just had to keep reminding myself he wasn't *my* normal, worried Alpha.

As if he was summoned by my thoughts, the buzzer

sounded. Walking to the intercom by the door, I checked it was him. "Hello?"

"It's Rio."

My heart pattered a little faster at the sound of his voice, but I squashed it down. It would have to get over it. I'd tell him tonight, at the end of this meeting, that I was transferring him to a different support group, and I'd give him more resources for Paloma. Then I'd make a clean break.

Later.

"I'll be right down." Grabbing my wallet and stuffing my feet into my sneakers, I tried not to run down the stairs. Instead, I made my way slowly and leisurely, keeping my composure. I needed some professionalism right now.

I stepped out the security door, and Rio was there, eyeing the security cameras with disdain. "These aren't even pointing in the right place," he grumbled, and I laughed.

"I'll let the Super know. Where are you parked?"

He pointed a little down the street, where he'd double parked, his hazard lights blinking. "I didn't want you to have to walk too far in the dark."

I raised an eyebrow at the large Alpha. "You do realize I run every day? I also take MMA classes and self-defense refreshers once every month. I'm not helpless."

Rio flushed. "I understand that, logically."

Rolling my eyes, I followed beside him to his car. "I know. Alpha instincts and all that. But I promise you,

I'm safe and capable." I kept my voice soft, because shouting at him wouldn't make the point any more than gentle understanding.

He opened the door for me, and I chastised my preening Omega. He was not for us. *They* were not for us. But just like it was Rio's instinct to protect, it was my Omega's instinct to find the biggest, burliest Alpha who would provide security and keep us safe, and Rio had that in abundance.

When he climbed into the driver's seat of his SUV and pulled out onto the road, I broke the silence. "How has your week been?"

He shrugged. "A bit of a rollercoaster, if I'm honest. She's so lost. She oscillates wildly between fascination with everything that's new, and grief at all the time she lost. Plus, she's beginning to smell sweeter and sweeter every single day. Her heat isn't far off, so you coming tonight is going to be a relief, I think. I promised I wouldn't lie to her, and if she'd asked me straight out, I would have told her, but I worry she'll be scared of me."

I nodded. Your first heat was scary, even when you were raised knowing what to expect. For it to come out of the blue, and not understanding the emotion involved, it might sound a little like you'd be losing control of your body and your free will.

Rio's jaw clenched, and it was obvious it had been playing on his mind. I could smell the stress in his scent.

I resisted the urge to squeeze his hand reassuringly. "And how is she dealing with being bonded?"

A small smile crossed his face like the way the dawn lit the sky—slowly, until you were sitting there, suddenly mesmerized by its beauty. "I can't explain it. Separately, they are two damaged people, but together, they have such happiness." He cleared the emotion from his throat. "Watching them together heals something in me too. Llew treats her like she's the only thing in the world that matters, and she gives him strength and normality. There haven't been any negative effects of their bonding, but we've been playing it safe anyway. One of us is always at home, or we take Paloma out with us. I don't think Llew would hurt her; actually, I'm positive he wouldn't. But after I got back... Some things would send him into a frenzy, and I don't want her to be scared either."

I mulled over his words. I didn't think Llew would hurt her either. I'd seen him with her. His Alpha was fully hers now. He really would put himself down first.

But damage like the kind the Barrie Pack had suffered was insidious. It festered below the surface, and sometimes odd things could trigger it to rise. It didn't help that Llewellyn Barrie had been sequestered away all this time, refusing the help that he needed to feel okay again.

Maybe all he needed was an Omega, but putting a patch over it like that, without working on the deeper issues, could be a recipe for disaster.

We pulled up in front of their large house, where I was surprised to see Paloma on the front porch, waiting for us. Behind her stood Llew, leaning against the doorframe, an amused smile on his face.

When we pulled to a stop, she bounded down the steps. "August!"

My heart did that clenching thing in my chest again, my Omega purring at her greeting. *What the fuck?*

I climbed out of Rio's car, and she raced up to me, bouncing on the balls of her feet. I could tell she wanted to hug me, but I kept my hands to myself, no matter how much I wanted to hug her too. She had to make that leap.

"I made dinner with Max. Did you know you can make ice cream at home? I'd never had ice cream until this week, and I think it might be the best thing I've ever had. And chocolate. Why did they not have chocolate at the Homestead?"

I wanted to frown at that, but I didn't want to dampen her enthusiasm. Finally, she leaned toward me and gripped my arms, pulling me closer. How few hugs had she had in her life that she felt so awkward making this connection?

I reached around her back and squeezed her tightly. "I love ice cream. Is that what you made for dessert?"

She was nodding and smiling. *Fuck,* she was beautiful. Achingly beautiful. "With chocolate chips and chocolate sauce."

"Best of all worlds, then."

She dragged me up the front steps, and I smiled at Llew as I walked past. He nodded respectfully. "Evening, Omega."

I nodded back. "Alpha." But that was all the conversation I could get in before I was in the kitchen with Paloma, staring at the ice-cream maker churning away.

She wasn't talking, just sharing her wonder, and in that moment, I wanted everything for the Omega in front of me. Happiness. Security. Good Alphas, and a great Pack. It solidified my need to pull away after tonight, because this Pack was the best of them—exactly what she needed. It didn't matter that I wanted them too.

Her need trumped my want.

Max appeared, smiling fondly at us both. "Hey, August. I see you've been introduced to the ice-cream machine."

I grinned back at him. So fucking handsome. When he wrapped an arm casually around Paloma's waist, they were so attractive together, it stole my breath. What would it be like to be between both of them during my heat?

The thought pulled me up short. Not only were those thoughts completely inappropriate, but it was a slippery slope. My own heat was merely a month away, and if I fixated too much on this Pack, I was bound for disappointment, which was never fun during a heat.

"Paloma was just telling me about her flavorings. I have to admit, I'm excited for her creation."

Max looked down at her fondly, and jealousy reared its head again. "Come on through to the living room. I'll grab you both a drink." He led us both into the living room, where Rio and Llew were already on the couches.

Paloma bounced over to sit on the giant Alpha's lap, and Llew immediately wrapped her up in his arms, pure bliss on his face.

I could see what Rio was talking about now. Llew's Alpha dominance felt immense now that he wasn't trying to suppress it, but it wasn't a chaotic sensation anymore. No, it pulsed with happiness, and I *knew* it came from his bond to the woman in his lap.

I listened to Paloma chatting about her week, about the public library that she'd signed up for, and her cheeks went pink. "I couldn't sign up under my own name, because I don't have any identification. Or a last name."

"You're a Barrie now. That's your last name forever, or as long as you want it," Llew said, nuzzling her cheek.

I nodded. "Yes, once you bond to a Pack, it's traditional to change your last name to theirs. If that's what you want. Nothing is set in stone. You can change your first name too. Everything is your choice now."

She blinked at me. "I wouldn't have to be Paloma anymore?" She stared at me with open-mouthed shock.

"Not unless you wanted to be," I informed her gently. "Would you like to change it?"

She chewed her lip. "My friend at the Homestead, Nimah, used to call me Polly. I called her Nim. We weren't meant to shorten our god-given names, but it felt like a secret between the two of us. I think I'd like to be Polly now."

I saw Rio stiffen beside me, but I patted his leg gently. He couldn't react negatively to these little tidbits;

otherwise, she'd stop dropping them completely just to keep the peace. We needed the information she had stored away in her brain to stop these people for good, information she might not even know she had.

I smiled softly. "Polly is a beautiful name. Bright and happy. It suits you." She gave me a half-hearted grin. "Was Nim an Omega too?"

Paloma—I mean, Polly—shook her head. "No, I was the only Omega after the last one died, maybe three years ago? It's hard to know. Nim's a Beta. She is the sweetest person. The only one there who showed me love, despite me being marked by Melize. We were raised in the same house."

"Could you be sisters?" Max asked, and she shook her head.

"No, she had beautiful golden skin and almond-shaped eyes. Her mother was definitely Sister Alita, because she was the only one there who looked like Nim, but we weren't allowed to say so. We were all children of the house. Sister Alita didn't show any favoritism toward Nim."

I resisted the urge to grind my back teeth as her scent soured. When she turned her face into Llew's chest, he stroked her back gently. "We'll rescue your sister, Polly. We'll bring her home here and open up the world to her, so she can be the decider of her own fate. Just like you."

Well, I guess if we were having hard conversations, it might be good to get them all out of the way in one go.

"There's actually something else the guys invited me over to talk to you about."

She frowned at me, biting her lower lip. "You didn't just come to visit me? Visit us?"

Her hurt wafted toward me on her scent, and my Omega whined. "That too. I didn't want to overstep while you were settling in. Some Omegas can find that uncomfortable, especially at this time."

She looked between us all. "What time?"

"When you're close to going into heat. Now that you're off your suppressants, I think you'll have your first heat within the next ten days."

Sixteen
Polly

I wasn't an idiot. When I'd gotten my library card, the first book I'd checked out was about designations. It was a guide made for teens just coming into their designation, but it had helped. Most people grew up knowing this stuff. They'd met dozens, if not hundreds of Alphas, Betas and Omegas before they went through their own transition.

Then I'd gotten books on religion. On cults. On modern technology. On social and cultural norms. Politics. I'd spent hours curled up on the couch with Rio, or in Llew's suite, or at the breakfast bar while Max cooked and I read. I consumed all the knowledge I could lay my hands on, like a greedy little sponge.

So I knew Omegas went through heats. And I knew that they tended to start when Omegas were just a little younger than my age. I'd just never had one, so I thought that perhaps I was just a little defective. The guys didn't seem to care—not that I'd ever brought it up—or if they did care, I wasn't ready for them to kick me to the curb yet. I would happily stick my head in the sand.

So I knew what heats were in theory, but how did they know that I was going to go through a heat in ten days? And what did it mean? What would it be like?

The books didn't go into specifics on that. I knew sex happened, and that if people didn't have a Pack, there were clinics where an Omega could go and get clinical help. The book hadn't been very specific what kind of clinical help you'd get.

I looked at August, the only other Omega I knew. "I wasn't on suppressants."

"Did you have daily vitamins? Supplements? Anything like that?"

I realized exactly what he meant. We'd all had morning vitamins given out by Sister Roberta. I'd always gotten an extra one, because I was the child of Melize. They'd said it was to rid me of her taint. Of *course* it had been suppressants.

"Yes. I feel like such a fool."

Llew squeezed me reassuringly. "How could you have known? You are bright and beautiful, Sweet Thing. You can't know what you don't know." I wasn't sure about the logic around that statement, but I still nodded.

August leaned forward, and I got caught in his pretty brown eyes. "You were abused, Polly." I flushed, my gut feeling sour at his words. "None of this is your fault. The people who were supposed to love you, supposed to care for you—they hurt you, emotionally and physically. Llew is right; why would you question the people who were supposed to care for you?"

In my head, what they were saying made sense, but it might take my heart a little longer to catch up. "So my heat... What does that mean?"

August wet his lower lip, dragging it between his teeth in a way that was entirely transfixing. I wanted to taste that lip. I wanted to drag it between my teeth. I wanted to feel it against my skin.

Llew rumbled beneath me, and someone groaned.

August's face looked flushed. "It means that you'll find yourself feeling more aroused by your mate, and his Pack members and, uh, anyone else you find attractive. You'll want to arrange your nest—the guys have explained your nest?" I nodded, and he continued. "You'll want to make it and remake it. You'll feel irritable, and things will annoy you more. Irritating smells and sounds will make you want to overreact. I once threw my clock out the window, because the ticking sound made me irrationally grumpy just before my heat."

I laughed softly, thinking about the crunchy peanut butter I'd tried this morning. And the feel of the cotton balls in the bathroom. Both had made me gag. "Okay. I knew that from the book at the library. What isn't in the book? During my heat itself, what happens?"

The guys all looked uncomfortable, but also maybe a little intense? August sucked in a deep breath, his gaze bouncing around at the guys too. "So when your heat starts, you'll be in pain. It's like a deep cramp low in your belly, and your Omega knows only one thing will ease it. Alphas. An Alpha's knot, to be exact. You're lucky—your Omega is smart. She knew that Llew was a good Alpha, and she made him yours. He will ease the pain as soon as you let him. Consent is key, *always,* so if you want to go to a clinic for your heat, I know this Pack would support your wishes," he said with steel in his tone that invited them to argue, so he could eviscerate them.

"Of course we would. Whatever Polly needs," Max agreed quickly.

I noted again that they were immediately all using the name I'd chosen. They respected my wishes as soon as I voiced them. I felt safe with them; I wouldn't want to go to some clinical setting with strangers for my heat. Not when I could have my Alpha.

My eyes drifted to Rio. My Alphas.

So I shook my head. "No, I want to be here. I trust these men."

August inclined his head. His eyes were warm and maybe possessed something like longing? I knew longing. I'd longed for a different life for an eternity.

Shaking my head, I looked at Max. "And Betas? Can I have Betas with me too?"

"You can have anyone or anything you like during your heat. It's your moment."

My Omega lurching in my chest, I looked at August from beneath my lashes, wanting to climb into his lap. "What about another Omega?"

August froze. It was like he was a statue, his eyes flying wide. "That's unusual, but not unheard of."

I knew what I wanted, but it wouldn't leave my lips. I wasn't brave enough. I dragged my eyes away from August's and looked at the other men in the room. "Okay. And the heat itself, I'll want to have sex a lot?"

August's face slipped back into its professional mask. "Yes. Orgasms will ease the pain. You'll be insatiable, and it's the job of the people you pick to join you in your heat to tend to you. To give you countless orgasms and, uh, the proteins in male ejaculation can also act to ease the pain. It might be worth considering going on some birth control immediately. I'm sure the guys won't mind going to get tested so you know they're clean."

"Free from sexually transmitted diseases, because they've had sex before." And that was the sticking point for me. I was untouched. Well, maybe not so untouched now that Llew woke me up every morning with his mouth on my nether parts, but still.

As if he could sense my thoughts, Llew turned me on his lap so I was facing him. There was just me and my Alpha in the room. "I can feel you through the bond, Sweet Thing. Whatever you decide is the right course of action. If you want to be... more present when you make love for the first time, I will worship your body and the gift you're giving me. If you want to wait until your heat, that's okay too. If you aren't ready for any of this, we can find a way to put it off for however long."

"More suppressants?" I asked softly.

Llew nodded. "Probably. They're illegal, because they're really bad for an Omega's endocrine system, and long-term use causes serious, sometimes irreparable harm. But this isn't a normal case, and if you need more time, I'll get you more time. You've been through a lot; this is just one extra thing for you to deal with."

What they'd been giving me had screwed with my system? "What kind of harm?"

August gave me a reassuring look. "It's nothing to worry about right now, I promise, but it can cause damage to your hormones, which govern all sorts of things like your immunity, your growth, your reproductive systems, your metabolism. I can help you book an appointment with an endocrinologist, if you wish. But you've been off the suppressants for a little while now, and I'm sure the Alphas can sense the change in your scent that indicates your heat is coming soon."

I looked between Rio and Llew, who both nodded softly. *Huh.* "Do I smell better or worse?"

Llew snuggled into my cheek, inhaling me deeply. "Better. So delicious, it makes me want to eat you up."

I gave him a small grin. "More so than usual?"

"Like I would happily die between your thighs, then in my will request the Pack puts that I died eating out my Omega on my headstone, so everyone knows how irresistible you are."

Max groaned. "Laying it on a little thick there, aren't you, Llew?"

He shook his head, his little grumble-moan spreading through my body. "Not thick enough."

Rio held up a hand. "Before this devolves into a lot of sexual double entendres, do you have any other questions?"

I had more questions than I could possibly express. Or that I wasn't scared to express anyway. I knew that I didn't want my first time to be during the haze of the heat. I wanted to know what to expect, to be in my right mind. I wanted to enjoy what was happening, not just because my Omega was screaming that I was in pain.

I also kind of wanted to see what a penis looked like, especially one with a knot. Could I ask Llew to show me? Could I ask Max to show me his too, so I knew how they compared?

The idea of seeing their cocks made desire slowly drip through me like hot coffee, which was *insane,* because last week I would've been horrified if some Alpha had shown me his dick. Now, not only did I get excited by the idea of seeing it, I also wanted to know what it would feel like—in my hand, in my mouth, inside me.

I rapidly shook my head, trying to push down the dirty thoughts. "Uh, not right now. Can I call you and ask if anything comes to mind?" I asked August.

"Absolutely. I can get you a phone, if the guys already haven't, and you're welcome to call or message me day or night. I'm here to support you."

A ball of emotion lodged in my throat. It had been a lot, this whole week. This whole month. This Omega's kindness was like a balm across the aching wound of my betrayal. "Thank you, August."

Reaching over to me, he stroked my arm softly. "You aren't alone in this. You're not alone ever again. I promise."

Silence dropped over the room, but it wasn't awkward. We were all lost in our own thoughts, memories, dreams.

Max cleared his throat. "So, uh, you have around ten days, and if you're feeling up to it so soon after the mall, Rio and I had an idea of an outing you might enjoy. I think maybe even Llew could come to this one. August as well, if he isn't busy tomorrow, or wants to play hooky from work." His smile was wide and bright, and I was reminded once more that he was beautiful, in case my eyes had forgotten.

"Don't leave us in suspense, Maxie," Llew rumbled.

"I thought we might take our Omega to the zoo."

I gasped, excitement buzzing through my veins. "The zoo?"

"The zoo. There's one about an hour from here. It's midweek, so the place shouldn't be too busy, but it's got some cool animals. I thought you might enjoy it."

I launched off of Llew's lap and straight at Max. You could tell he was military-trained, because he caught me easily, his reflexes ensuring he quickly plucked me out of the air and into his arms.

When Rio grumbled about it being his idea too, I reached across and pulled him into the hug. This was what happiness felt like. I might not have chosen them purposefully, but I wouldn't change them for the world. The people at the Homestead might have believed that being an Omega was Melize's curse, but right now, it felt like she'd given me a gift.

I was going to hold onto it tightly with both hands.

SEVENTEEN
LLEW

Being inside the car was making me feel claustrophobic. My Alpha snarled and whined grumpily, but I held onto control. It helped that they'd put Polly right beside me, her small hand wrapped in mine, her happiness beating down the bond between us, pushing back the panic. She'd looked over at me with worried eyes once, but I'd given her a tight smile. Then she'd cuddled into my side, wrapping her body as far around me as she could while remaining buckled in.

It also helped that August had been convinced to take the day off from work, and he was on her other side, filling the cab with his warm, sweet scent, and I could feel its calming effects on my limbs.

"How long since you've been to the zoo?" Polly asked me, her excitement contagious.

I squeezed her fingers gently. "Not since I was a boy

on a school trip. Though I was with Rio and Maxie then, too."

"Max tried to climb in with the kangaroos, so we got sent back to the bus before we even got to the lions," Rio grumbled.

Grinning, Max looked over his shoulder at me. "I still reckon I could have petted it. It was a real chill dude."

August raised an eyebrow. "You guys have been a Pack that long?"

I tensed beneath Polly's hand, but she sent another wave of reassurance to me. She'd become accustomed to the bond so quickly. She left it wide open, maybe because no one had taught her to close it, and I wasn't in a hurry to do so. I loved that I could feel every fleeting emotion. I wanted to know her inside and out.

It was Max who answered. "I met Rio in the third grade, when he was placed with his foster parents down the street from me. We were the same age, so my parents thought we'd enjoy each other's company. I think his foster parents just wanted to ensure he stayed out of trouble. They were elderly, and honestly, should have given up fostering kids ten years earlier, but I was glad they didn't. You were one of the last, though, right?"

Rio nodded. "I was more than enough trouble by myself, and instead of making sure I stayed out of trouble, you got me in even more mischief."

I chuckled, because it was true. Young Max had been wild and adventurous. He had two parents who doted on him, and that adorable face, which made authority figures believe butter wouldn't melt in his mouth.

Max's laugh echoed around the cab of the SUV, and it was its own balm. Such a happy, carefree sound that I didn't hear nearly enough anymore. "Then Llew moved to town in the fifth grade, and we connected in a way that's hard to explain. Even though none of us had come into our designations yet, we just *fit*. I was happiest when I was with them, and I like to think they felt the same."

I remembered the day perfectly. I was this huge kid already—there wasn't much doubt in people's minds I would be Alpha. But my dad had been a pacifist, telling me that it was better to solve arguments with empathy and words, rather than fists. I had a girly name that some brave, but stupid kids had decided to use to put me in my place on my first day. John Herman had me backed into my locker, taunting me that I had to have a vagina, because what boy was named Ellen? I'd been doing the "turn the other cheek" thing when he swung a punch at the back of my head like a coward.

Rio had crash-tackled him to the floor, Max joining the fray, before I'd even realized what happened. I'd just stood there while these kids, half my size, pounded on John Herman and his friends until teachers broke it up. We'd all been sent to the principal's office, and then I'd been sent home from school.

When my mom had found out what happened, she'd made an extra large batch of tiddly oggies to share with them. Because while my dad hadn't approved of violence,

my mom wasn't above some bloody comeuppance, especially when it came to someone hurting me.

"Tiddly oggies?"

I hadn't realized I was talking out loud. "Little
pastries filled with cheese, onions and potatoes. My
parents were Welsh."

Max and Rio both groaned. "Fuck, I loved your
mom's oggies," Max whined.

Rio snorted. "Pretty sure we were only friends with
you for that first month on the off chance your mom sent
more of them." He grinned in the rearview mirror,
meeting my eyes. "You grew on us after that."

The history I had with these men meant more than a
broken bond. We were brothers. Closer than brothers.
We were three parts to a whole. "We bonded young, and
designated within a year of each other. It felt like we were
meant to be together, and when Max designated Beta, we
moved out of home."

"The raging testosterone between just the two of you
in our teen years was enough to choke a rhino. You
needed balance." He'd always said as much; there hadn't
been any jealousy when he hadn't designated Alpha. Max
was just Max. Confident in himself and his place in the
world. He'd become our center. The unfortunate recipient for all our overprotectiveness, and later, the glue that
held us all together.

I could feel the questions in August's gaze. How had
we gone from that to what we were now?

Maybe that was selfishly something I adored about

Polly's naivety. She couldn't tell how fucked up we were. She had no touchstone for what a healthy Pack looked like.

But August did, and he knew we'd been irreparably damaged, even if he didn't know how.

Luckily, I was saved from the possibility of more questions by our arrival at the zoo. Polly bounced in place excitedly. We piled out of the car, and she kept a firm hold on my hand. I didn't know if I was her security blanket or she was mine, but either way, I had no intention of letting her go. Max went up and bought our tickets, while Rio hovered around August and Polly protectively. I watched the way he eyed both of them.

There was so much longing in his eyes when he looked at them both. An old residual kind of desire when he watched August, and a newer, hotter want when his gaze landed on Polly. How long had Rio wanted his group therapist? Why hadn't he ever said so?

I knew the reason before the question even settled in my mind. Me. I was the reason he'd never tried for the Omega in front of us.

And maybe a little himself too. Between the two of us, there was enough fucked-up mental health to write a textbook. We were probably a therapist's nightmare Pack really, like bringing your work home with you. But Polly hadn't had any options, and it felt like fate had placed her here in our laps, so we could each be what the other needed.

Max walked back over, handing us each a ticket.

"Okay, Polly. What are we hitting first?" He handed her a map that had all the animals listed and their locations in this big botanical garden.

"Rhinos still exist?" she breathed, pointing to an area on the map. "My magazine said they were extinct."

I led her into the zoo, the kid at the gate eyeing us warily as he scanned our tickets. Some people were sensitive to the fractured sensation of my Alpha, but now that Polly was here, he felt a lot less feral.

Max looked over her shoulder at the map. "Some are extinct, and depending on how old your magazines were, it would depend which one they were referring to. The Western Black rhino was declared extinct in 2011. The Northern White rhino was made functionally extinct in 2018 when the last male died. So while some subspecies are dead, it's not necessarily the whole species. These ones look like Southern White rhinos."

August looked at Max, like he'd grown the horn from his face. "How do you know that?"

Max nudged him with his shoulder. "Information is my thing, remember?"

August and Max were of a similar height, and they looked good together. I looked down at Polly, who was watching them hungrily. Her question last night, about whether Omegas could join the heat of other Omegas, was playing on my mind. Anyone with eyes and a heightened sense of smell could tell she wanted August. It was odd, but given that he was here instead of at work, that he seemed so at ease, it led me to believe that perhaps August wanted my Sweet Thing too.

"Well, looks like we're doing the chubby unicorns first," Rio said, heading off in the direction of the rhinos.

Polly stood up on her tippy toes, pulling me down closer. "Unicorns aren't real, right?"

I kept the amusement from my face. I didn't want to make her feel bad. "No, beautiful girl. They're just myth." She nodded solemnly, or maybe a little sadly. I hugged her close, her body fitting against mine perfectly.

Rio looked back over his shoulder at us. "Hurry up, you two, or I'm leaving you with your brethren in the sloth enclosure!"

Laughing, Polly skipped away, but she never let go of my hand.

Eighteen
Polly

This had been the most magical day of my life. I couldn't remember another moment in time where I had been this happy, not even as a child. No birthday or celebration, no single moment in my life had been filled with as much joy as going from enclosure to enclosure, seeing living animals that I'd thought I could only ever read about.

Galapagos tortoises, Lowland gorillas, tigers—they were all there, in large enclosures, but close enough that I could touch them. In all the scary moments of realizing that I'd been in a cult and that everything I'd ever learnt was wrong, this was a sparkling silver lining.

I didn't have time to be scared, or worried, or overwhelmed, because I was surrounded by four men I knew would jump in front of a bullet for me.

Max and I took turns trying to one-up each other with animal facts, while Rio rolled his eyes. August spoke to me like I was a normal person with a normal history, making conversation like we were getting to know each other. I guess we were, really. I knew he was the youngest in a family of girls. I knew his dad had been in the army, and his mom had been a kindergarten teacher. Two of his sisters were also in the army, while the other one was a dental hygienist. I knew that he loved his job at the VA; he loved helping people find solid ground after they left the armed forces.

The more he spoke, the more the feelings in my chest grew and stretched toward him. Desire. Longing. By the time he bought me ice cream at the end of our first lap of the zoo, I wanted to pull him closer to me and kiss him. I wanted to kiss all the gentle places and all the jagged ones too. I wanted to hold him close to me, breathe in his reassuring scent, and listen to his sweet voice.

And I wanted to do it all naked.

Okay, there was definitely some merit to his statement that my heat was coming. The thought thrilled and terrified me in equal measures. One part of my mind was purring at the idea that all these big, strong men would be mine.

But the other part—the one who'd spent her whole life shying away from the touches of the Alphas she knew —was terrified. If I had barely any control over my Omega, what if they lost control of their Alphas? They felt good, but how would I even know? I knew nothing. That was well established now.

August nudged my arm with his. "What's wrong?"

I gave him a bright smile that probably didn't reach my eyes. "Why do you think something is wrong? This day has been the best one of my life."

He tapped his nose. "The scents don't lie, Omega. Tell me why your scent suddenly soured, only if you'd like."

Because while August had basically told me his entire family history, he hadn't pushed me for information. I mean, it had poured out anyway, but he never asked me any direct questions. He never pressed me, and I never felt interrogated. He was a calm presence in a hectic world, and I wanted to cling to him.

"I was just thinking about my heat. Old fears that I *know* won't happen, but I can't shake the unease anyway."

He reached out and grabbed my hand, the connection calming the budding anxiety in my chest immediately. The others were looking at the meerkats in the enclosure by the ice cream cart. "Your emotions are valid, Polly. Your first heat is a scary uncertainty."

Before I could stop myself, the question burst from my lips. "Would you be there too?"

Embarrassment immediately washed through me. He'd shown no interest in me like that—why would he want to be part of my heat? What if he was one of the territorial Omegas that the books had talked about? What if he felt obligated, just because he was a nice guy?

"I'm sorry. That was rude of me to ask. I mean, you

don't have to participate or anything. Maybe you could just check that I'm okay. I don't know any—"

He stopped my words with a kiss. His full lips brushed across mine, and he groaned in a low voice. "Polly, I'd be honored. But you don't know how you'll feel until the heat is closer. Your Omega might be resistant to other Omegas being around. So how about we play it by ear?"

He wrapped me in his arms. He wasn't huge like Llew, or tall and rangy like Max. He wasn't stacked with muscle like Rio. But something about the way August held me felt so *right* that I knew me and my Omega were on the same page. August felt like ours, and we wanted him at our heat.

"Even if your Omega doesn't want me there, I'll make sure you are safe and cared for. The draw I feel toward you isn't the norm, but neither is our situation. Besides, normal is overrated." He kissed the top of my head and stepped away.

My eyes felt too wide, my body leaning towards his like he was the sun and I was a light-starved flower. "Okay," I mumbled.

I could feel eyes on me. When I looked over my shoulder, the hungry gaze of Rio met mine, and they flicked between me Dond August. I realized with a shock that Rio also had a crush on the other Omega. I acknowledged that I should probably feel bad about that, jealous or something. But honestly, it was understandable.

"I think Rio would like you to be there too."

Red flushed along August's cheeks, and I couldn't resist lifting my hand to chase the changing color. "It doesn't matter what Rio would like—it's your heat. You're the only one that matters for those few days." Like he couldn't help himself, he kissed me once more.

I smirked at him. "I think I'd like to watch you and Rio together. Is that strange?" My nose twitched, and then suddenly, I could scent it too. His desire. It was like a highlight to his already sweet scent. Like coffee in chocolate.

He groaned again. "I'm trying to be a gentleman here, Polly Barrie, and you're making it difficult not to pull you into my lap and kiss you senseless."

Uh, why was he even resisting?

Then his words pierced the haze of lust that swamped me, and I grinned. "I have a last name."

He looked down at me, his brows pulling together. "What do you mean?"

"I have a last name now. I've never had a last name before; I was just Paloma. There were no other Palomas in the Homestead, and we didn't need last names. But Polly Barrie isn't Paloma anymore, and she has a family name, because she has a *family*." I burst into tears. August gathered me up in his arms as the Alphas appeared, and I realized they'd been giving us privacy.

Rio was there first. "What happened? Polly, baby, what's wrong?"

August laughed low in his chest, a joyful noise. "They're happy tears, I think?"

I nodded against his chest, then turned in his arms, wrapping my own around Rio and making grabby hands towards Max and Llew. My family. The Barrie Pack. *My* Pack. "I'm just... It's just really nice."

Llew chuckled, because I guess he could feel my happiness. "You make us happy too, Sweet Thing."

Max kissed the tears from my cheeks and stepped away. "Come on, Polly, let's go ride the carousel. No more tears." Tugging me along behind him, he headed over to a carousel, which was huge and shone gold in the midday sun. It was turning lazily, empty except for a few parents with their toddlers. Instead of carousel horses, they had zoo animals, all intricately painted. Ostriches, giraffes, gorillas, rhinos, cassowaries—there were so many to choose from.

Max wrapped an arm around my waist. "There's only one good choice here, obviously."

I looked up at him like he was crazy, because there were at least fifteen different choices. "Oh?"

"The tiger, of course. The king of the jungle."

I screwed up my nose. "It's a good choice, but..."

He raised an eyebrow, the smile across his face infectious. "Oh. All right, which one are you choosing?" I pointed to one, and he laughed. "Well, I didn't see that coming." He leaned down and brushed his lips across mine. "I didn't see you coming either, Polly, but I'm so glad you're here."

The previous ride ended, and we climbed on board. Max lifted me gently onto my animal—a whooping crane—and settled in beside me.

This day had felt like a dream, and the men I'd shared it with were a gift. My past was behind me. There were nothing but good days ahead for Polly Barrie.

Nineteen
Max

Some days seemed like perfect snapshots of the future, and seeing August and Polly together had sparked something in my chest that refused to be doused. I wouldn't interfere, but I had a feeling our sweet little Omega wanted a big, brawny Omega of her own, and I was here for it. I hadn't thought our Pack would ever get this lucky, yet here we were, on the cusp of our Omega's heat.

I wanted to do more. I wanted everything to be settled, with the Homestead, with our Pack. I wanted her happiness more than I'd wanted anything in a long time. Except the return of Llew as the man I'd fallen in love with. And this beautiful woman had given me that gift too.

There was literally nothing I wouldn't do for her now.

Including deep diving into the dark web to find and

punish the people who'd treated her like a dog to be kicked around on their puppy farm from Hell. I would find them, and I would make sure her "Leaders" wished they'd never been born, that they'd wish they'd never thought of something as horrendous as the Homestead.

I'd stood close by yesterday while she talked with August, listening as they unraveled themselves piece by piece, and using my training to sort through what could be important in my search for the Homestead. I hadn't been allowed to interrogate Anthony Smalls, the Alpha who'd bought her, as he awaited trial.

Although Rio and I would be waiting for him as soon as he got out of jail. There wouldn't be a dark corner that fucker could hide in where we wouldn't provide the most painful retribution that US military training could provide.

It wasn't fast enough, though. The stories that Polly just casually dropped, of indentured servitude and child marriage and all sorts of other atrocities—stories which she didn't even realize were terrible—told me everything I needed to know about The Homestead and its founders. The way she talked about the girl she was friends with, Nimah, who was still there in that shithole, scrubbing floors and barely eating. I wanted to save her, save them all, for Polly.

None of my searches for the Homestead had brought up any results. Nor did any of the names of her gods or goddesses, or Leader Malakai, or the other Leader names, which was understandable. An organisation that was off-grid to this extent wasn't going to have a digital footprint. But we lived in a digital world, so there had to be something somewhere that would give me a hint.

I wrote some script to search through the web. They had to have dealt with Anthony Smalls somehow, so no matter how off-grid they were, they either had to have a wifi connection or an intermediary on the outside to negotiate with third parties.

Also, selling Omegas wasn't something you could just do casually, like selling cookies in a grocery store parking lot. I'd have to scan some of the more unsavory places on the web for mentions of people selling or wanting to buy Omegas.

The more I thought about it, the more I was sure that they had to have connections on the outside. Polly had been unable to use our television, but had known that the coffee machine worked with little pods, although she'd never used it. It was only for the Leaders. They obviously had electricity, and I very much doubted they were growing and roasting their own coffee beans.

It was very hard for a community that large to be completely self-sufficient. Someone was doing resource drops, probably under the cover of darkness. Someone knew, and I'd find them.

I also thought about what Polly had said, about the lack of Alphas being born into the community. There was something wrong with that. Growing up, there'd been six kids who'd designated Alpha in my elementary class. The population divide was pretty split; although most were Betas, there were very few Omegas, but there were more than enough Alphas.

Some should have been born in the Homestead. Where were all the young Alphas going?

I called up a friend who might not play on the legal side of the road, but he jaywalked between pretty frequently. He'd been dishonorably discharged from my unit for giving himself leave approval and getting caught. Toledo was not wise, but he sure was smart.

Pressing his number in my phone, I waited for it to ring out and for him to call me back. He never answered his phone.

Sure enough, it rang back within fifteen seconds of the call ending. "Max. How are you?"

Toledo wasn't his real name. His real name was apparently John Smith, but given what he could do, I highly doubted that was real either. It had been a good enough alias to get him into the army, though, and I didn't think he was a spy, so we all called him Toledo and let it go.

"Good, my friend. I was just wondering if I could call in that favor."

There was silence at the other end of the line, so I knew he'd heard me. There was a slight squeak and the clack of computer keys. "Okay, what do you want me to find?"

I snorted a laugh. "How do you know I didn't want you to babysit my house or something?"

I could almost see him rolling his eyes. "I'd be the last

person you'd give unfettered access to your house, and we both know it. Besides, it's not every day a friend busts an animal cruelty ring and releases the data and video to national news networks. I assume you need something to do with that."

Frowning, I opened my own laptop. "How'd you know it was me?"

I could almost imagine his shrug. "Digital fingerprints. Plus, I know the sound of your voice and the small freckle you have at the base of your left thumb that appears in the video provided to the news outlets."

They really should have kept Toledo in the military. He'd have been scary on the wrong side. "That's creepy."

He snorted derisively. "It's why I get paid the big bucks." I didn't want to think about who paid Toledo now. He might make dumb decisions, and he might be super smart, but he'd always had a very black-and-white moral compass. Civilians were off limits, but step one foot over that line he'd drawn in the sand, and you were fair game.

"That animal cruelty bust from the other day? Turns out that animals weren't the only thing they were intent on selling." I said it matter-of-factly, like the very idea of Polly ending up in the hands of someone who'd *buy* an Omega didn't make me sick to my stomach.

"Prostitution?" he asked lightly, though I could hear the note of disgust in his voice.

"Omega trafficking."

The clack of his keys went still. "He was trying to sell

Omegas?" I knew he'd heard me, but he was just clarifying, like a good little hacker.

"Yes. We rescued her from beneath the warehouse. She was from some cult, and..." I trailed off. How did I sum up how fucked up her life had been in a concise way, without laying all her own stories bare? "They didn't respect Omegas. They sold her to Anthony Smalls, like she was a runt from a litter of puppies."

A soft growling sound came down the line. I suspected Toledo might be a Beta, but he was hard to pinpoint, and honestly, his designation was the least mysterious thing about him. "You want me to back-end his communications, find out who he was talking to? Maybe who the middle man was?"

See. Smart. "Ideally, but the cops will already be knee-deep in all of Anthony Smalls' technology. I don't want you to broadcast that you're looking. We didn't exactly tell the cops we found her. She was so fucking traumatized, Toledo. The idea of handing her to the cops, for them to grill her about what happened, and potentially send her back? It wasn't a risk she wanted to take, and neither did I."

His fingers were still flying across the keyboard; I could hear the soft noise of them in the background. "I'm going to ignore the fact that you think some lazy cop would even see me coming, but I'll be careful. I'll check the usual places for mentions of selling Omegas, but it'd be hard to narrow it down to your girl."

That was the point that really hurt. Because Polly

might have been saved, but a lot of Omegas weren't. It made my stomach turn. "I hate that."

There was a pause at the other end of the line. "Me too. We should do something about it."

I tilted my head. "Perhaps we should. Let me secure my Pack first."

"Your Pack?" There was a sharpness in his voice, and I knew my next answer would decide what side of Toledo's Line of Good and Evil I stood on.

"She knew nothing about how to be an Omega, or the urges and behaviors she might experience. She accidentally force-bonded my Alpha, Llewellyn."

The soft gasp was the closest I'd ever come to hearing Toledo shocked. "She attacked him?"

I screwed up my nose. "I wouldn't say attacked. More like her Omega knew that he was injured, uh, emotionally, and wanted to fix it in the most basic way possible. Like I said, she didn't understand the urges in her body. They were taught that Omegas were worthless, and that giving into the urges was basically sacrilege." I rubbed a hand down my face. "I can't even tell you how fucked up it was, Toledo."

He hummed his agreement. "But everything worked out okay in the end?"

The bubble of happiness in my chest wanted to shout our contentment from the rooftops. "Yeah. Turned out her Omega was smarter than all of us combined. They became each other's safe place."

But Toledo was silent on the other end, only the

gentle hum of computer fans and the soft clicking of keys audible for a few moments. "Okay, I'm in. I'm just copying the case reports from the Anthony Smalls trial, including from Forensics. Is there anything else you want me to look for, while I'm playing here in Big Blue's backyard?"

Jesus, he was so casual about hacking the police databases. I was pretty sure that if he was caught, it'd be guaranteed jail time.

"Actually, there is one more thing. Can you search for any reports over the last twenty-five years where kids have been dumped with no known ID or relatives? Perhaps in the same place repeatedly. They'd be from twelve up to seventeen or eighteen, I guess. My bet is most of them would already have been designated Alpha, if that helps you narrow it down."

"What the *fuck*, Max?" Toledo sounded beyond outraged. I had him invested now. The abuse of kids, animals, and Omegas? That was in the pitch-black area of his moral compass.

"They're evil, Toledo. Help me bring them down, and I'll owe you one."

There was that soft growl again. "I'll do this one for pleasure. You owe me nothing. Give me four days."

TWENTY
POLLY

The warmth of the sun was making my skin itch where Doodles lay curled up beside me. I was on a quilt in the Packhouse's backyard, and the little dog was in heaven. He'd tried to lick the inside of my mouth at least a dozen times before he calmed down and fell asleep in the sunshine.

The guys were all busy, even Llew, and I found I didn't mind being alone for a moment. I could feel Llew's bond right there, pulsing in my chest. Max was working in his office, and Rio had taken Llew to an appointment with his financial advisor, now that our bond had settled him enough that he could leave the house without going feral.

The last week had been almost normal, which gave me hope that this would be what my life could be like forever now.

"Rufio..." the bird cooed beside me. He'd crooned at

me until I'd let him out of the cage, and when I told him we were going outside, he kept screeching "FLYYYY HIIIIGH FREEEEE BIRDDDDD YEAHHHHHH!" but kind of melodically, like he was singing. I'd grabbed a handful of the nuts he enjoyed, and some kibble for Doodles, and we'd gone outside for a picnic.

When Rufio had flown from my arm to the tree, I'd panicked, but he'd come right back. I'd given him a nut as a reward, and we'd repeated the process several more times, until I was pretty convinced he wasn't going to take off and I'd have to tell Max that I'd lost his pet.

Now he walked along the ground, ripping up the grass and combing his beak through my hair and Doodles's fur.

I had a book on twenty-first-century technology, which was both amazing and terrifying, as it read like a science fiction novel rather than a textbook. Rufio kept trying to chew the corners, his thoughts on the advancements in robotics clear.

The backyard of the Barrie Packhouse was large, filled with trees and shrubs and curated gardens that I never saw anyone tending to, though someone must, because it was beautiful. There were fruit trees in the back corner and eight-foot-tall fences, so I couldn't even see the houses on the other side. It was like an oasis, and I decided it was my new favorite spot outside my nest.

Rufio flew back to the closest tree and sat there, preening himself happily. Maybe that was his problem, and why he cussed so much. He didn't like his cage.

Me either, but we were both free under the clear blue sky right now.

I listened to music from the streaming app that Max had put on my phone. The fact I could take pictures, search for information, communicate with all the guys, and listen to music on this one tiny device was mind-blowing. I loved it.

"Surprise, motherfucker!" Rufio squawked, and I raised myself up onto my elbows to see Max coming down the stairs. He was in a tight tshirt and a pair of shorts that hugged his strong, tanned thighs. His glasses were perched on his nose, the dark frames highlighting the heavy lashes around his eyes and their brilliant blue irises sparkling in the sunshine.

He looked at Rufio in the tree. "Surprise indeed."

I smiled up at Max. *So damn pretty.* "You've trained him well."

He shook his head. "I didn't train him to do this. Must have been his previous owners. Did he try to fly away?"

He grabbed a nut from the little bowl beside me and held it out to Rufio, who promptly flew down for his snack, screaming, "Fly high free bird, yeah!"

Bursting out laughing, Max scratched his head softly. "Lynard Skynard fan too." At my quizzical look, he sat down on the quilt beside me. "They're a band. 'Free Bird' is a song." Picking up my phone, he searched in the music app, and a moment later, a rock song played through the tiny phone speaker.

Rufio flew back to his tree with his newly obtained nut, while Max lay down beside me, on the opposite side to Doodles, who hadn't moved at all. Even when I shuffled over to give Max some space. Was he okay?

I ruffled his fur gently, but he didn't wake. A little more firmly. "Doodles? Are you okay?"

Max reached over and shook him harder. *Oh god.* Was he dead? I mean, we'd had livestock at the Homestead, and sometimes they'd died—sometimes I'd even had to slaughter them, though that usually wasn't my job —but this was different. This little dog was the first thing I had ever had to care for and it had died within a month?

"Doodles, wake up!" I said, desperate now. I lifted and dropped his floppy head once. Twice. On the third time, he lifted it up himself, giving a deep-bellied groan of annoyance. Relief swamped me.

Max flopped back on the blanket. "I wish he'd stop doing that. I swear, every single time, I think this is it." He squeezed my shoulder reassuringly. "He's very old, and given his three legs and missing teeth, he's probably had a really hard life until now. So if he does, uh, pass on, it wouldn't be your fault, okay? It's just the natural way of things."

I knew that, but I wasn't sure I was ready for the moment to be now. Snuggling closer, I placed my head on Max's chest and listened to the steady beat of his heart. My hormones were wild, and even knowing Doodles was alive and kicking, my eyes still misted over.

Wrapping both arms around my waist, Max pulled

me until I was lying across his chest, my body pressed right along his, and suddenly, sad was the last thing I felt. Desire so hot coursed through me like an inferno. I guess this was what August had meant by mood swings.

Unable to help myself, I let my legs slip to either side of his hips and shifted around, the friction feeling too tempting to ignore. Max stiffened, his arms tightening around me, but he didn't stop me.

"Omega..." he breathed, his eyes hooded, his lips slightly parted.

"Max," I whined back. Why did I feel so hot all of a sudden? "Can I tell you something?"

His fingers traced distractingly up and down my spine. "You can tell me anything, Beautiful."

"I've never done it before. Had sex, I mean."

His fingers paused, but picked up again quickly. "I know. Llew insinuated as much. He expressed that everything had to be at your pace, or he'd toss us off the second-story balcony." There was a hint of humor beneath his gentle words.

I wasn't embarrassed. Not anymore, anyway. If anything, I was relieved that if I was going to give myself to someone, it would be someone I chose—not someone chosen for me by the Leaders at the Homestead.

I nuzzled my nose into Max's throat, his scent as comforting to me today as it had been when he'd dragged me out of that hole in the ground. "I don't want my first time to be during my heat, either. I want it to be..." I didn't even know what I was trying to say.

"You want it to be special?"

I nodded. Looking down at this man—this Beta who would be a part of my heat, but not integral to it—I knew deep in my chest that I wanted it to be with *him*. How did I ask someone to take my virginity?

As Rio would say, fuck it. "I want it to be with you."

Max's whole body froze. I wondered if I shook him and lifted his arm, whether he'd be as unresponsive as Doodles had been a moment ago. He wasn't even breathing, but I could feel his heart thundering beneath my cheek. Maybe he was trying to formulate a way to let me down easily.

Putting my arms on his chest, I pushed myself up so I could try and read what was going on inside his head. His eyes were wide. "Me? You want me to—" He swallowed hard. "Are you sure you don't want Llew? I know you guys have been intimate, and he's your Alpha. Or Rio?"

I shook my head. The more he tried to find reasons why he wasn't good enough, the more I knew he was the right choice. "There will be enough time for Alpha and Omega sex during the heat. For my first time, I just want to be Polly. Polly and Max. The person who changed my life and held me steady every step of the way. That was the first day of the rest of my life, and I want you to be there for this first step too." I paused, because I was telling this to him like he was winning a prize. What if he didn't want to be my first? "I mean, if you want that too."

Without answering, he rolled me to the side, laying

me back on the quilt. Leaning over me, he kissed me hard. "I've never wanted anything so much in my life." He tasted like mint and something sweet. "You just tell me when."

His lips brushed across mine again, and my hard nipples pressed against his chest in a way that made all my nerve endings catch on fire. "Now?"

He pulled back, shock making his lips part. "Now?" he repeated. I nodded, kind of enamored by how shocked he was. "Now." He repeated it one last time, climbing to his knees. "Okay. Yes. Okay." He grabbed a nut and put an arm out for Rufio. "Give me ten minutes. I'll put the bird away, and make something perfect." Rufio landed on his arm, and Max began walking back toward the house, talking softly to the bird, like they were discussing plans for my great deflowering.

Flopping back down on the quilt, I stared back up at the sky, feeling equal parts nervous and excited. It felt right, though. It might have been a spur-of-the-moment thing, but my instincts agreed.

August had told me to trust my instincts, and he hadn't led me astray yet.

TWENTY-ONE
POLLY

In the end, I gave him closer to fifteen minutes before I summoned the lady balls to go inside. I'd talked myself in and out of the whole thing at least ten times in those fifteen minutes, but the certainty I felt that Max was the right person—and wouldn't care if I had no freaking clue what I was doing—prevailed over every other possible embarrassing scenario I imagined.

The house was still silent, and my bond with Llew told me he was annoyed and bored, but still not home. I was kind of relieved. Not that I thought he'd be mad about what was going to happen, but because I wanted to avoid the awkwardness of... everything.

"Max?"

"Down here!"

I walked through to the back of the house, where my bedroom was. When I didn't see him in my suite, I walked further down the hall to the main bathroom. I could smell the sweet scent of flowers, and the gentle splash of water. Opening the door, I stepped hesitantly inside.

There must have been twenty small candles lit around the room. The tub was filled to the brim, the sweet-scented water milky, with rose petals floating on top. In the soft glow of candlelight, it looked *magical.*

A shirtless Max stood beside the tub, a soft smile on his face. "This is a little cliché, but it's cliché for a reason." He moved around toward me, mesmerizing me with the way his muscles all seemed to flex. "Are you still sure? I promise you, if you've changed your mind, I won't be mad. I'll walk out of here satisfied, knowing you're enjoying the bath I provided."

His concern only solidified my decision. Nodding, I reached out and stroked my fingers down the strong muscles of his abdominals. Llew was the only naked man I'd ever touched, and while he was all hard muscle, he wasn't defined like this. He was solid like a tree. Max was more solid like one of those Grecian statues.

He stood still as my fingers explored the ridges and lines of his body, his breathing even, but the heat in his eyes almost burning against my skin. I traced the line that went from his hip, angling down towards the waistband of his shorts, and he grabbed my wrist, letting out a low grunt.

"Beautiful, if you explore down there, we're never making it to the tub." He cleared his throat, heaving in some deep breaths. "Can I undress you?"

I licked my lips, my mouth dry, but I nodded. I was wearing a pair of yoga pants; the Leaders would have had a heart attack if they'd seen me in these back in the Homestead. They hugged every part of my lower half in a way that was almost obscene. Maybe that's why I liked them so much. They were a giant *fuck you* to Leader Malakai and the hell he'd created. Plus, they were super comfortable.

All thoughts of yoga pants and Leader Malakai fled my brain as Max's fingers brushed beneath the bottom of my tank top. I held my breath as he dragged it up, his knuckles brushing up along my sides until he was tugging the top over my head. I stood there in my new cotton bra and tried not to blush.

"Fuck..." he breathed. "You're so fucking beautiful, Polly. It's taking every ounce of willpower I possess not to just tear your clothes off, prop you on the vanity, and fuck you senseless." He wrapped his hands around my sides, then trailed them back down my body until he hooked the waistband of my yoga pants. Lowering himself to his knees and dragging the band down, he kissed little lines across my stomach. My lungs were burning, and I realized I was still holding my breath. I sucked in a much-needed breath, and when he tapped the back of my knee, I lifted one foot, then the other.

My heart was racing a million miles an hour. I stood before him in my plain cotton underwear, and he was on his knees in front of me. He was so beautiful down there, his eyes trained on my face, even as his hands moved their way up the back of my calves, then my thighs, until they were cupping my butt.

He dropped his head and groaned. Then he got to his feet, his hands still on my ass, and lifted me until we were mouth to mouth. I wrapped my legs around his waist, and it wasn't my imagination how perfectly we fit together. He kissed me with so much... I couldn't even describe it. He kissed me like he needed me to live. Like oxygen wasn't as important to him as the taste of my lips.

I kissed him back, fumbling and not nearly as practiced, but he didn't seem to care. I gripped his strong shoulders as he walked me back toward the huge tub, which could fit us both easily in its depths. He held me like I weighed nothing, kissing me deeply, for so long that I was seeing stars.

When he finally pulled back, he let me go. His hands went to the waistband of his shorts, and I watched with rapt attention as he pushed them down, his hard cock springing free as they slid down his thighs.

Transfixed, I stared at his cock. Like his body, his cock was different to Llew's. Not as giant, but still thick and hard. And long. So long. I reached out, stroking my hand up its length. He hissed between his teeth, his eyes closing as he dropped his head back to stare at the ceiling. Had that hurt him?

I dragged my hand back up, and he wrapped his fingers around mine. "That feels so fucking good, but if you keep it up, I'm going to come already and embarrass myself." He lifted my hand to his neck, stepping closer.

His arms slipped around my back, unhooking my bra. It fell down my arms, baring my boobs to the air, and he moaned. Like he couldn't help himself, his hands slid to the front, and he cupped their weight. "Oh, baby. Fuck, these are some beautiful tits. Can I taste them?"

I nodded. *Uh, heck yeah.*

His lips slid down my collarbone to my chest, then over my nipple. He sucked gently, and I moaned so loudly, it echoed around the bathroom. I was almost too distracted by his mouth to realize he was slipping me out of my underwear.

At least, until his fingers were swiping through my slick lips. He groaned again, popping his lips off my nipple and resting his forehead against my chest. "You're so slick for me already. I haven't been this close to losing control since losing my own virginity." As he was speaking, his fingers were stroking gently across my clit, making it hard to concentrate on his words.

Without another word, he swooped me up into his arms and stepped easily into the tub. He lowered us into the water, which felt like an impressive feat of core strength. The water was a perfect temperature and scented with something floral. Once I was in the water, he spun me gently until my back was to his front, letting me lean back and use him as a backrest. It was both intimate and casual.

The tub was deep enough that my body could float gently without touching the bottom or the sides, with Max's arm wrapped around my torso. I was wedged hard to his body, his cock nestled between my ass cheeks. He hooked his calves around my ankles, pulling my knees apart. Then he did nothing but let us soak.

I was both relaxed and electrified. Every lap of water against my sensitive core felt amplified tenfold. His hand running over my torso was lazy and unhurried, and my nerves turned into something more languid. More sensual.

His slippery fingers slid back over my breasts, rolling the tight buds between his thumb and forefinger. His lips pressed against the nape of my neck, right over the pulse point, that place that made my Omega whine in my chest.

"Max..." I breathed.

"Yes, Polly?" The way he said my name was like a prayer.

"Touch me?"

He growled deep in his chest and pulled me further up his body, until the hand that had been playing with my breasts slipped between my thighs. He strummed my clit, circling it achingly slowly. "You're so soft. I bet you're sweet too, aren't you? I can't wait to taste you on my tongue. Open wider for me," he murmured.

I did, spreading my thighs, close to begging for his fingers. He didn't make me beg, though.

"Has Llew been playing with this sweet little pussy? Has he been stretching it, preparing you for your heat and his knot?" He slid one finger inside me, curling it gently, stroking with the same languid movements as he stroked my skin. But so much better, especially when his thumb brushed across my clit at the same leisurely pace.

I wanted to hurry him, to chase down that pleasurable feeling inside me like a wolf chasing its prey, but I didn't. I trusted my Beta, and I let him play my body like an instrument. He slid another finger inside me, which was more than I'd done with Llew. Llew liked to use his tongue to fuck me, which I enjoyed.

But the feeling of Max's two thick fingers inside me was different. More. He moved them faster now, and my moans began to echo off the wall, especially as he plucked at my nipples with his other hand.

Oh god.

"I can feel your pretty, wet pussy squeezing my fingers, baby. You're getting close, aren't you? Can you feel that pleasure right there?" I nodded vigorously, and he stroked his fingers faster. That feeling, that low ache that stole my breath, was *just* there. "Reach out and take it, Omega. I want you to come for me," he growled, and I did.

I clenched down on his fingers so hard, I wondered if I might break them. I came in long waves that shook my body and made my toes curl. He stroked me through it, and when it was almost too much, he pulled out his fingers. He kissed across my shoulders, whispering things that my blissed-out brain couldn't really comprehend.

"I want to slide my cock inside you right now, sweetheart, but the first time I have you, I want to see your beautiful face."

He stood, climbing out of the bath and grabbing a towel. He was beautiful, naked and wet, with water dripping down his body like a work of art. When he returned, he scooped me out of the water and wrapped me in a towel.

Then he kissed me with so much feeling, it made tears well. I wasn't sure how I knew what he was telling me, that this meant everything to him, but I did.

He swept me up into his arms. "I'm going to make love to you now," he whispered, and there were a million promises in his words.

TWENTY-TWO
MAX

I was so fucking nervous, though I was trying to hide it. Ever since she came on my fingers, I'd been holding back the urge to come. But I'd control myself. I would make it good for her, even if my balls exploded in the process from back pressure.

She was still small in my arms, but the irony didn't escape me that I'd held her just like this when rescuing her from that pit a couple of weeks ago, and now was walking into a room to make love to her. I laid her down on the bed, which I'd made with soft sheets and a water-proof mattress protector, because I intended to make her come, and come, and come again.

Her skin was soft from the milk bath, and as I set her on her feet, I took the towel and dried her gently. Reverently. As she moaned at the coarse feeling of the towel over her hardened nipples, I bit the inside of my cheek and thought about insider trading laws. The Espionage

Handbook. Every color of beige paint I could conjure in my mind's eye. *Anything* but coming on the floor while I dried her off.

When I fell to my knees in front of her, I was nose to pussy, helpless to do anything but hook her leg over my shoulder and have a taste. I groaned as it hit my tongue. She was definitely nearing heat, because she was addictively sweet. Biology was wild.

I lapped and sucked until she was coming on my face, and it was too much. The taste, the way she fluttered against my tongue. I blew without even touching my cock.

Fuck me. I hadn't come this quickly since Llew and I had decided to take each other's virginity when we were sixteen. That had been like a crime scene of bodily fluids, but I wouldn't have had it any other way.

I wanted better than that for Polly, though, so I gave my dick a stern talking-to, hoping that she didn't notice that my cock was currently on rest mode.

The taste of her, and the scent of her that just flowed through the room, meant it wouldn't be soft for long. *Thank fuck for Omega pheromones.*

I climbed up her body and between her thighs, kissing her until I was almost fully hard again. "You're so perfect for us, Omega. Our Omega. My Polly," I breathed, and she kissed me back without any hesitation. If she was worried, I think it was lost in the haze of pleasurable endorphins that had to be rushing through her body.

"Please, Max," she begged softly, and I groaned.

"This might hurt a little, and I'll stop anytime you say the word. This moment is yours, Polly. *You're* in control." A nice female Omega doctor had given her the Omega rod earlier in the week, and I hoped to god it was effective, because when I slid inside her, I swear my vision went white.

I held myself still with burning muscles as I took it slow, clenching my back teeth until I was pretty sure I was going to have to get dentures. Inch by inch, neither of us breathed, and I leaned forward to kiss her. I wanted to soak up any millisecond of pain she might feel and take it into myself.

Finally, she whooshed out a breath, wrapping her feet around my ass and pulling me in tightly until I bottomed out. *Holy shit. Holy shit.*

I kept myself still as my gaze ran over her face. Her eyes were scrunched shut, and I started to panic. "Polly, are you okay? Do you need me to stop?"

She shook her head. "No... I need you to *move*, Max," she moaned, and relief flooded my body. Taking it slow, I moved shallowly inside her, just enough friction that I could build up to what I really wanted. I wanted to drive my cock in and out of her, wanted to flip us over so she could ride me and I could watch those delectable tits bounce.

Instead, with willpower I didn't know I possessed, I took it slow and steady, and soon she was curling against me, chasing the pressure and the pace. I was more than happy to provide. I kissed and sucked at her neck, over the little scent gland that one day I was going to sink my teeth into and bond her.

When I scraped it with my teeth, her eyes went wide, her mouth going slack. "Oh... *oh,*" was all the warning I got before she clamped down so hard on my cock, I stood no chance of holding back my own release. She moaned my name as her sweet little cunt milked me, and I buried my face in her shoulder, exercising all my willpower not to bond her.

When I collapsed over her, she gripped my back muscles almost frantically, and I was worried I was squashing her. But when I went to roll off, she held me there. "Don't move," she said softly into my neck. "I'm not ready for this to be over yet."

This sweet woman, this Omega who I knew we didn't deserve, melted my heart. "Don't worry, Polly. This is only just the beginning."

Despite the sultry looks she was sending me, and then the pouting, I gently refused to have sex with her again. It was hard, but her body needed a little break. It didn't stop me from exploring every inch of her body, and letting her explore every inch of mine too.

That's what she was doing right now, and my military training hadn't prepared me for this level of torture. I was mentally listing off every variety of bird I could think of right now to stop myself from dragging her back up my body and fucking her senseless.

Especially when she was staring at my cock like it was the most fascinating thing she'd ever seen. "Is your penis like Llew's and Rio's? Or August's?" She screwed up her nose. "I'm trying to remember to use the slang words for uh, nether regions, but it still sounds kind of wrong. Cock. Dick." She flushed. "Pussy."

I let out a strangled laugh, and despite the fact it was just biology, my face still heated. It was more complicated to talk about anatomy when someone was staring at your hard cock like a bug under a microscope. Still, I would do the best I could to answer.

"Uh, Llew's is a little bigger; he's a big guy. I'd say Rio and I are equal, length and width wise, but both Llew and Rio have a knot at the base." She reached out and gripped my cock. *Jesus fucking Christ.*

"A knot where?"

I moved her hand down to the base of my cock. "Here. It expands when they come, an evolutionary quirk to keep their cum inside their pretty Omega. That would be you," I teased, hoping she couldn't see the strain I was under not to thrust up into her hand.

"How big does it get?" So curious, my pretty Polly.

I looked down at her fist wrapped around me, and lifted my chin. "About the size of your fist, I guess. It would probably look much like that," I choked out.

She gave me a wide-eyed, worried look that chased

away some of my lust. "That can't fit inside me, Max. You barely fit inside me."

Snorting a laugh, I pulled her further up my body so she was draped over me. "They fit, sweetheart. Omegas were made for Alphas, like two pieces of a puzzle that just fit. Your body will stretch over their knots, and they'll fill you in a way that's intensely pleasurable. More pleasure than I could give you."

She frowned. "You're perfect."

I rubbed my cheek on hers. "Thank you, Omega. I don't doubt I can bring you unimaginable pleasure in other ways, and trust me, I'm going to spend every day of the rest of my life trying to outdo those damn Alphas anyway, but the pleasure an Omega gets from taking a knot—especially during the heat—is something else. Omegas have a reverse knot, I guess. It's called a fib. Did you read about that?"

She nodded, but motioned for me to continue. There were things that you couldn't really get from a textbook.

"It will hold an Alpha, and even a Beta, tightly inside your body and pulsate, milking your Alpha of every last drop of cum. That's what I mean about how perfect you are together."

She hummed softly, her lips nibbling on the skin of my pec. "And what about male Omegas? Do they have a fib?"

I kind of wished August was here for this conversation. Naked too. Actually, there were quite a few of today's activities that could have been fun with August here. Not that it wasn't perfect with just the two of us; I wouldn't have changed a moment.

I selfishly hoped that Polly's Omega wanted August during her heat. The more the merrier, but seeing the two of them together... I bit my lip at the thought.

Then I remembered she'd asked me a question. "Uh, male Omegas have a lock. It's kind of the best of both worlds. A knot for female Alphas, or in rare cases, female Omegas." I winked at her, making her flush that pretty pink. "And a fib-like muscle in their ass, to lock their Alphas in that way, even though I don't think there's a biological imperative there—it just feels really good."

She leaned up and stared down at me. "People have sex in their butts?"

I blinked. And blinked again. Now I *definitely* wished August was here for this conversation.

TWENTY-THREE
LLEW

On the way back from the accountant who took care of all our business affairs, I asked Rio to stop at the VA. I wanted to see August. I thought that perhaps it was time we talked. Rio hadn't argued; I was fairly sure he was just excited to see the handsome Omega. That made two of us.

As we walked in, shame washed over me. This place had been a second home to both Rio and Max since they'd returned from duty. I should have been here too, helping them, supporting them, but instead I'd been lost to my own madness.

The smell of anger and sadness permeated the walls of this building, which was little more than a converted church hall. "There are offices out the back that August works out of for private sessions. We'll see if he's in and has time," Rio murmured softly. He hadn't asked why I wanted to visit August yet, but I could see the burning questions in his eyes. He was probably worried he'd spook me.

I gripped his shoulder and squeezed, and my Packmate jolted. How long had it been since I'd physically touched him?

He looked at me with wounded eyes, and I pushed down the guilt once more. I hadn't broken our bond to hurt him—I'd done it to save him. But the after-effects were the same, this distance between us that had seemed insurmountable, until one sweet little Omega had launched herself into my arms.

The door to August's office was slightly ajar, and his name was on a piece of copy paper beside the frame. Rio looked at that piece of paper hard. "This branch of the VA hustles hard to provide as many services as they can. I know August does shit in his spare time without being paid." Like visiting us at home.

"We'll do what we can." I'd talked to the accountant; I could absolutely do something. I had the money. I might have been out of it, our Pack might be a mess, but my accountants and finance guys were excellent. They'd taken my generational wealth and quadrupled it. I'd already been rich when we'd formed our Pack, but now, none of us had to work unless we wanted to.

We could fund something like this. I'd talk to August about it... if he still wanted anything to do with us after this.

I knocked gently on the door. "Come in," August called, and when we pushed the door open and entered, his smiling face greeted us. "I thought it was you guys. To what do I owe the pleasure?"

It was impossible not to smile back at him. His energy was so light, his scent so sweet and comforting, it was like being embraced by the sun.

"I thought maybe we could take you out to lunch?" I asked him softly. Rio was looking at me from the side of his eye, but didn't contradict me.

August grinned. "I'd like that. I'm starving. There's a deli just around the corner." He hesitated slightly. "Unless you want to go somewhere fancier?"

Stepping back, I shook my head. "I could ravage a Cuban sandwich right now."

Grabbing his wallet—which he definitely wouldn't need—and his jacket, he led us from the room. We followed along behind him like two faithful hounds. He really did smell fucking amazing. If he came to Polly's heat, the combination of their scents would be intoxicating.

I watched as he smiled and talked to every person we passed, his tone gentle at times, and teasing at others, depending on the person he was talking to. I watched the load on people's shoulders lighten with only a few words.

As we emerged from the building, I smiled down at him. Not too far down, because for an Omega, he was very tall, probably around six feet. I was huge, though, so almost everyone was shorter than me. "You're excellent at your job."

August laughed. "I think there are quite a few

damaged people who would disagree. I can't tell you how many times someone's told me I was a quack during a session."

"Hurt people want to hurt people," Rio added, and I wondered if my Packmate had been one of those people, but instantly disregarded the idea. Rio wouldn't raise his voice to an Omega, even someone as large as August.

August reached out and squeezed Rio's hand. "That's true, but it's never too late to heal." He pointed down the street. "It's just around the corner, and it's a nice day to walk."

Agreeing, I waved at him to lead the way.

It didn't take too long for him to break the companionable silence. "Is everything okay with Polly?"

"Polly's fine. She comes more and more into herself everyday and she's..." It was hard for me to express everything Polly had become to me in such a short amount of time. It was how it happened for mates, I think, but even among mates, the connection we had was fast. Fated mates—that would have been the old name for it, and it certainly felt right. "She's like the light at the end of the tunnel, you know? She makes the world brighter just by being in it."

August gave me a small, sad smile. "I know what you mean."

"Polly isn't why I wanted to visit you today." I pointed to a bench seat near a bus stop and indicated we should sit. The wood was rotting, and when I sat, it groaned ominously. "Well, not entirely the reason. I'm unsure if you know this, but my Pack is quite attracted to you."

"Llew!" Rio hissed, but I waved a hand.

"It's true. I have nostrils, Rio, and the smell of your desire makes me sneeze every time anyone even mentions August." August's cheeks pinkened with embarrassment, and it was oddly adorable. "It's not just Rio. Max looks at you like you're the last cookie in the jar, and he just wants a bite. And Polly... Well, Polly hasn't been raised with the ideas that permeate our society about Omegas and what they're supposed to do and be. Not that I agree at all with the way she lived before." A growl rumbled up in my chest, and August rested a calming hand on my forearm, settling my Alpha. That one small gesture cemented what I was going to say.

"Sorry. The idea of what she went through riles the beast and the man." I cleared my throat. "As I was saying, Polly wasn't raised on the idea that a Pack only gets one Omega, that she's meant to see other Omegas as competition. She wants you just as much as the rest of the Pack. At her heat, but also after, I believe. She misses you."

August remained silent, and I worried I'd pushed too hard, but there was no going back now.

"My own Alpha feels quite interested in you. Even before Polly, when the madness still rode me, you made him feel clear-headed when we'd barely gotten moments of clarity in years. I think what I'm trying to say is that if you feel willing, my Pack would like to court you. After Polly's heat, I mean. I don't want to rush you, and I feel like you should have all the information before you decide."

Rio was stiff beside me, but he didn't try to stop what I was saying. He hadn't interrupted at all, and I knew I'd been right. He wanted August, but would never have made the move.

August's gaze was running all over my face, and I wondered what he saw. Did he see the wounds beneath the surface? Did he see the mental shrapnel damage?

A small squeeze of his hand on my arm told me he was listening. Sucking in a deep breath, I ripped off the barely healing scab and let my wounds bleed. "I came into my designation young. I was an extremely strong Alpha, and Rio and Max felt like Pack really early on. I bonded both of them before they even came into their designation. It was a big scandal, but we never understood. How could they not see that we were the same person spread over three bodies? Bonding between Alphas was a little more taboo a decade ago, and bonding when you were a teen made the society Packs clutch their pearls. But what was done was done, and no one could say anything about it."

Our parents had been disapproving at first, but there was nothing that could break a Packbond, and it wasn't like Max and Rio had been unknowns. We'd been close for years.

I cleared the lump from my throat. "I think it was because we had the bond *before* his designation that my connection to Rio was different to other Alpha Packs.

Stronger. His Alpha had always felt like an extension of mine, or mine was an extension of his. They were intertwined. I'd seen it spark to life down our bond, and it was just... different, I guess."

That's what all the Pack theorists had said. Under strict NDAs, at least.

I was surprised when Rio spoke up. "Ever since I'd been a kid, I'd always wanted to join the army. I wanted to be the strongest, most badass person in the room. I wanted to never be weak and small ever again. Joining the Forces had always been my goal, and Llew always supported me. Through basic training and then specialist training, he was there, a constant source of strength, both within the Pack and down the bond. When I was weak, I could draw on his strength, perhaps more than what would be considered normal."

I could see the moment August began to put together the pieces. He knew Rio's story. He'd been there for his recovery. But I still wanted to put it out there, to air our damage and hope that it would help it heal.

"When he did that second tour and was taken by insurgents, it was the worst fucking time of my life. I could feel his pain down my bond." I licked my lips. "They tortured him for information that first day. I felt every second of his pain." The demons threatened to creep in, but there was a huge pulse of happiness down the bond between Polly and me. I sent her the biggest wave of love back, almost an avalanche. We hadn't said the words, but I always wanted her to know the depths of my feelings. She gave me the strength to continue.

"By day two, I couldn't take it anymore. I was the lead Alpha in our Pack. I deserved to feel the pain. I took control of the bond—of his Alpha—and essentially, knocked him out. He was there, but he wasn't. He'd mentally checked out, and I pressed my bond around his and sheltered him from what was happening to his body."

I'd been there for it, though. Every tiny hurt, every way they tried to extract information from him.

I tried to swallow past the lump in my throat. "But bonds aren't meant to work that way. It was just circumstance that ours did. The doctors said it was a form of control akin to barking at an Omega. That because I was there at the formation of his designation, I had control over his Alpha too. So when I knocked him out by taking control of the bond and blocking the pain, he was essentially in a coma."

I clenched my back teeth. "It burned through the bond. By the time he was rescued, the bond was hanging on by the finest thread. The relief of setting him free from his comatose state was the last straw. Our bond broke. It was destroyed, and so was my mind. I turned feral."

Poor fucking Max. He'd borne the brunt of it all. He'd felt his bond snap, and that pain had been the worst feeling of all, worse than the weeks of torture. He hadn't slept for weeks trying to find Rio, and when he did, I lost it.

"You survived through his torture, so he didn't have to," August said softly. His scent wrapped around me, soothing and sweet. "You would have both had to feel it, except you were able to save the Packmate you loved so much from that pain." He gave me a sad smile, filled with empathy, which made me want to break down. "You're a good Alpha, Llewellyn."

I gave him a shaky but sad smile. "That madness was there for years, although it settled eventually. The rage settled. Memories of the pain dimmed. But the loss of my bonds was always there, a yawning chasm in my chest that nothing filled, not even their presence. We tried to re-bond, but it didn't work. It was like we'd had this gift and we'd broken it, so we didn't get a second chance. And then Polly came along."

"And she filled the chasm."

My smile this time wasn't sad. "She did. The madness began to recede immediately. But even with you in the same room as me, the madness ebbed away. The Alpha's feralness eased, like he hoped you'd come to save him." I let out a shaky breath. "So that's it. The big secret. Our baggage laid bare. I wanted to lay it all out before we officially requested to court you."

I stood, reaching down to squeeze Rio's hand, hoping I hadn't overstepped and fucked everything for him. He squeezed it back, and a tension I didn't realize had been stretching down my spine finally relaxed. I looked down at him, and he nodded, his eyes shining.

We didn't talk about what had happened. Not ever. Not when he first came back. Not when he went to therapy. Not when I was lost to the memories and flashbacks that could set me off every day. It was this big bad thing that had sat in the center of our Pack like a grenade.

Apparently, all we'd needed was a sweet little Omega to put a pin back in it, and now we could all move on with our lives.

Rio cleared his throat, thumping me gently on the back as he stood. "Let's go to the deli. We owe August lunch after all that."

Maybe now we could heal. I hoped August would be there to see it too.

TWENTY-FOUR
POLLY

I'd been nervous to tell the guys that Max and I had... had sex? Made love? That he'd deflowered me?

But Max had just told them matter-of-factly over dinner, and they'd all been really supportive. Honestly, it was kind of bizarre, but it was like they were used to operating as a single entity. Rio had inferred as much; as long as I felt cherished, he didn't care who was doing the cherishing.

Some things were odd about my new life. The internet. Popcorn that you cooked in the microwave, but not for too long or your house would explode. Infomercials.

But the weirdest thing was that Omegas were beloved. Coveted. They wanted to hear my opinions. Wanted to look me in the eye as I spoke. Wanted to involve me in every aspect of their lives.

So when they sat me down on the couch for a Pack

meeting, I wasn't even nervous. I didn't expect them to punish me, which was the only reason I'd ever been sent to a meeting back in my old life.

Llew reached for me, so I could take my normal place on his lap, but Rio grabbed me first. "Dibs."

Max raised an eyebrow. "You can't call dibs on a human being, Rio."

He snuggled his nose into my hair. "Just did."

I laughed and leaned back into him. I could feel the semi-hard bulge beneath my thighs, and I wiggled a little. Now that I'd lost my virginity, perhaps I felt a little more brazen? I'd had a taste, and I wanted more.

So, so, so much more.

Rio growled in the back of his throat. "If you don't stop wiggling, my sweet little Omega, I won't be held accountable for my actions."

I looked over my shoulder at him. "What are you going to do?" I teased.

He put his lips next to my ear. "I'd bend you over the back of this couch and eat your pretty little pussy until you're all I can taste. Then, when you're screaming my name so loudly that the neighbors will hear, I'll slide my cock inside you until you're wrapped like a tight little fist around my cock."

My lips parted, lust roaring through my body on the heels of my Omega's enthusiastic *Yes, please!* Someone groaned as I perfumed, and Llew threw his head back to stare at the ceiling like he was physically in pain.

Max tutted, but his pupils had blown wide. "Rio.

Come on, man. We can't have this conversation when all the blood has left my head and landed in my cock."

Rio chuckled evilly behind me and wrapped a tighter arm around my middle, snuggling me close to his body. "Not sorry," he rumbled, but waved a hand for Llew to start.

Llew leaned forward, his elbows on his knees, making his biceps bulge out. His forearms were thick and veiny, and I didn't know why that drove me so wild, but it did. I whined softly beneath my breath, but they all heard.

"Fuck this. Postpone the Pack meeting—I'm going to eat our girl out." Max was already on his feet, and I laughed, shushing him. The power I had over these three men was heady; I'd never had *any* control over another person, and it was both intense and pleasurable at the same time.

"Sit back down, Max. We can get to that part later." I would have been impressed with my sassiness if I hadn't turned bright red as I spoke.

Max slumped back with a disgruntled sigh. "Fine. I think you're an addiction, Beautiful. I can't get enough."

There was a joy in being this desired. They were vocal about how badly they wanted me, and molten desire mixed with the bigger feelings flowed down my bond with Llew almost all the time. Those bigger feelings felt a lot like... love.

Was that what this feeling was? Like I couldn't breathe unless they were with me? Like I was being warmed from the inside out? Like the heart in my chest felt too big to be contained by my ribs?

Llew cleared his throat, his eyes filled with emotion. "We went and saw August today."

I stilled, thoughts of sex disappearing. No, that was a lie. My libido was still in a frenzy around all of them. But my Omega and I were of the same frame of mind when it came to the other Omega. We were intensely interested in August.

"Oh? Why?"

"I wanted to explain a little of our history to him. I'll explain it to you also, if you'd like. Now, or one day, whenever you're ready. It's not a nice story, and it's in the past." Licking his lips nervously, Llew continued. "You're the most important person in the world to me, but Max and Rio are too. They are my life and my heart, and they kept me going through some of the worst days of my existence." He hesitated again, and I could see him struggling. I wanted to appease him, but I thought perhaps he needed to get this out in his own time. "Do you like August?"

I nodded. "Of course. He's sweet and kind, and so smart."

"And handsome?" Rio prompted. "Your Omega likes him?"

I chewed my lip. Was this a trap? Would they tell me to leave if I admitted to desiring someone out of our Pack?

Rio stroked a hand up and down the outside of my

thigh. "Be honest, Sweetheart. Nothing you could say now would change how we feel about you. You're a part of this Pack forever."

"Uh, yes. I find him attractive. I asked if he'd consider being at my heat," I reminded them.

"Would you like him to be a part of every heat forever? Would you like for him to become part of our Pack?"

The happy little whine that burst from my lips wasn't entirely from the human part of my brain. I cleared my throat. "Yes."

"Your Omega too?" Max asked. "Really embrace her and see how she feels about another Omega in her Pack. Kissing her Alphas. Sharing her nest. Taking her knots?"

My cheeks heated at his words. I wanted to see a knot. Taste it. I imagined August beside me, licking at Llew's knot, and my whole body flashed with heat. Someone groaned, and I realized my blush had travelled from my face down to my chest.

"I think I'd quite like that."

Llew laughed. "So I can scent, Sweet Thing. God, how are you so perfect?" He adjusted his cock in his sweats. "Rio and Max have had a crush on August for a long time. I was the problem with their pursuing him— well, my illness more specifically. Though I think perhaps it was fate that made us wait. Fate was bringing us you, and we just had to be patient. We would like to discuss the possibility of courting August to join our Pack."

I screwed up my nose. "Courting?" I'd read the term

in *Omegas for Dummies,* but the book hadn't been very specific about what courting actually entailed.

Llew frowned, and I kissed Rio's cheek before wiggling from his lap and crawling across the couch toward my big Alpha. Rio groaned, and I felt his fingertips stroke across my butt as he mumbled something about how perfect my ass was, making me grin.

Straddling Llew's thighs, I looked up into his rough-hewn face. "Why do you smell distressed, Alpha?"

"You deserved so much more than you were given, Polly. You deserved to be loved and coddled. You deserved to be courted by Alphas. You deserved to experience everything life had to offer, and I feel guilty because selfishly, I'm glad you bonded with me. I couldn't imagine my life without you now."

I tried to imagine the life he was describing. Tried to imagine a world where I'd been rescued and instead of coming home with Rio and Max, I stayed with OJ and her Pack. Where I had to meet strangers, go out into the world without the security of Llew's bond deep inside my chest giving me strength. Without Rio solid at my side, without Max talking me through things.

I imagined meeting Alphas like the ones who took me from The Homestead again. Ones who didn't have the moral compass of the Barrie Pack.

"I deserve the best Pack." It was a simple statement, and Llew nodded. Smiling, I leaned forward and kissed his full lips. "Then I'm lucky, because that's what I got. I've seen the worst the world has to offer, and I know what you are. So, back to courting August. What does that involve?"

It was Max who answered. "Gifts. Dinners. Dates. Showing him we can provide."

"Showing you *both* what we can provide," Rio added.

I didn't need material things, and I doubted that August was overly worried about the things that money could buy either. "And what happens at the end of the courting period?" I had a few guesses, but I wanted to hear it out loud.

Max steepled his fingers under his chin. "We'd formally ask him to join the Pack, we'd have an official bonding ceremony, and then we'd share mating bonds."

The idea of having a mating bond with more than just Llew set my heart racing. "Could I share mating bonds with you guys too?"

Rio launched toward me, landing on his knees at my feet. There was something oddly thrilling about this big man, who was eye height with me even on his knees, looking at me with such hopeful desperation. "Anytime, Polly. You say the word, and I'll make you mine." He seemed to get control of himself, and I could almost see him struggling with his Alpha. "But you deserve the grand gestures and the declarations just as much as August. I can wait, and we can do this the right way. Bond or no bond, I'm yours, Omega."

His eyes were burning with something so hot, so possessive, that it stole my breath, and I was moments away from telling him I wanted it now. I didn't need grand gestures or ceremonies. I needed *him*.

Unfortunately, Max's phone broke the moment. Pulling from his pocket, he looked down at it. "I need to take this."

I reached out, and Rio leaned into my arms. For a moment, I was pressed between two Alphas and hooboy, my Omega liked that. A lot. She sent me a rapid barrage of images where we were in this exact position but naked. More and more, my thoughts devolved into pure filth, which seemed to track with how close to my heat I was.

"Omega, you smell so divine right now," Llew murmured into my ear. "I'm dying to know what you're thinking—" He paused, cocking his head and looking toward the door that Max had gone through.

Max reappeared, his face more solemn than I'd expected. "My informant has a lead. He thinks the Homestead is in Arkansas, although he hasn't narrowed down where exactly." He came and sat next to me. "He found other survivors."

"Survivors?"

"He found the Alphas. The ones who designated."

I shook my head. "There weren't any Alphas born, only Betas and very rarely, Omegas. Alphas stopped being born after the..." I trailed off. There was no apocalypse. No world-changing phenomenon. There were only old men on a power trip. "They got rid of them."

Max grabbed my hands and held them in his own. "Yes."

"And they're alive?"

He chewed his lip. "Some are." He hesitated. "Some didn't make it. Toledo—uh, my tech guy—thinks they were murdered to tie up loose ends."

I sucked in a breath that felt like acid. Just when I thought the Leaders couldn't get any more reprehensible, they did.

"Toledo reached out to a couple who'd managed to find each other. They want to meet you, and see if you have any knowledge that can help them bring down the Homestead."

"No." Rio's tone was firm. "She can't go and meet random Alphas from her old life."

Max gave him a heavy look. "That's not your decision. It's no one's decision except Polly's."

I didn't know what I wanted. Crawling back beneath the strong arms of my Alpha, I breathed in his scent until my heart stopped thundering out of my chest. His hand worked up and down my back in soothing lines.

"You don't have to make a decision now, Sweet Girl. In fact, it would be... safer to wait until your heat is over completely."

I nodded, thankful for the reprieve. This was too much. I was happy, but could I continue to be so, knowing that out there, the Homestead was killing off kids who were Alphas?

The answer was no. I couldn't be happy with that. I'd do what I could to stop them, including meeting with the ghosts of my past.

TWENTY-FIVE
RIO

I could punch Max in his annoyingly beautiful face. Polly was walking around subdued, her scent edged with something burnt and sad, contrasting with the sweetness of her oncoming heat.

She'd been happy. We'd made her happy. Hell, I'd seen her face when we suggested we bring August into the Pack too—like I'd given her a puppy, a kitten, and a lifetime supply of chocolate all in one day.

Then Max had gone and ruined it with the harsh realities of fucking life. If I could save her from the ugly things about the world, I would. Max and I had argued about it, after she'd gone off to bed with Llew last night.

He said she'd been lied to for her whole life; she deserved the truth. I argued that she'd seen enough of the evilness of humanity, and didn't need to be subjected to more. It was an impasse, and we'd gone to bed angry.

I hated that too.

When we found this fucking Homestead, I was going to burn the whole fucking thing to the ground. I couldn't even go to the VA and talk through the growing anger in my chest, because we'd propositioned August and he still hadn't given us an answer. Talking to anyone else about it would feel almost wrong.

Sighing, I slumped back on the couch. It didn't help that my Alpha was so close to the surface that it was a constant battle for control. Riled by the proximity of Polly's heat and the ongoing threat to her safety, I felt like I was ready to crawl out of my skin.

A knock on the door had me groaning and getting to my feet. Checking the security cameras on my phone, my heart thumped harder in my chest at the sight of August at our front door. Had I summoned him with my thoughts?

Fuck, he was beautiful. Delicate and sturdy at the same time. My Alpha just wanted to chase him, run him down, and fuck him into the lawn. Chase, bite, bond.

Dammit. Maybe I shouldn't open the door, and instead go and have my third cold shower for the day.

Another knock had me gritting my teeth and pushing the Alpha down. I was in control. I sucked in a deep breath before I opened the door, but it was useless. As soon as his scent hit my nose, the Alpha roared back to the surface.

I growled deep in my chest, making August's pupils blow out. His scent surged up at the sound, and I stepped back, giving us a both a little space before I reached out, grabbed him, and kissed the fuck out of him.

He cleared his throat. "You okay, Rio?"

It was only practiced vulnerability with August, a trust built over months of therapy, that had me saying, "No, not really."

Worry shadowed his gaze, before it was gone again. My Alpha huffed that he was being weak in front of his Omega, but the man knew that it wasn't a weakness to have feelings. If anyone had taught me that, it was the Omega in front of me.

"Can I come in? We can talk about it." August reached out, stepping closer to me, and I held my Alpha tightly. His Omega scent washed over me, calming the Alpha, and giving me space to breathe.

"You're welcome here anytime. Just walk in." *And never leave. Stay forever.* I led him through to the kitchen. "Do you want a coffee? Max is out, and Llew and Polly are still sleeping."

August nodded. "That would be great."

I put a pod in the coffee machine and sucked in a deep breath. *Don't fuck this up for us*, I chastized myself.

While the coffee brewed, I turned back around to face August, pushing the worry down. Instead, I reveled in the happiness of seeing August in my kitchen. I couldn't pinpoint the moments he'd gone from someone who was helping me through the worst parts of my life, to someone who I looked forward to seeing every week, to someone I missed when I didn't see him, but it had been gradual. If Max hadn't felt the same way about him, I'd worry that I was projecting my healing onto the Omega in an unhealthy way. But there was something about August that just meshed with us both.

I'd had fantasies of making him ours for so long, had imagined knotting him and marking him so many times in the shower, that it would be way too embarrassing to ever admit.

"What's happened?"

I kept my voice even and professional as I told August about what Max's tech guy had found. About the murder of Alpha teens. About survivors wanting to see her. Her spiral. My fears. My argument with Max. It all just poured out of me.

I gave him a sad smile. "We have more baggage in this Packhouse than JFK."

August stood, stepping in front of my chair until his legs were between my knees. And then he pulled my head to his stomach and hugged me. Pulling me tight against his hard abs, he buried his fingers in the short lengths of my hair and just held me. His breaths were even and regular, his scent so reassuring that I could feel the anger, the turmoil, just floating away.

I admitted something to myself that I would never admit to August for fear of pushing him away. At some point in the last year, I'd fallen in love with him. It was a soft glow in my chest that always turned into an inferno in his presence. I'd kept it hidden, locked away, because he deserved better than a broken Pack and an even more broken man. But it hadn't stopped me from loving him, wanting him.

As I shuddered in his embrace, I couldn't help the feeling of rightness that settled in my soul. I was greedy; I knew that. I had Polly, who I wanted with a longing that stole my breath. My feelings for her had struck me like a bolt of lightning.

But my feelings for August had been like a steady warmth in my soul.

It was selfish, but I wanted them both, and I would do everything in my power to have them both. To make them happy and content.

I tilted my head up to look at August's pretty dark eyes. "Thank you."

"Anytime." He leaned down and brushed his lips across mine. I froze, not moving, in case this was actually a dream. When he deepened the kiss, I leaned hard into it, chasing the kiss until I could taste him on my tongue. He pulled back, and his pupils were so wide, it was like looking at pure darkness. "Forever."

My heart thundered in my chest. Was he suggesting that he was considering us? Allowing us to court him? God, I hoped so.

His smile was sweet, and I couldn't help but kiss him once more. I held him tightly to me, unwilling to let him go just yet. "Why'd you come over? I'm pretty sure it wasn't to hear my woes, for once."

He laughed and sat in my lap, and I gave my cock a stern talking-to about what was appropriate courting behavior. Stabbing him in the thigh was not appropriate behavior.

"I wanted to check on Polly, and, uh, tell you that I accept your courting suit."

I whooped, leaping from the chair and spinning him around, even though we were basically the same height, so his feet dragged on the ground. I kissed him again. "You won't regret this, August, I promise."

The sound of my shout drew a sleepy-looking Polly and a mussed-looking Llew from his bedroom. He had her tightly just behind him in case of intruders, and I loved that man more than anything.

When Polly saw August in my arms, a bright smile spread across her face, the first one I'd seen since last night. "August!"

She ran towards him, and he caught her easily in his arms. He lifted her up to bury his nose in her neck as she clung to him. She began to scent mark him, though I wasn't sure she was aware she was doing it. They looked so happy together, that any last fears I had about them eventually becoming adversaries in the same Pack disappeared.

"Beautiful girl, you smell so fucking delicious right now," August groaned, and I realized he was right. She smelled sweeter, and given the haggard expression on Llew's face, he'd had to sleep beside that sweet scent all night.

"She had a rough night. Little heat waves, I think, and then she'd settle. But not long now, I don't think."

Llew went over and kissed August's cheek. "It's good to see you, Omega." His voice was husky, and Polly whined. But not in discomfort at her Alpha kissing another Omega. She grabbed him closer, like she could drag her big Alpha into her Omega cuddle pile.

Fuck, I wanted to be in the middle of that cuddle pile.

When Polly turned her head and kissed August, I swear, all the blood rushed to my dick until I was light-headed. She kissed him like she wanted to swallow him whole. Their scents intertwined, and I stared at the ceiling, breathing through my mouth so I didn't go into rut.

Fuck.

August finally pulled his mouth away from hers. "You better get Max back here as soon as possible, because Polly is going into full-blown heat. I give it a few hours, at most."

I grabbed my phone from my pocket and moved out the back door to the patio. I couldn't think in there, with the pheromones so thick in the air, I could almost taste them. I hit Max's number, and he answered almost immediately. "Hey. Everything okay?"

"She's going into heat. August says get your ass home ASAP." We were prepared; Max had seen to that. We had snack foods and sports drinks, waterproofed bedding, nesting supplies—basically everything we thought she might need.

Max swore softly. "Show her the nesting supplies in

the cupboard. She'll want to nest. I'll pick up the instant meals and be home in forty minutes."

He hung up, and I knew I could leave the details in his hands. I was going to be worse than useless for days now. I only had one objective: to please my Omegas.

With that in mind, I sucked in some clear air and walked back into the house. I had this.

TWENTY-SIX
AUGUST

I hadn't really known how a heat with another Omega would go. There was a chance that her heat would push me into mine, but it wasn't guaranteed. There was also a chance that when she reached the stage of her heat that was more instinct than cognizance, she'd throw me out.

What I hadn't really expected was her dragging me into her nest and making me help set it all up. All the research I'd ever read told me that even when there were two Omegas in a Pack, nesting was an intensely personal experience.

But not for Polly. She'd dragged me and my armful of soft furnishings into the small room and pushed me into the middle of the low bed, then nested around me. It was like I was becoming part of her safe place, especially when she would come over and rub her body over mine, scenting me and herself. She'd grind herself down on my dick, until it took every ounce of willpower I had not to flip her over and fuck her senseless.

Soon enough, though, she'd break the fevered kisses and go back to setting up her nest. I realized she was creating a safe place for both of us, and my chest clenched. It was so easy to fall in love with this little Omega.

When she lay next to me and whimpered softly, I gathered her up into my arms. I just wanted to soothe every hurt, every clench of pain. Stroking her back, I made soft noises in my chest. "I know," I crooned. "For a little bit, it will feel like your body is trying to turn itself inside out through your ovaries, but your Alphas will give you their knots. You'll feel better than you ever have in your life."

She rubbed her sweet little body against mine, making me grit my teeth. "I hurt *now*, August," she whined, so pitifully that I was helpless to resist the words that sprang from my mouth.

"Want me to ease you a little? It'll stave off the cramps for a little while."

She nodded furiously, but then cocked her head at me. "Ease me?"

My own dick was leaking at an alarming rate just from her pheromones, and if I didn't also go into heat this week, it would be nothing short of a miracle. "I'll make you come, so your heat will ease a little." Her eyes hooded, and I growled in my chest like I was the Alpha here.

"I'd like that," she whispered. "I'd really like to have sex with you, August. And it's not just the heat talking either. You're the most beautiful man I've ever seen."

Any semblance of control I had disappeared in an instant. I rolled on top of her, caging her between my forearms before dropping down to kiss her. I made out with her, a desperation I hadn't felt since I was a horny teen driving my mouth to plunder hers, my tongue twisting and sliding, my body wedged between her thighs.

She arched up, chasing the friction of her core against a pair of soft sweats Rio had lent me when it was obvious my dick was being choked in the meatlocker of my Levi's. I could feel my slick leaking through my boxer shorts, dampening the front of the sweats. I was going to have to wash these before I returned them.

She was shoving against her soft pajama shorts, and I wanted to tear them off with my bare hands. Was this fever what Alphas felt during their Omegas heats? This complete loss of any higher reasoning? I just wanted to be buried deep in her body as soon as possible, and all the reasons to wait had escaped me completely.

She finally managed to wriggle them off, then her dripping pussy was sliding up and over my abs. Continuing to whine, she shoved at the waistband of my sweats. "August," she panted. "Please. I need someone inside me." Shaking her head, she spun on my stomach until her back was to me and she was bending forwards, pushing her ass in my face and my sweats down my thighs.

Oh fuck. The sweet scent of her slick made me feel high, and I groaned. "Take what you need, Omega," I choked out, warning my dick to hold it together. Not to blow on her before she'd even taken us in. My brain was screaming about foreplay, about connection, but my little Omega knew what she wanted and it was to take my cock, place it against her entrance and slide down it with an excruciatingly slow pace.

Holy fucking goddess. "Polly, fuck, you feel so good that I'm going to..." I came inside her, painting her inner walls and filling her up. She shuddered around me, her own orgasm spurred on by mine, but I didn't soften at all. The joy of being a male Omega. Holding her hips, I fucked up into her, watching intently where her core stretched around my cock, cum leaking out with each thrust.

I was going to need dental care with the amount of force I was grinding my teeth to prevent myself from coming again. I was dying, but it was the only way I ever wanted to go. I levered myself up, wrapping an arm around her waist, restricting her movement but hitting new places inside her.

Fuck. I played with her clit, and then she was coming again and I was barrelling right after her. My lock thickened inside her, swelling and holding me tight inside her entrance.

"Fuck, Polly. Fuck," I breathed, and she finally

slumped back against me. My arms and abs felt like jello, so without taking my cock from her, I rolled us both to the side in her nest.

She was breathing heavily, her body lax in my arms. "That was..." She waved her hands like words were too hard to summon. I agreed with a grunt and maybe a tiny thrust inside her. The primal part of my brain liked the fact that my release was trapped, soaking into her womb.

By the time my lock went down, some functional part of my brain caught up with me, and I slowly eased myself from her body. "Come on, beautiful. Let's get you cleaned up." I stroked my fingers through the mess I'd made and tried not to just thrust myself back in again. "There'll be plenty of time to be dirty later."

Polly's nest had lower ceilings than the other rooms, so when I picked her up, she had to hold onto me like a baby koala.

She giggled as she wrapped her legs around my waist, and I tried not to die of lust as my own release smeared across my abs. That shouldn't be so fucking attractive. I was basically a barbarian.

Her suite had an attached bathroom, for which I was eternally grateful, because if I'd had to walk ten more steps with her wrapped around me like that, I would have pressed her against the wall and fucked her again.

I was surprised someone had run a bath, and I held her close with one hand while I checked the temperature with the other. It was perfect for her overheated skin. She was definitely having a heat spike, if she wasn't going into full-blown heat. I thought I'd have about fifteen minutes before she was climbing back out of this bath and begging for release.

She sank into the water with a contented sigh. "Do you ever feel like fate just owes you one?" she whispered softly to me. "I didn't even believe in the concept of fate until I got here. I thought my life was at the whims of some vengeful gods who had an unfortunate love triangle millenia ago. But I was reading a book that Max bought me, about sexy vampires." She smirked, and I fell in love.

Maybe it was the pheromones or the elation of what we'd just done fucking with my emotions or whatever. But that tiny smirk, the way her head was tipped back in the water as her body was lax, while she smelled so good, it was like a match to the powderkeg of emotions inside me that I was barely holding back.

Dumbstruck, I said nothing, and she continued completely oblivious to the fact she now held my heart in her dainty hands. "Anyway, these vampires had fated mates. So I Googled the idea of fate, about how the world seems to maneuver us until we end up at that one moment where everything just falls into place. Someone on the world wide web called it the 'invisible string theory'. I kind of like that idea."

Kneeling beside the tub, I brushed the hair from her forehead, as she floated there happily. "I like that idea too." Because it certainly felt that I'd been waiting for this moment for so damn long. She was the string, drawing us all together.

She yawned, her eyes closing. "I feel so tired, like my limbs are made of stone."

I stood up, climbing into the large bath behind her. Resting her against my chest, I twined my fingers in hers and rested them on the soft curve of her stomach. "It's your body trying to conserve energy for the heat. Rest, beautiful. I'll hold you safe until you wake up."

I kissed the top of her head, and she purred for me, but it was a sleepy sound, and soon enough she was lightly snoring.

Without a shadow of a doubt, I knew my decision to allow the Barrie Pack to court me was the correct one. Hell, they didn't have to court me at all; I knew deep down in my chest that this was right. But part of me wanted to show Polly what to expect, what she deserved.

How to be coddled and loved properly. Protected. I knew that the guys wouldn't court me and exclude her. If they were doing it for me, they would do it for Polly too. That was part of the reason I knew they were the Pack for me.

A soft knock at the door had me looking over my shoulder. Max stood there, his cheeks flushed and a crooked smile on his face. "How is she?" he whispered, stepping into the room.

There were hardly any bubbles left and the water was starting too cool. "She's perfect."

He sat on the edge of the tub, reaching over to run a finger down the soft curve of her cheek. "On that, we can all agree. Heat symptoms?"

"She was ramping up in the nest, but I managed to ease her enough that she could get some rest. But today is definitely the day. How are you?"

He looked wild, his eyes shining and filled with anticipation and worry. "Stressed that I've forgotten something. Worried that this will somehow be traumatizing for her despite the fact that none of us would do a single thing that she didn't want. Excited to be a part of something so primal that it makes my dick hard if I think about it for too long."

I huffed a small laugh. "So all the usual things then. And the Alphas?"

"Wearing a hole in the carpet. Even I can smell your combined scents from the hallway, and it's a heady damn elixir. You could bottle it and put Viagra out of business."

Polly whined softly, squirming beneath my hands. Our respite was over. Her skin was beginning to heat up all over again, and I knew that the moment she got out of this bath, the sweet scent of her slick would flood every crevice of the room.

I looked at Max, my face serious. "I think the carpet will be safe. Tell the guys to get their shit under control because our Omega is about to go into heat and it'll be a long, exhausting few days. Carb load while they can." I traced my fingers across her cheekbones. "Omega? Polly? Time to wake up before you turn into a fish."

Her eyelashes fluttered open, and she looked up at me, then at Max. "You're back." She smiled, then curled into a ball with a groan as a heat cramp hit. She was breathing through her teeth by the time it released. "That was... not fun. Is it supposed to cramp like that?"

I nuzzled her head. "Yeah, remember the miserable part? Welcome to the heat, my sweet Omega. Don't worry, it won't be for long."

Max reached into the bath and lifted her into his arms, only putting her down briefly to wrap a towel around her soft curves. He hesitated at the door, like the idea of leaving me behind felt wrong. Smiling, I shooed him back into her suite. "I'll only be a minute."

He left, and I pulled myself out of the bath. I took a moment to breathe before the air was so thick with pheromones and nothing but the need to be inside her.

This was the first night of the rest of my life with my Pack. I knew that much in my soul.

TWENTY-SEVEN
POLLY

Oh god. August hadn't been exaggerating about the way the heat would be a terrible balance between pain and pleasure. As a wave of pain did its best to shred my uterus, Max placed me gently in the middle of the nest, then walked away to stand outside the doorway once more.

I mewled pitifully, and he gave me a soft smile. "Can I enter your nest, Omega?" he asked quietly, and I growled at him.

"Yes! But your clothes have to stay out there." I grinned, before the next cramp had me curling up like one of the little wood bugs that we used to roll down the paths as kids.

Max must have shed his clothes in record time, because he was right there seconds later. He sucked on my nipples, which took the edge off the pain, but my

Omega was screaming at me that what would *really* help would be a big knot from one of my Alphas.

I had to agree, but Max felt so nice between my thighs, and I wanted him inside me. Right now. I wrapped my legs around his so he couldn't disappear, and when he slid himself inside me, my body went lax. *Yes.* This was what I needed.

His nose bumped against mine, and he swiped a kiss across my lips, before gripping my thighs and pressing back up to his knees. He spread me wide, moving his hands up to my hips to hold me tight, and then he *fucked* me. There was no other word for the sweaty slapping of his body against mine, the way I could feel every inch of his cock pounding inside me, and I adored it. I'd been the fortunate recipient of Max's lovemaking, and that wasn't this. This was raw and carnal, and oh so *perfect*.

"Max!" I screamed, my fib starting to flutter, ready to catch him and hold him inside my body. But he wasn't done, my beautiful Beta. He pulled almost all the way out, fucking me in shallow thrusts that seemed to hit just about every nerve ending I possessed. I came with the force of a tsunami, and my slick gushed across his body, running down onto the bed.

But my Beta, he wasn't done. He pushed back inside, and this time, he didn't hold back. He fucked me until I was coming again, my fib gripping him inside me as he came, and he collapsed on top of me.

He groaned, his face pressed into my hair. "Fuck, Polly... You have no idea how good that feels," he grunted, and I grinned, wrapping my arms around his waist.

"I might have some idea," I teased. My body felt hot, and my mind was increasingly foggy, but I wanted to get this out before I was too far gone. "Max?"

Pushing up onto his arms, he looked down at me. "Yeah, baby?"

"I want you to bond me. I want you all to bond me. August said I might ask to be bonded during my heat, and that I wouldn't know what I'm saying, but I do. I want you all to be mine. I want what I have with Llew with all of you. So if I ask... don't deny me? Unless you don't want it."

Now my face was hot, and it was only partially because my whole body felt like it was on fire. Mostly, it was because I was still embarrassed at asking for what I wanted, like I deserved anything more than whatever they deemed necessary to offer.

Max stiffened, and I worried I'd fucked up, but then his whole body melted against mine. "Are you sure?"

I nodded vigorously, my core clenching around his penis that was still inside me. His cock. I wasn't a biology textbook.

He kissed all over my face, every inch of my sweat-soaked skin. "Then I would be honored to bond you, my sweet Omega. My Polly," he groaned, kissing me deeply with so much... love. That was what his adoration was. Love. And I loved him back.

My skin was tight on my bones now, and even

though Max was still inside me, I needed him to move. I needed *more*.

My whine was barely a thready breath, but Max knew. He kissed my cheeks again, then slid out of me, still semi-hard. I looked over to see my Alphas standing at the door. Llew was looking at me with so much heat, it felt like it was raising my core temperature. Rio stood beside August, who'd put pants back on, which made me feel outraged. I frowned, reaching a hand out to him.

He smiled down at me, like he knew why I was pissed. "What's wrong, beautiful girl?" he teased softly, and I gripped the waistband of his sweats and tugged. He laughed as I dragged them down his legs, uncaring that Max's cum was leaking out of me. When August finally stepped out of them, I stuffed them at the edges of my nest, his delicious scent settling something.

Yes. Perfect.

Looking over at the other guys, I made grabby hands, and they dutifully undressed. Rio even passed me Max's discarded clothes. I smiled up at him, and he groaned. "Beautiful, don't look at me like I just gave you a diamond ring instead of Max's dirty underwear."

Max chuckled from where he was lying naked in the nest, August pulled down beside him. My eyes took in all that skin greedily, and now I wanted more.

As if it was throwing a tantrum, another cramp punched me in the gut. *Alphas. I need my Alphas.*

Llew was right there, like he was seconds from

launching himself at me. "Omega, can we enter your nest?"

"Yes! Please, Alphas. Fuck me."

Rio looked at the sky like he was praying for strength, and Llew pushed him inside the nest in front of him. My big Alpha, always taking care of his Pack.

Rio came down onto the nest and bundled me into his arms. "You smell amazing, Omega. Like home." He kissed me as he pulled me into his lap, a dirty, messy kiss. "Like happiness." I ground down on his hard dick and was rewarded by his hands clenching tightly around my hips. "Fuck, your body feels so hot. Is she meant to be this hot?" he asked someone, but I didn't look up.

No, I was entirely focused on his cock jutting between our bodies, large and hard and straining. I reached down and stroked it, feeling the large band of... not spongy. But like something that was both firm and hard. My brain was too fried to think of a good example.

When I squeezed it, Rio yelped and groaned, his cock flexing in my hand. "Fucking hell, Omega. You're going to kill me."

I already felt like I was dying, and with his knot in my hand, I was whimpering with need. "Want. Now." Higher reasoning was lost. I gripped his cock, put it where I needed it the most, and slid him inside me.

Almost instantly, the pain eased, my body immediately going languid. *This. This is what I need.*

But then I needed more again. I whined, and Rio growled low. His eyes were hooded, the look in them wild. He rolled onto his back so I was straddling his hips. "Ride me, my Omega, and then I'm going to knot you like the good girl you are."

Yes. I laid a hand on his chest and did what he suggested. I rode him like he was the only way to get where I was going. I was so far gone that I didn't care if I was doing it right, or if I looked stupid. The only thing that was right was that he was there, below me, filling me.

I came on his cock, and his growled, "Keep going. Take more," was the most beautiful thing I'd ever heard. He was big and hard, and he chased away the pain, replacing it with a bliss that was almost indescribable.

Someone knelt beside me, capturing my lips. I realized it was Max purely from the taste of his tongue. I kissed him hard, my movements messy, but his hands on my hips helped to keep me steady.

Rio looked like he was in physical pain, and I could feel his knot nudging at my entrance. Suddenly, I was wild. Feral.

"Mine," I groaned, striking at his chest with my teeth. I bit him as I forced myself down on the wide knot, and then I felt him everywhere.

His blood was on my tongue. His knot was stretching me impossibly wide. His thoughts, his happiness was banging down the newly formed bond between us. It was... everything.

He sat up, his arms banding around me, holding me tight to his body, and his knot hit new places inside me that made my vision flash white. He buried his face in the crook of my neck and then the sting of his bite was quickly chased away by the third orgasm from his knot. I milked him dry, all pain disappearing, to be replaced by nothing but love.

"My little Omega. My mate," he murmured against my skin as he licked at his bite. Every time his tongue moved over the wound, I felt it in my clit. "I'm going to love and cherish you forever."

I knew it; I felt the certainty of it in my soul now. I blinked rapidly, my head flopping forward until I was pressed to his chest, and then exhaustion dragged me into blissful darkness.

Pain roused me from my sleep, and I reached for anyone who could help. I peeled my sweaty skin from someone around me and whined.

Big hands gathered me up, and I sighed contentedly. I knew who this was. I knew his scent like my own. Knew his taste. Knew the feel of his hands.

"Llew," I breathed, tilting my head up for him to kiss me. He slid inside me, but didn't move. Just sat there, his huge dick filling me up and chasing away the pain. "So big…" It definitely wasn't a complaint.

He chuckled softly, his hands tilting me back so he could kiss my overheated skin. "You're good for my ego, Sweet Thing."

"Hurts," I grumbled, and he made a soft, soothing noise.

"I know. I'm going to help you fix this right now. But I thought you might like to see something while I do." He lifted me up off his cock, ignoring my whine as he spun me, then slid me right back down. I closed my eyes at the sheer perfection of him inside me. Would anything else ever feel as good as my Pack like this? He leaned in close to my ear. "Look, my Omega," he murmured.

I looked over to see August pressed between Rio and Max. They were kissing his body, sucking sweet little pink marks all over his skin.

I wanted to add my marks to theirs. I clenched hard around Llew's body, making him grunt. "They've been at that for nearly an hour. They want each other, but they want you to be there for the first time. To watch what you helped create. Would you like to see your Omega stretched between your Pack?"

"Yes!" I shouted it, making the three men in front of me pause and look at me with wide eyes. I flushed, but made grabby hands, scrambling to hold Llew close. "I'm sorry. Don't stop. Please," I groaned, especially when Llew bucked up inside me as a reward. "You're like a dirty dream."

Max got to his knees, leaning across to kiss me gently. "Do you want to watch us fuck your handsome Omega while you're trapped on your Alpha, my dirty girl?" I nodded so hard, it was a wonder I didn't get a concussion, and he laughed. "You got it. Thank you for letting us share a taste."

I pushed at his shoulder. "Kiss him."

He raised an eyebrow. "Where?"

I blinked. "On his cock," I mumbled with a little less sass, my cheeks flushing. I hadn't given oral, though I'd received a lot, and I wanted to see. Wanted to watch how it was done.

Max crawled between August's legs and licked up the insides of his thighs. He flicked his tongue over his tight sac before running it up the length of August. A length I knew the feel of so well. Rio leaned back against the edge of the nest and dragged August into his lap. He whispered something into his ear, and I watched him drop August down onto his cock.

Their combined groan made me come, just the sound. Llew panted behind me, but didn't divert my attention, just moved in slow, shallow movements that made pleasure build like the ebb and flow of a tide.

When August was fully impaled on Rio's cock, Max readjusted himself in between their combined thighs and sucked the head of August's cock into his mouth, making him shout something entirely incomprehensible. I could feel Rio's waves of pleasure like they were my own; combined with Llew's, it was like I was being bombarded with endorphins. I felt high.

August opened his eyes and held my gaze, hot and filled with lust, and Llew decided we'd had enough of being silent spectators. Gripping my hips, he moved me up and down his cock in time with the pace of Max on August's cock.

I was panting, my eyes never straying from August's

like we were fucking each other, our Alphas just the instruments we were using to achieve release. It was... transcendent, and I lost count of the amount of times I came. Over and over, I fluttered around Llew's cock. Over and over, I watched August's face scrunch up until his cum poured from the corners of Max's mouth.

I must have made some noise, because Max crawled toward me and dribbled the sweet taste of August's cum across my own lips. He fed it to me slowly, until I grabbed his hair and pulled him down, chasing the taste from every corner of his mouth.

Then I pulled back and bit my Beta. Right there on his throat so everyone would know he was mine. My Max. He bit me back, on the top edge of my breast, just below the brand that marked me as property.

I wasn't property anymore, but I did belong to someone. Several someones. My Pack.

As Llew's knot filled me with an orgasm that had me losing consciousness, I knew that this happiness was worth every torment I could have ever endured.

This was fate. This was where my strings led.

TWENTY-EIGHT
MAX

I felt like a raisin, wrinkled and dehydrated, but the happiest fucking raisin on the planet. The last four days had been intense, but the best four days of my life. Rio had both Polly and August in the bath, washing them down like the gifts that they were.

Pulling my phone off the charger, I looked down at the dozen calls, messages and emails I'd missed. Some were from work—there was one notable message from Lance of an irate-looking Rufio throwing a tantrum.

Lance had come and collected both Rufio and Doodles at some point after Polly's heat had started. They needed to be cared for, and with two Omegas, I wasn't sure any of us could have been pulled away. I'd promised to return the favor when they needed it next.

There were quite a few calls from an unknown number and one message from Toledo which merely said *Call me.* Frowning, I dialed the encrypted number we always talked on. It rang and rang, and I hung up, knowing he'd call me back.

Which he did, within two seconds. "Where have you *been?*" His pissy tone relaxed me somehow. Toledo always sounded a little pissed at the world.

I kept my voice neutral as I replied, "Something came up here that I had to deal with." I wasn't going to tell Toledo that Polly had gone into heat and I'd spent the last four days balls deep in an orgy.

"There's been a development. You should have told me someone else was working on this for you. Some little hacker on the dark web found what I was sifting for and tried to backdoor me."

Shit, J3wel. I should have warned him. "Sorry, Toledo. My bad."

He huffed. "Whatever. Anyway, once I convinced her that I wasn't the mark and was working for you too, we combined resources and came up with something." He paused. "Max, it's bad."

A chill went down my spine. "How bad?"

"Looks like they've been spooked by the arrest of Anthony Smalls and they've decided to clean house. J3wel found a few feelers in out-of-the-way places, peddling everything from slavery to illegal adoptions. They're cashing in the people at the Homestead and disappearing."

I ground my teeth. *Fuck.* "Any luck finding the place?"

The pause at the other end was heavy. "Yeah, the

group of Alphas who survived know some things, but they still want to meet with your girl to see if she can shed any light on how the place is set out now. Most of their information is old. If they want to do this with the least amount of civilian casualties, they need better intel."

I hated this. Hated that I'd have to put her in that position. But I'd seen her face when she discovered that they'd been murdering the Alpha kids. There was no way that she wouldn't want to help where she could.

"I'll talk to her, and to the guys. We'll get back to you."

Toledo let out a long breath. "We're all in Charlotte."

Both of my eyebrows hit my hairline. "Already?"

"When we couldn't get hold of you, we came down here, hoping to limit the amount of downtime once we tracked you down. I can't stress enough that we are in a life-or-death time crunch, Max."

Well, fuck. Breathing in through my nose and holding it, I straightened my shoulders. The timing sucked, but that was life. "I'll let you know by lunchtime, but Toledo? She's been through enough. I won't force her to relive that trauma if she doesn't want to. It sounds harsh, but I don't care who lives or dies, as long as she's happy."

Toledo grunted. "Love makes people fucking stupid, but okay. I'll wait for your call."

He hung up, and I pulled my phone from my ear and resisted the urge to throw it at the wall. I just wanted a little longer to stay in our bubble of happiness, where deranged cults and murders didn't exist.

Grabbing a couple of sports drinks from the fridge, as well as a prepared charcuterie board, I made my way back down the hall to the Omega suite. I was surprised to find August and Polly not in the nest, but back on the freshly made bed. Llew had Polly on his lap as he leaned against the headboard, and August was squished between him and Rio on the other side, bracketed by the Alphas who wanted to make him theirs. We might have skipped a few steps, but he looked like he was exactly where he was supposed to be.

Not bonding him as well during Polly's heat had been the hardest thing I'd ever done.

Frowning, Polly saw straight through my fake smile. "What's wrong?" She was an intuitive little thing, probably from the trauma of growing up with psychopaths, as well as our newly minted bondmark.

The tension in the room ratcheted up to ten. "Toledo called while we were otherwise occupied. The Homestead is trying to clean house."

Polly frowned, not getting the idiom. "The Brothers and Sisters have always cleaned."

Llew held her tighter, and August gripped her hand. "No, it means that they think that they've been caught out, so they're going to try and get rid of any liabilities and disappear."

"Liabilities?" she asked, her voice shaky.

"Probably everyone but the Leaders," August said

softly. "They don't want to leave anyone behind who could talk to the authorities."

Polly shook her head, like she could shake out the terrible reality. She turned her face into Llew's chest, and the scent of her distress washed through the room, crawling across my skin like acid.

Rio growled. "Tell them to forget it. I won't have them stressing out Polly like this. She's been through enough."

August scent marked Rio gently, attempting to calm him, and the sight almost made me smile, despite this shitshow. "I know you want to protect Polly, but you can't do that by taking away her choices, Alpha," August said gently.

Llew looked distraught, and whatever was pouring down their bond looked like it was testing his control. I could feel it too, her wild swirl of fear and anger. I needed to get this figured out, fast.

"No one is asking her to go and confront the people from the Homestead herself. She just needs to talk to these survivors, and a single, tiny piece of information squirreled away in that beautiful head of hers could save lives. You know this, Rio. You know how information can make or break a mission. We'll go and meet with Toledo and these people, but if we even so much as suspect that it's causing her undue stress, we'll pull her out of there."

I crawled up the bed toward my Pack, hating that I had to be this voice of reason. "I don't want her to wake up in ten years time and have regrets." I rested my hand on Polly's thigh, addressing her directly now. "You're so strong and brave. I know you can do this. But if you can't, that's okay too. It's up to you. We are *your* Pack. Your wellbeing is the only thing we care about."

Her silent, heartbreaking crying was like a stab to the chest with every single sob. Finally, she sucked in a shuddering breath. "I'll do it. Nim is still there, and the kids who don't know any better. The rest... I want Leader Malakai to die a horrendous death. Does that make me a bad person?

Rio reached over and gripped her hand. "It makes you human, Beautiful. And I'll personally make sure that happens." I knew that if they were going to bring down the Homestead, Rio and I would be right there with them.

I squeezed her thigh, leaning across Llew's broad chest to kiss her. "I'll make the call. Eat something and rehydrate." I ran my nose over her cheek. "I'm sorry this ruined the day."

She shook her head. "It's not your fault. And the people who are at fault need to be punished."

Yeah, there was my little fighter.

Toledo had rounded everyone up super quick, and less than two hours later, we were in a hotel bar on the outskirts of Charlotte. In the end, the whole Pack came, including

August. We were a show of support, and maybe a show of force, in case shit went sideways. Given how upset Polly had been earlier, I doubted any of us could have just stayed home while she was out here, confronting her past.

I noted Toledo in the back corner, and beside him was a girl with mermaid-blue hair. I could also see the back of two male heads. I raised an eyebrow at Toledo; that was a lot of people to subject my Omega to.

When we neared, he reached out and shook my hand. "Max, it's good to see you."

I'd never seen him so... not snarky. He was obviously on his best behavior, but for who?

He indicated the woman beside him. "You know Jewel."

I raised both eyebrows at the tiny little thing with the brightly colored hair in front of me. She was the hacker that some of the tech guys at the CIA jerked off to? Well, her work, anyway. Though if they'd seen her, probably to her visage as well.

I reached out and shook her hand. "Only professionally."

Polly appeared beside me, her eyes taking in Toledo and Jewel. And then she went inhumanly still beside me. "*Henry?*"

The man to my left was young, around Polly's age. He had a wide smile, eyes that were a little too far apart, but not enough that he looked like Sid the Sloth. It just kind of made him look sweet.

"Hey, Paloma. When they told me..." The guy shook his head. "I hoped it would be you."

She stepped around me and when he stood, she wrapped her arms around him and cried. "They said you'd died. They said you got a fever, that you passed in the middle of the night, and by the time Nim or I got any answers, they showed us your grave." She was sobbing again, and I resisted the urge to pull her back into my arms.

"I designated Alpha, and they kicked me out. Is Nim... Is she okay?"

"She was when I left." Stepping back, Polly rubbed her eyes with the back of her sleeve. "Now? I don't know."

Henry stepped back and introduced the other man beside him. He was older, around my age or probably a little older. "This is Pieter. He has the safehouse where we go when they rescue us."

The man in question reached out and shook my hand, then Polly's. "It's lovely to meet you, Paloma."

She shook her head. "I go by Polly now."

Henry looked over my shoulder, and I turned to see a big Alpha appear, his dark eyes taking in our group with almost military precision. "And that's Kross. He's our de facto leader."

Polly turned, the polite smile on her face dropping and the color in her cheeks draining. Her scent soured, and suddenly, her Omega distress pheromones could have suffocated a horse. She shook her head wildly. "No!"

I didn't ask questions. I just swung.

TWENTY-NINE
POLLY

Max landed several solid punches before *he* got out of the way. The Alpha from when I'd been sold by Leader Malakai. The one who'd barked at me to be calm. It was him. He was *here.*

Llew had me and August stuffed behind him, his big body a shield from the brawl that was occurring in front of us.

It was clear that the Alpha from that night had military training too. He stepped back, his hands raised. "Wait! Wait! I can explain. *Please.*"

But my Alphas weren't listening.

Henry's eyes met mine, wild and fearful. "Paloma! Call them off."

Something about his terror shook me from mine. I whined, and Rio's head snapped toward me. I held out a hand, and I could see the indecision in his eyes. He wanted to eliminate the threat, but his Omega needed him.

"Llew, do something," I hissed, and then the soothing scent of August's pheromones spread through the room. The bartender looked like he was ready to call the cops; someone would have to go talk to him so we didn't all end up in a jail cell.

As if he'd read my thoughts, August went over there. I could hear him saying it was just a misunderstanding, that it was all okay. His Omega presence would soothe the Beta bartender, even if he wasn't quite as susceptible to the pheromones.

Llew stepped forward, grabbing the Alpha by the throat and lifting him straight up in the air. Sometimes I forgot how huge my Alpha was. "Speak. If I don't like what you say, I'll snap your neck and never lose a wink of sleep over it."

Okay, that shouldn't be so hot.

The girl with Toledo looked up at my Alpha. "He's not going to tell you much if he can't breathe." I stared at the girl with the blue hair, and that little voice that was my Omega hissed at the way she was looking at my Alpha.

Oh, shit. She was an Omega too.

"Llew," I said softly, and he put the guy down. I pressed myself into Llew's spine, both for my comfort and for his.

The dark-eyed Alpha from the worst night of my life rubbed his throat. His eyebrow had been split open, and he was definitely going to have a black eye from the hits he took. "I deserved that, I know. But I promise it will all make sense in a moment. Come and sit down. I'll sit right down at the other end."

I looked over my shoulder. Would the other Alphas appear too?

As if he could read my mind, the dark-eyed Alpha—I guess his name was Kross—leaned forward in his seat. "They won't be here. Anthony Smalls is behind bars, and the other Alpha... well, he's somewhere a lot more permanent. You'll never have to look at either of them again." He sucked in a deep breath. "I'm just sorry that I caused you some kind of grief."

Rio growled. "Some kind of grief? You're sorry you caused her *some kind of grief*?" Oh, he was about to lose it. "You sold her off, had her branded with a hot iron, rendered her mute with a bark that could only be undone once she was rescued, and you're *sorry*?" he hissed, his cheeks flushing with anger. His Alpha was rising so close to the surface, the dominance was suffocating.

I reached over and wrapped my fingers in his. My Omega preened that my Alpha was defending me against this threat, but the logical side of my mind knew that if I wanted to get to the bottom of what was happening, I had to let this person speak.

Kross, to his credit, cringed. "I tried to get them to skip the branding; I really did. But I also knew that if I protested too much, I'd blow my cover, and then dozens more lives would've been on the line."

"Explain." Max seemed like he'd calmed down, and when August appeared with a sandwich bag filled with ice for his knuckles, he even managed to smile thankfully at our Omega.

I pulled August closer to me. I could lean on Llew's strength and August's calm, and they'd prop me up until we sorted through this whole situation.

Kross licked his lips. "I was nine when my parents joined the Homestead in the nineties. They were a pair of Betas who'd become disillusioned with the world and their place in it. My dad had always been a little unhinged, but my mom was worse. My grandmother told me later that once she had me, she went a little crazy. She'd had miscarriage after miscarriage, and when I survived to term, her post-natal depression turned into neurosis. She was convinced that everything would harm me. Plastics in the food. Radio waves from cellphones. Television giving me subliminal messaging. Later, it became chemical weapons testing and mind-control agents in the milk.

"Then John Parris came along and convinced her that she was right, that there were chemicals controlling us all, and the only way to protect me—and her future children—was to join them in the middle of nowhere in Arkansas at an off-grid commune. I found out this all later; at the time, all I knew was that they made me leave everything behind, even my favorite teddy bear. I went to Arkansas with the clothes on my back and nothing else." He sounded calm, like telling this story was no big deal, but I wanted to cry for the little boy who couldn't keep his teddy bear.

"When we got to the Ozarks, there were dozens of people. Older people who no longer knew how to operate in the world, younger people who were disenfranchised. Mentally ill people, who definitely skewed more towards women than men. The first year or two was kind of idyllic, I guess. There were a bunch of us kids, and we just ran around the woods like wildlings.

"And then they put up the fence. They locked us in. There wasn't even a gate to go out, even if we wanted to leave. They told everyone that there was a world war and that nuclear weapons had gone off. They played news programs that said there were viruses killing people, that nuclear fallout had finished off almost all of the world. That those who remained were forever altered and contagious. That it was best to stay safe inside, in small groups."

He took a sip of his drink, and the blue-haired girl looked at him like she wanted to crawl across the table and hug him. His distress was obvious, even to me. But he was still a man who'd stolen me from my home. I'd thought he'd been in his late-twenties, but given his story, I aged him up a little in my mind. He'd have to be mid-thirties by now.

"Babies began to be born, the first wave of kids just before you and Henry. The Leaders decided that they wouldn't tell the children of what had happened outside the walls. That we'd alter their history so they would never have to know the world's evils. Leader Malakai went into a trance for days, and when he came out, he managed to convince everyone that he'd talked to some unknown gods and we were now their children. That they'd protect us from the shit outside the walls." His lips twisted. "What we needed protecting from was the evil *inside* the walls."

I was clutching onto Rio's hand for dear life, but I could hear the truth in these words. I lifted my chin, asking wordlessly for Kross to continue.

"People who were skeptical just... disappeared. The Leaders said that they were taken by the threat outside the walls, but I think they had them killed. Then my best friend, Alex, designated Alpha. The next night, he was gone. I found out later that he'd been shipped out in the night by the Leaders, and he was buried somewhere in the woods outside the walls. Unsurprisingly, when I designated as Alpha, that very night I was dragged from my bed and smuggled out of the compound through the tunnel in the ceremony room. Ian, the Homestead's guy on the outside, picked me up from the older Betas, took me to Oklahoma City, and shot heroin straight into my veins. They overdosed me, and it was only by sheer luck that an off-duty paramedic with Narcan in her purse found me. She took me to the hospital, and I was shipped off into foster care."

He wet his dry lips. "Eventually, they tracked down my grandmother, but no matter who they asked or how hard we searched, they couldn't track down my parents.

They weren't missing persons; they hadn't been abducted. They'd joined this cult of their own volition. The search was eventually given up, and my grandmother raised me. I joined the army, then when I was discharged, I had all this *rage*. I was bigger, and uglier, and scarred, and when I remembered what they'd done, I couldn't let it go.

"So I went back to Arkansas, and I watched. I researched. I got Jewel involved by chance. We chased down police reports and rumors and overdose cases. We chased down talk of preppers in the Ozarks, and message-boards on the dark web. I remembered Ian, so I tracked down every Ian in the Ozarks for the right one. Eventually, I got lucky. *We* got lucky." He looked over at Jewel, and there was something in his expression. Gratitude? Adoration? I wasn't sure.

"I found the right Ian, and I put a tracker on his car. It'd been five years since I'd been dumped by then, and they were getting pretty lazy. When Pieter designated, they barely drove him over the Oklahoma border before ditching him in a gas station bathroom with a needle in his arm. Then they got even lazier of the next five years, throwing them from moving cars. That's how we got Henry. He was thrown from a car on the side of Highway 49 just before crossing over into Missouri. He was in hospital for a month, healing his broken body."

Henry gave him a sad smile. "It wasn't the best time of my life, that's for sure."

Kross nodded. "I decided to up my game after that. I

couldn't let any more people die, waiting for them to be tossed out like garbage before I could rescue them. I moved to the town where Ian lived. Grew a beard just in case they recognized my face, but I should have known they wouldn't; self-obsessed bastards didn't see us as anything more than waste to be discarded. I looked nothing like the boy I'd been. I went to the bars he liked, the diner where he had breakfast. I became his friend and managed to bug his phone. When Jewel picked up a communication that they needed to 'take out some trash,' I disabled his car, then happened to be nearby when he realized, inviting him to a cookout. He was in a state of near-panic and had me drive him to this location in the middle of nowhere.

"We picked up a kid, then dropped him at a gas station just outside of Springfield. Ian made it sound like he was rescuing this kid from a bad situation. Said it was his nephew. It was all bullshit, and when Pieter scooped up the kid less than ten minutes later, Ian had thrown half a bottle of sleeping pills down his throat and left the bottle there with him in a dirty bathroom stall." The rage in his voice was barely tamped down, and I bit back the small fearful whine that wanted to escape. "For the next few months, I ingratiated myself with him, and when word came that we had to bring someone in—someone who wanted to buy an Omega—I knew I had to be there, if for no other reason than to protect you."

Max's lip pulled back in a sneer. "Great job at protection, asshole. She was down in that hole for a week before we found her. If we'd killed that little weasel before he confessed she was in there, we would have burnt the place down around her."

Kross looked aggravated. "It wasn't perfect. I lost her once she went with fucking Anthony Smalls, then shit went sideways and I had to kill Ian." He said it so casually, like murder was just something he did after getting takeout on Thursdays. "By the time Jewel tracked down the warehouse, she was gone, and there was nothing but smoldering rubble left. We thought she was dead. At least until you popped up on the dark web, asking questions."

Silence fell over the table, and my head was whirling with information that I didn't know what to do with. I looked at Henry, who'd basically risen from the dead, and his soft expression was so like the boy I'd known.

Nim had always had the hugest crush on Henry. She used to think that once they both designated as Betas, she would choose him as a partner. When he'd died—or rather, didn't die—she'd been inconsolable for weeks. I thought of other members of the Homestead who'd died or disappeared with little explanation. "How many have been saved?"

Henry reached over and put his hand on mine. Rio growled, but I squeezed his knee, reassuring him that it wasn't like that. Henry, Nim and I had been raised in the same house, almost like siblings. Well, for me it had been like a sibling bond; for Nim, it had been something else. But I definitely didn't see Henry as a new prospective Alpha, no matter how happy I was that he was alive.

"Including Kross, but not including you"—he shot an apologetic look at my Alphas—"there've been nine survivors. We've buried eight more in a cemetery outside of Pieter's farm, about an hour outside of Little Rock."

Sadness echoed around me, mine and theirs. People I'd known, people I'd loved, discarded like they were little more than waste.

Sucking in a fortifying breath, I steeled my spine and looked at Kross. "What do you need me to do?"

THIRTY
LLEW

Being in a room with this many other Alphas was grating on my control, but there was no way I'd leave my Omegas alone in here, or leave my Packmates outnumbered. So I sucked it up and when we got to their hotel suite, I sat on the furthest wall with my eyes on the door and Polly in my lap. I also had August tucked close. Neither of them protested, like they could sense I needed this.

In the end, all the others needed from Polly was information. Things that had changed in the years since Henry had left. The routine. Where people slept, ate, and the weapons they possessed. It was hard watching Polly now second-guess everything she'd seen. The guns that rested on the sides of the building hadn't been to keep out monsters. They were to prevent people coming to help, because the Leaders were the monsters. The people she'd regarded as parental figures had all had lives outside the walls of the Homestead, and suddenly, she was questioning every single interaction.

"They all lied so easily," she said to me softly, and I held her tighter, pressing her closer to my body like I could absorb her pain through symbiosis.

August kissed the side of her head. "It's likely that they've detached from reality and truly believed the things they were telling you."

She looked completely wrung out by the time they circled back around to things she'd already told them, and I decided that was enough. I was taking her home to our Packhouse, where she was safe. I stood, not letting her out of my arms. "We're done."

Kross didn't protest, merely stood as well. The rest of the Pack gathered at my back, and Polly wiggled until I set her on her feet. Walking over to stand in front of her, Kross dipped his head. "I'm sorry that I caused you so much trauma, Omega. I'm not perfect, and neither was the situation. I was doing the best I could, but I'm Alpha enough to admit that my best just wasn't good enough." He looked at me and the men around me. Her Pack. "I'm glad that you actually have a chance at happiness now. From what Henry's told me, the Homestead's views on Omegas have only gotten worse since I left. I wouldn't wish that on my worst enemies."

Polly was more gracious than I ever could be. I doubted I could ever forgive someone who caused her even a moment of pain. But she wasn't me; she was better than us all. "You did what you thought was right. It's all any of us can do."

Shaking my head, I envied her that sweet nature right then. Because we all knew there was more that could be done, and if I judged by Kross's cold expression, he was going to do it with extreme prejudice.

I let Polly go long enough for her to walk over to the other Alpha, Henry, and hug him. My Alpha didn't like it, though I kept telling myself that there wasn't anything romantic between them. Looking between them, though —Henry with his straight, dark brows and blue eyes— they looked almost like siblings than friends.

August leaned in close. "Do you see the similarities too?" I nodded. He cleared his throat. "So, you guys don't know who your parents are?"

Henry shook his head. "No, they believed that children belonged to the village. I assume there must be some record somewhere, if they had any foresight, and some of the older members would obviously know, but if we ever asked, we were quickly shut down."

"And you guys are the same age?" August pressed, and I watched Kross tilt his head, understanding dawning on his face.

"There were several of us raised in a group, though I couldn't tell you our actual ages with any certainty. I'm only basing mine off a guess and the age I went through my designation," Henry answered.

Jewel was eyeing them too now, and that little Omega had a sharp mind and a fierce gaze. Where Polly was soft,

I doubted Jewel had any softness left. She looked over at August appraisingly. "You think they're twins?"

August nodded. "Even their scents are complimentary. Jasmine, but hers is kind of sweet, where Henry's is a little spicier, maybe woodsy?"

Jewel tilted her head and nodded. Omegas were very sensitive to scents, even more so than Alphas. But now August mentioned it, I could sense the similarities in their scents, as well as their appearance.

Polly blinked up at Henry, looking at his face as if she'd never seen it before. "We didn't have mirrors; I never knew what I looked like to know if we looked similar. But Nim never said anything, nor did any of the other kids."

"Nim was raised with us. We probably looked wildly different to someone who'd seen me try and grow a moustache at twelve," Henry joked, but I could see the sadness on his face. He was clearly holding it in for Polly.

She threw back her head and laughed. "It looked like dirt on your lip. Nim was planning to shave it off while you slept if you let it go much longer." She looked over at us, then stepped away. "I don't know if we're related, or twins, or anything like that. But I'd like to know later—after we get Nim out of there."

Henry gripped her hands. "I'll bring her back to us, Paloma. I promise. I won't stop until we're all safe and happy."

Polly nodded, her eyes getting shiny with tears, and I'd had enough. I walked over and wrapped her in my arms, before reaching out, putting a heavy hand on Henry's shoulder. "I hope it's true, but it doesn't matter either way. You're family to Polly, which means you're family to us."

"I can't bury you again," she whispered, which broke my heart once more.

Henry nodded solemnly, but he didn't promise. I respected him more for it. Things could go sideways on missions like this, and Polly had been lied to enough for one lifetime.

I bundled both Polly and August out of the suite, holding open the elevator doors as Rio and Max brought up the rear. I moved over to the corner where, unsurprisingly, Polly turned into my body and climbed me like a tree, wrapping her arms and legs around my body as her tears soaked the curve of my neck.

"You held it together so well, my brave Omega," I crooned.

"It's so bad, Llew. So much wasted time. So much needless hurt," she sniffled, as I stroked up and down her back, holding her close. I looked at Max and Rio, seeing the helpless anger on their faces. They would do what was right for our Omega, and put down the people that hurt her.

The Leaders and the Homestead would receive their retribution, and it would be all because of an Omega they'd thrown away like trash.

. . .

In the end, Rio and Max only came home for long enough to get Polly settled and grab their gear. August insisted he had to return home, because he was due back at work, but I hated having him out of my sight when things were so uncertain, even knowing that there was no threat to him. To my Alpha, August was already ours, so he needed our protection. It was a hard pill to swallow that he didn't really need us, and despite going through Polly's heat together, he wasn't officially Pack.

Yet.

Everyone had left less than two hours ago, and I knew it would be a long few days. Rio and Max would meet Kross and his group in Arkansas, and it would take at least a half a day or more to get there. They'd take the long route, checking into a hotel in St. Louis, but not staying there for long. Then they'd drive through the night to a town just over the border and head down to where the Homestead was buried in the mountains. From there, the others had called in a few helpers, who had strong feelings on the mistreatment of children and Omegas, as well as less-than-stellar morals. Together, they'd go in and shut down the Homestead for good.

According to Max, the plan was to deliver the Leaders—and those who'd wilfully looked the other way—on the doorstep of police in Little Rock, along with so much irrefutable evidence, they'd be forced to open an investigation. I just hoped it didn't lead back to Polly.

Right now, though, it was just me and a scared Omega in my Packhouse. We'd retreated to my suite, and

I was showing her all my favorite movies from the last two decades. Max had stored enough food in the fridge that we wouldn't have to do anything more strenuous than reheat stuff in the oven.

"Why didn't you and the guys have a bond?"

I wanted to brush off the question, distract her with something else, something happier and more pleasant. But I'd promised myself I'd never lie to her, even by omission.

"When Rio was in the military, his humvee was blown up, and he was captured by enemy insurgents. He was taken and tortured for information for a little over ten days. Much like our connection, my bond with Rio was rare. It meant that I felt every moment of his pain. I worked out that using our bond, I could shield him from that, and I did. However, when they brought him home, our bond had burned out, as well as my one to Max. It had worked so hard to protect our Pack that it just... fizzled. I was worried that I wouldn't be able to bond you back after your Omega went rogue, because no matter how we tried after Rio returned, it was too broken to repair."

She didn't say anything for a long time, her head just resting on my chest. I could see the fluttering of her eyelashes on her round cheeks. She looked less gaunt and starved already, her soft Omega curves making her even more irresistible. Finally, she rolled over so she was looking up at me. "I think I can do it. I *want* to do it."

"Do what, Sweet Thing?"

"Bond us all back together. Our bond is strong, as is my bond with Rio and Max. I think if you try to bond them again, maybe it'll work because the links are already there, if fainter for you. When the time is right, we should try and bond again." A smile curled her lips. "Maybe when we bond with August. It's meant to be, Llew. I can feel it in my soul."

A wave of pure gratitude washed over me. "I believe you. There's nothing you can't do, Polly Barrie." I hugged her tightly. "Now, how are we going to court our Omega? I vote you just turn up naked, dipped in chocolate sauce, and say 'Be Mine?' We should practice that now."

She giggled and slapped my chest, and I held her close, this angel that I didn't deserve.

THIRTY-ONE
RIO

Despite being honorably discharged over a year ago, preparing for a mission still felt like second nature. I wouldn't say I felt at home doing it, but it was something I was good at—hell, something I'd excelled at for a long time.

Having Max beside me was new, but I also knew he was highly skilled and we weren't going up against an armed militia. We were liberating a bunch of brainwashed people from the hands of some truly evil sociopaths.

I sent a quick message to the group chat I'd created with everyone, including August and Polly, telling them that we were about to go dark. That I loved them.

I was coming home with closure for my Omega. There were no other options.

I turned back to Kross. Toledo had gotten some satellite footage of the compound, and I wasn't surprised it had never been found. They'd managed to camouflage it beautifully with the surrounding national forest—even the rooftops—making it hard to distinguish it from the surrounding terrain. There were no vehicles, any farm-land must've been worked in between the trees, and even the fence was a drab green that looked like it had been reclaimed by nature long ago.

All in all, if the others hadn't led us to their doorstep, we would never have found them.

"We go in through the entry point here"—Kross indicated where the tunnel came out in the ceremony room—"and we scale the walls here and here." He pointed to the south and southwest corners, which were closest to the access road. "Minimal casualties is the aim of tonight, people. They'll be scared and confused, and unless you are in immediate threat of grave injury, keep your phasers set to stun."

Max looked at me with wide eyes. "Did he just make a *Star Trek* reference?" he muttered under his breath. My Beta Packmate had been a little bit of a nerd growing up, and I didn't want to tell him that I'd scrolled on my phone the entire time I was meant to be watching *Star Trek*.

Llew would've known, though. He was one hundred percent supportive of anything we ever wanted to do. When I'd tried to play baseball in seventh grade? He'd been at every game, right there with my foster parents. Max had taken up close-up magic in eighth grade, and Llew had watched with rapt attention, applauding every trick. Though I think we'd all been glad when that phase passed.

We went over all the small details once more. When we'd call the cops to clean up. Who would talk to the cops. Who the hell would get the fuck out of there—that was us. We'd fuck shit up, Leader Malakai would conveniently "disappear" before the cops arrived, and then we would go home to our Omega.

I looked down at my watch. It was go time.

I hugged Max close. "Be safe."

He slapped my back a couple of times, already in the zone. "You too. No revenge is worth not going home to our Pack." It was a timely reminder, because my Alpha was already snarling underneath my skin.

Finally, we rolled out, and we hiked the short distance to the wall. It was at least fifty feet tall, with an almost perfectly sheer face. If there had been a forest fire in this part of the Ozarks, the whole place and everyone inside it would have perished.

We split, and I kept Henry with me. He had a bit of hand-to-hand training, but he was mostly here to keep people calm. I'd happily kept him on my team, because it was obvious that Polly loved him, and if we were right, he was her brother, at the very least. I wanted to keep him as safe as possible.

Throwing my grappling hook over the wall, I hoped that the night sounds would muffle the noise. After a few moments of waiting for any calls to ring out in the darkness, I started climbing up the wall. I'd check out what was happening on the other side, and if I thought it was safe, Henry would come up after me.

The solid top of the wall was enough for me to rest on, and I got my first impression of the place where Polly had been born and raised. There were four low, wide, flat-roofed houses in different sections of the compound. The entire place had basically been built beneath the canopy of the trees. There were only dirt paths, and even the agriculture had been spaced in natural fields.

It was pretty genius, really. A prepper's wet dream. I could respect *how* they'd created the place and still hate *what* they'd created.

Nodding down to Henry, I waited until he climbed up—a little slower than I had—and then anchored our ropes so we could belay down the other side. Again, I went first, pulling my gun and waiting for Henry to land beside me.

He indicated the house on the far right. "That's our old home. Leader Malakai's house," he whispered, and that rage that had been simmering in my chest quieted. We had a lock on our target. We would make him pay for what he'd done to Polly, and Henry, and every other poor kid who didn't fit with his agenda.

I could see other dark-clad figures moving towards the houses. There were sixteen of us in all, but only a few would still be here when the cops arrived. More than enough for us to clear out this nest of depravity.

Two more guys joined us—another Alpha from Kross's little rescue, along with a huge Alpha, almost as big as Llew, who didn't speak and had brutal scars than spoke of violence, but not the type you'd get from war.

I lifted my hand, indicating they should go around the back, and we'd enter through the front. Of course the door was unlocked, because why would it be locked out here? Creeping through, I looked over at Henry, who indicated we should travel down the main hallway to the back portion of the house.

Reaching the master suite, I opened the door silently, noticing a girl curled up on the furthest edge of the bed, her eyes wide with fear. I lifted a finger to my lips, telling her to be silent. Fuck, she had to be younger than Polly. I indicated she should leave, slowly, and she slipped from the bed.

If I had any doubt about what a piece of shit this guy was, the fact that a barely legal girl was terrified in his bed in her underwear would've been enough to warrant the bullet between the eyes I was going to give him.

But not here. Not right now.

Picking up a dirty sock, I waited until I was standing over him. "Rise and shine, fuckhead." The old guy's eyes snapped open, his sallow jowls hanging down loosely. He opened his mouth to yell, and I slammed the sock in there, muffling the sound. And then I punched him in the face. "Night night, you piece of shit."

While he was out of it, I hog-tied him facedown on the floor. He was naked, his liver-spotted ass and shriveled mole dick sure to haunt my nightmares for years.

"Go, wake the rest of the house's occupants," I told

Henry. "Get the big guy to disarm anyone he thinks might cause a problem and herd them all into the main living room. From there, we'll work out who's a victim and who needs to meet their god, other than this piece of shit."

With a nod, Henry disappeared out of the room, and I looked down at the man who'd caused so much hurt. He looked like any other old guy, gray-haired and soft around the middle, like he should be complaining to the barista at Starbucks that his coffee didn't taste the way it used to, not leading an underground cult that dipped its toes in human trafficking.

He'd be so easy to kill, and holding back my Alpha from stomping on his frail neck was taking every ounce of willpower I possessed. Once I was sure he was properly secured and probably in a little bit of pain, I dragged him into the bathroom and threw him into the bathtub. It had three different shower heads and multiple hot tub jets.

To think, Polly hadn't even been able to use her shower that first day because they'd always had to haul water from the well to bathe, while this piece of shit had a bathroom like the penthouse of the Hilton.

Setting the water as cold as it would go, I put it on full blast from all three shower heads. The icy blast brought him back to consciousness.

"*Argh!* What the hell?" he screeched, and he sounded like someone's grandpa. I hated him even more.

"Have a nice sleep, Leader Malakai? I can promise

you, you've woken up to a nightmare, but don't worry, it won't be for long." My earpiece let me know that Kross was on his way here. "You're about to meet your maker, and it isn't some fucking made-up god that you use to exploit other people."

"Who are you?" he hissed.

Squatting down in front of him, watching him shiver beneath the frigid water, I smiled. "I'm just an Alpha who loves a woman you threw away."

He screwed up his nose. "Paloma. That fucking little *bitch* was always trouble. I should have had her killed instead of—" I kicked him in his pudgy stomach for even saying her name.

Behind me, the door to the bathroom opened and closed. My Alpha was acutely aware that it was Kross. I looked over my shoulder at him, and as if he could see how close the Alpha was to taking control, he gave me a wide berth.

Malakai looked up at the man. "*You?* What the... You double-crossing son of a bitch!"

Kross squatted down in front of him and pushed away the stringy gray hair that was across the old man's face. It would've almost seemed gentle, if the other Alpha's eyes weren't promising death. "Not the son of a bitch, actually. The son of Robert and Leslie Kross."

The Leader frowned. "Christopher?"

I raised a brow at the Alpha beside me. "Your name is Chris Kross? No wonder you just go by Kross." I couldn't wait to tell Max. He'd get a kick out of that.

Ignoring me, Kross nodded. "You do remember me. I'd almost feel honored, if I gave even the smallest shit about your opinion." He rocked back on his heels. "I'm going to level with you, Ken. You're dying tonight. However, the amount of pain you'll feel beforehand will be dependent on your answers to my questions. Answer everything, and this guy here"—he indicated me—"will put a single bullet between your eyes, and that's the end."

He leaned forward, the expression on his face menacing. "If you don't answer, I'm going to remove a limb for every broken Alpha teen that I had to scrape up off the side of the highway, or nurse back to health from an overdose, or had to watch spiral into depression in a world they didn't understand. And there were a lot. In the end, you'll either tell me what I want to know, or you won't. But the outcome is the same. You're dead, and everything you've built is gone."

The old guy had nothing but hatred in his eyes, but I knew the face of a coward when I saw one. I was quickly proven right.

"What do you want to know?"

Sighing unhappily, I turned from the bathroom door. "I'll go help the others. But Kross? His death is mine."

Kross nodded, but didn't take his eyes from the guy in front of him. I grinned at Malakai—or I guess his real name was Ken—and it was a demonic expression. When Kross was done, my face would be the last one he'd ever see.

THIRTY-TWO
MAX

Teamed up with Pieter, we made quick work of two of the houses, clearing them out and ushering people to the central building. I let Pieter deal with the Leader of the second house, and if I wasn't incorrect, the guy looked like his father. The similarities were too prominent to be anything else. How could a man order his son to be killed, just so he could maintain his own power?

I left him to it; they were his demons to appease, and no matter what the outcome, it'd be the right one.

Moving from room to room, I woke up the people inside. Some looked at me with fear, others with anger, and honestly, it made it easier to sort them. I rounded them up into the living room.

"Evil!" an old woman shrieked. "A test from Izuny—that's what you are."

Smiling at the old battle-axe, I smirked. "If I was the

vengeful tool of any of your fake gods, it would Melize. You chose the wrong fucking god to follow, and I'm your retribution."

Preaching back at her about her own fucked-up religion seemed to shock the old bat, because she shut up. I left her with two other guys, their faces covered by masks, and went to the last bedroom.

A girl launched herself from the shadows, and I spotted at least three children in the corner behind her. "You can't have them!" I pulled her off me gently, watching her swinging fists, though one still clipped me in the ear.

"Woah, I don't want anyone. Calm down." Gripping her hands, I pried her off me with as much care as I could. She was a Beta, that was obvious, and also undernourished. It didn't take much to hold her. I looked closely at her face, with the almond-shaped eyes and olive tone of her skin. "Shit, are you Nim?"

The girl froze, her eyes going wide and her lips parting. "What did you say?"

"Are you Nim? Nimah?" It had to be her, right? "Polly sent us."

All at once, every ounce of fight left her body, and she slid to the floor before I could catch her. "She's okay? Paloma's okay?"

I smiled, crouching down in front of her. "She's better than okay. She's happy. She'll be even happier when I tell her you're okay. I can take you to her, if you want?" The woman looked back over her shoulder at the kids, and I could tell she didn't know what to do. "They can come too. We aren't leaving anyone behind." I paused. "Actually, there's someone else I think you'd like to see." I led her from the room, ushering the kids along with her. There was a preteen boy holding a toddler, and a little girl around six. "Do these guys have parents?"

Nim shrugged. "Somewhere. But I wouldn't know who. They have babies in... well, batches I guess, and then disperse them across the different houses. No one ever really knows who belongs to who."

I ground my back teeth, glad there was no one in punching distance. "Anyone you'd trust them with while I take you outside?" Her hesitation broke my heart. "It's okay. They can come with us." I looked at the boy. He had to be around twelve, with soft features. "Are you okay carrying the little one?" He nodded, his eyes still wide and fearful where they landed on my gun. "It doesn't feel like it, but I promise everything will be okay now."

We walked up to the house that Rio and Henry were meant to breach, and I could see people being ushered out of there, into what I assumed was the ceremony room, which had an exit that we could direct emergency services toward.

I knew the moment that Nim spotted him. "Henry," she breathed. "But he's..."

I put a hand on her arm, immediately dropping it when she flinched. "There's a lot you won't understand, but we'll explain everything. But yes, that's Henry—he's alive and well. And I know for a fact that you're the reason he's here."

She looked back at the kids once more, obviously still reluctant to leave them behind.

"Go. I'll watch them and keep them safe. I swear it on my love for Polly."

That seemed to be enough, because Nim was running across the ground in bare feet. Fuck, I should have gotten her shoes. "Henry!" she yelled, and the Alpha in question turned, his eyes wide.

"Nim?" That was all he got out before the little Beta was slamming into his arms.

The rest of their conversation was just for them, and I looked down at the scared kids beside me. "Hey, my name is Max. I bet this is all scary, right?" The little girl nodded, but the boy just stared at me distrustfully. "A lot of things are about to change, but I promise you that they'll be for the better. I swear it. Do you remember Paloma?"

The boy continued to stare at me, his frown way too mature on his tiny face. "You know Paloma?"

I nodded. "Yep, I do. She's a beautiful, funny, intelligent Omega that I'm so privileged to call my mate. She wanted me to come and help you guys, because beyond those walls is a world filled with everything imaginable. An abundance of food, animals you've never seen before, and fun and other children and *life*. We'll be here every step of the way to help you, I swear it."

The kid clearly didn't understand, and how could

he? Polly was an adult, and she'd barely been able to comprehend the world outside the Homestead.

"But first, there'll be a bunch of men and women in cars who'll come to talk to you. They'll be police officers and paramedics. They'll keep you safe and make sure you're healthy. They'll support you in the world outside."

We reached the ceremony room, and I looked around. There had to be sixty or seventy people in here, including at least a dozen kids. *What the fuck?*

I walked over to Toledo, who'd been tasked with going through and mirroring everything on the computers of every Leader here. Yeah, they all had computers and satellite connections, while the rest of the compound believed they were the only people left in the universe. We'd leave the computers for the cops, but Toledo and Jewel wanted their own copies to peruse. Just in case they didn't like how the investigation was being handled and needed to get a little more vigilante in their justice.

He let out a sound that was almost a growl. "What a fucking shitshow. I'm tempted to just put down everyone who knowingly subjected these kids to this bullshit, and burn the place to the ground," he murmured. I understood the impulse. There were middle-aged men and women here, people like Kross's parents, who'd willingly moved their kids here and lied to them. Who'd had babies, knowing that those children would have to perpetuate the cycle, while being oblivious to a completely different world out there. Those weren't the actions of the sane or the innocent.

"We'll leave the cops and the courts to clean up who's guilty and who was just misled. We can't be the judge, jury, and executioner for everyone here."

Toledo grumbled. "And what about the kids? People like Henry and Polly, who are adults but had no idea that a world outside of this hellhole even existed? Your Alpha is a former foster kid. What do you think will happen to them?" Toledo was right; there was a chance that they'd be even more exploited in the outside world.

"We won't let that happen, man. We have money, space, and manpower. We'll figure something out and protect them all until they're on their feet."

He nodded his head distractedly. I knew it was true. These people, for better or worse, were Polly's family. Those who were innocent would get all the help Llew, Rio, and I could give. Hopefully August too, if the last two weeks hadn't made him want to run in the other direction.

Henry reappeared, holding Nim's hand. As they walked over to me, I could hear the shocked whispers of the older people, suddenly recognizing him. It wasn't that long ago that he'd "died" and he was more easily recognizable than someone like Kross.

He stopped in front of me. "Rio says it's time."

Nodding, I smiled at Nim. "I'll be in touch. Polly is going to be anxious to see you." I paused, looking between the two of them. "You can come with us, if you want?"

Nim hesitated, but shook her head. "Henry explained... a little. I'm not sure I completely understand, but the kids will need me." She looked up at her childhood best friend, back from the dead, with a little disbelief in her eyes.

"They'll need us. Don't worry, Nim. I'm not going anywhere."

Resisting the urge to say *aww,* I waved at Toledo. "I'll call you later." With one last look around the room, I walked out into the darkness. Rio was there, and so was some naked old dude. "Gross, man. Couldn't you have, I don't know, put some underpants on him or something?"

Rio nodded to a part of the wall that sat on the north side of the Homestead. As he stuck a long pin in a hole, there was some overriding mechanism, and a small gate opened.

"Fuck, that's handy."

The man in his arms swore at us as he stumbled into the darkness of the woods. When we were far enough away that I was pretty sure the people in the Homestead wouldn't hear any gunshots, Rio shoved the guy to his knees.

"Kross says that we can't torture you. Normally, I wouldn't give a fuck what anyone says—I'd peel the skin from your flesh in the most painful way possible, until you were screaming in pain," Rio said coldly. "But luckily for you, I have somewhere better I want to be." Pulling his gun from his holster, he held it between Leader Malakai's eyes. "Thank you for cooperating." He dropped the gun to the old guy's mouth, pulling out the sock and pushing the barrel between his lips. "Say hello to your fucking gods for me. I hope they drag you straight to Hell, where you belong."

Then he pulled the trigger.

Leader Malakai, the man who'd tormented our Omega forever, fell to the side like a wasted lump of human flesh. I quickly staged the kill to look like a suicide of a man who'd made a run for it in the middle of the night, wiping down any evidence we were here.

Getting to my feet, I looked at my Alpha. "Let's go home."

We walked off into the darkness and down to the place where we'd left our vehicles. As we drove down Highway 49, we saw the red-and-blue flashing lights of an entire convoy of cop cars flying in the other direction.

Thirty-Three

Polly

Nim's fine. She's with Henry. Everything went well.

That was the message I'd gotten from Max in the group chat at three a.m. last night. By the time I woke up this morning, the Homestead was on every major news channel on the television. August had come over early in the morning and sat beside me as I flicked through channels. I had to watch, especially when someone leaked bodycam footage from when the cops arrived. I looked at the faces I knew, searching for people, for Nim.

When I saw her, hugging tiny baby Brielle to her chest, the tight bands of anxiety relaxed. They'd need me. Could I really just hide here and do nothing? If I went to them, the authorities would ask questions, and I could expose my new Pack to the law, as well as Otille-James's Pack, if they discovered what had happened.

Leader Malakai's name was Ken Smythe. He'd been a corporate banker before he retired and decided to create a cult with his golfing buddies. He wanted to be the king of his domain. He wanted to play outside society's rules. Old acquaintances talked about what a kind man he'd been, if a little intense.

The news reporters talked about how he'd been found outside the compound's walls, having committed suicide from the guilt.

The relief and the guilt meshed together until I was a basket case. My emotions were at war with each other, and every news article just made it worse. The news anchor said that the police were interviewing all the people at the compound, and I knew Nim would be one of them. The reporter at the scene confirmed the children were being taken in by CPS, until it could be determined who their parents were, and if they had any other relatives that could be found in the interim.

I hated that they were going to be the victims in this too, innocents caught up in something that was completely out of their control.

August laid me against his chest, surrounding me with his warmth. "This was the right thing. I don't want you to ever doubt that this was the correct decision. They'll be scared and angry now, but they'll be able to grow up and live, fall in love, get an education, find their passions. They won't have to have sex with some old man, or have babies they don't want, or die if they happen to be an Alpha, or be shipped off to the highest bidder if they're an Omega. You've given them a *life.*"

I knew all that was true, but it still hurt. "It doesn't seem right that I'm safe and happy, while they're scared and alone, all because of something I did."

He clutched me tighter to his chest. "Listen to me, Polly Barrie. None of this is your fault. The fault lies squarely on the shoulders of men who wanted to play god. You might be happy now, but remember, the kids have something you didn't have. They have each other. They have you, and Henry and Kross. You had to navigate this world alone, so they won't have to."

"But what if they have no one, and they're forced into the system?" I asked softly, as Llew came into the room, a phone clutched in his hand.

"Then we'll take them." He said it so easily, like adopting a bunch of traumatized kids was the obvious answer. "There's someone on the phone who might make you feel better, though."

I was expecting Rio or Max, but when Nim's face filled the screen, I burst into tears. "Nim!"

"*Polly?* You're really okay?"

"I'm so okay." I did our hand sign for *I'm all right,* just so she knew I meant it. "Are you okay?"

She shook her head. "It's been... a lot. Cars, Polly. Cars exist. And Henry!"

Tears were streaming down my face. "I know. He's okay." Henry's face appeared over the top of Nim's head, and he gave me a happy little wave.

"I couldn't believe it. I thought I was seeing a ghost. And these cellphone things. And the world wide web!"

She had always been the most adaptable of us. It was Nim who'd come up with our hand language, when I wasn't allowed to speak in the Leaders' presence anymore. It was Nim's idea to sew the pocket in my ceremonial skirts, so I wouldn't be found with my magazines. It was Nim who'd built a small sculpture to put on Henry's grave, so we'd always know where he was. She was also the most pragmatic; she would conquer this new reality like every other hurdle.

"Are the kids okay?"

She nodded. "Scared, but the authorities agreed to put them all together in a single home, and they're letting me stay with them. Henry and his friend took the rest of us back to Pieter's farm for a while, until we get used to the idea that we were... that it's..."

"Not the end of the world out here? It's hard, but you'll adapt fast, Nim, I promise." I looked at Henry. "What about the Brothers and Sisters? And the Leaders?"

As he poked his head further into the frame with Nim, I smiled at how familiar it was, how perfect they looked together. Like a snapshot of our past, but aged up.

"The younger ones who have never been in the outside world were released immediately. They're the ones at Pieter's farm. The older Brothers and Sisters, like Sister Roberta, are being questioned by police and held in jail, until they decide if they're guilty of child endangerment, unlawful detention, and a bunch of other stuff. The Leaders are being investigated for murder and attempted murder. I already gave my statement earlier."

I wet my lips. "Do you think I should..."

Henry shook his head. "That's entirely up to you, Polly. Of all of us, your life was made the most miserable by the Homestead and the Leaders. You have the right to do whatever you'd like, and no one can say a damn thing about it."

I smiled. My two friends were there in front of me, safe and happy. That was all I'd ever wanted growing up. "Thanks, Henry."

He looked over to the side. "We have to go; the van is here to transport the kids. Stay in touch."

"You too. I'll help where I can from here." I paused. "I love you guys."

Nim's face softened. "I love you too, Polly. I can't wait to hug you."

Then she was gone, and my heart was both heavier and lighter.

For hours afterwards, I thought about Henry's words and Nim's face, and the thoughts that were going around and around in my head. Sister Roberta had known they were selling me. She'd branded me, while the other Brothers and Sisters held me still.

They should be punished too.

When Rio and Max finally arrived home, I ran into their arms and cried. I was so glad they were home and safe, that this nightmare was over. I dragged everyone into my nest and cuddled them close.

It was late when I rolled into Max's arms, my body still pressed tightly into Rio's body, August's hand resting lightly on my hip. Llew slept by the door, my big Alpha. My protector.

The others they'd rescued from the Homestead didn't have a Llew. Or a Rio and Max and August. No one to protect them the way a Pack could.

So I'd have to be that for them, until they could find their own Packs.

"Max?"

"Mmm?" he said sleepily, his eyes blinking open.

"I think I want to make a statement. They *sold* me."

He was silent for a long time, then he leaned forward and kissed me on the head. "If that's what you want, Beautiful. Whatever helps you heal."

I kissed his chin. "I love you."

He rubbed his face on mine, his low purr vibrating through my chest. "I love you too."

Two days later, I stood in front of the Rock Hill police station beside Truett Heathstone. Max had been true to his word and gotten me a lawyer, who happened to be OJ's Alpha, the very Alpha who'd allowed me to speak again. We'd talked on the phone for a few hours the night before, going over what I could and couldn't say to the police so that my Pack, and his, didn't get into trouble.

"Don't forget, you haven't done anything wrong. You aren't guilty of a single thing. You just give them the facts, and they can do with it what they will."

The guys had stayed at home, which I knew would be driving them mad. Truett was a happily bonded Alpha, twice over, but they still hated me going somewhere essentially alone. Truett had to swear on OJ's life that he'd protect me if anything happened before they'd even let me in his fancy car.

Nodding at his instruction, I gave him a small smile. "I remember." I paused on the stairs to the police station. "Thank you, by the way, for doing this for me. I know your time is valuable, and I can't pay you—"

Truett waved my words away. "Thank *you* for taking Satan's turkey and the zombie dog back. I swear, that bird has told me to go fuck myself more than any other living being has in my entire life. I think it's because it makes OJ laugh, and he does it for attention, the sneaky little birdbrain."

I laughed, because I could imagine Rufio doing that very thing. He was super smart—scary smart, even.

I straightened my shoulders, but nerves still ran up my spine. Grasping my elbow gently, Truett led me up the stairs. "If you can love that psycho, you can do anything, Polly Barrie," he murmured. "Let's go and make sure those who hurt you can never hurt anyone else ever again."

We walked into the bustling police station, and I took in the hard plastic chairs lined up in neat rows. An entire array of people were in there, from a woman who had no pants on, an elderly gentleman talking to the air beside him, two bored teens staring at their phones, and a woman in a business suit.

The officer at the desk looked stressed. "Can I help you?"

I swallowed hard, while Truett squeezed my arm reassuringly. "Hello. My name is Paloma, and I'm a victim of the Homestead Cult."

You could've heard a pin drop in the room. The police officer in front of me blinked a few times. "That's over in Arkansas, ma'am. This is South Carolina." His tone said he clearly didn't believe me, that I was just one more in a long line of crazies he'd seen today.

I looked him in the eye, despite my Omega wanting to run home with her tail between her legs. "I'm aware. I'm an Omega, and I was trafficked across state lines."

Still silence.

Finally, Truett interrupted. "Either get her statement, or she can tell it to the press with a nice little caveat that the Rock Hill PD didn't even believe her enough to take a moment to ask questions. I'm sure the Prosecutor's office would love that."

Another cop walked by and did a double take when he saw Truett and me. "Heathstone? Isn't one Omega problem enough?"

I almost felt Truett roll his eyes. "Frankie, this is Paloma. She'd like to make a victim statement about that cult in Arkansas."

Frankie's eyebrows almost hit his hairline. "Don't worry, Jerry. I'll take them back." He met us at a door off to the side and reached out to shake my hand. He was an Alpha, but he had non-threatening vibes. "Come on through. I'm Frankie Gunnar. It's nice to meet you." He led me down the hall. "You're pretty brave. That shit over in Arkansas is rough."

I didn't feel brave, but in the words of August, sometimes you just had to fake it until you made it.

For the next six hours, that's what I did.

THIRTY-FOUR
LLEW

In the end, they prosecuted fifteen people in connection with the Ozark Homestead Cult, as the media had dubbed it. The surviving Leaders, and more than a few of the elder Brothers and Sisters, were charged with crimes that ranged from child endangerment and false imprisonment, all the way to murder and human trafficking.

Truett Heathstone had managed to get the courts to agree to allow Polly her anonymity in exchange for her testimony, and along with most of the damning evidence of the younger generation, plus Kross and the survivors' testimonies, most of the older generation were going to get the life behind walls they'd always wanted. Except this time, it would be prison.

It was hard for Polly, though; the guilt warred with the need for justice, and she'd regressed almost all the way back to the unsure Omega she'd been that first week.

August had suggested a new therapist for her in the private sector, and that was really helping.

After two months of waiting for the hearing, the lead prosecutors managed to get the trial expedited, due to public pressure for justice. The only shining spot about having to attend this mess in Arkansas was that Polly would finally get to see her friend. Although they'd Facetimed a lot, Nim hadn't been able to leave Arkansas until the trial was over, and the drive was long and arduous, so Polly had decided to wait until she needed to be there for her testimony. I'd suggested a flight, but neither of us had been comfortable with the idea of flying. I would have done it for her, though.

She was nervous in the back of the hired SUV, and I resisted the urge to climb over the seats and hug her to my chest. August was back there, and he was hugging her enough for all of us. "It'll be fine, sweetheart," he murmured.

She nodded, but her next words defied her agreement. "What if they hate me for ruining their lives? What if they're sad and confused, and I'm the reason?"

He kissed her temple. "What if one of those babies grows up to be an Alpha and would've been put down because he didn't fit their agenda?" He squeezed her tighter to his chest. "In a year, or five, or a decade, they'll wake up and realize that all the things they have in their life happened because you were so brave."

This time, her nod seemed more sure.

We pulled up in front of a nondescript two-story

house on the outskirts of Little Rock. There was a pile of discarded shoes at the front door, and rose bushes that needed a trim. As soon as we got out, we could hear the sound of children laughing. It echoed up and down the street, and something loosened in my chest.

We all waited for Polly to climb from the car, and stood around her protectively. One or two of us would probably have been better, but none of us would risk not being here if Polly needed us.

The front door flew open, and out ran a girl with pretty almond eyes and long, flowing black hair. Polly sucked back a sob, tears spilling from her eyes. "Nim," she breathed.

"Polly!"

Nim barreled into our Omega, and I rested a hand on Polly's back to keep her steady as the two women hugged tightly. They were both crying, but they were happy tears. There was no distress in either of their scents.

Pulling back, Nim stared at my Omega like she was a wonder. "I thought you were dead. They told me that you'd choked on a piece of fruit, and they'd tried to save you, but it was too late. Sister Roberta wouldn't let me see your body. They wouldn't tell me where you were buried, *nothing*." The girl, who couldn't have even been over five feet, snarled like an Alpha. "It was because she was a freaking *liar*. They sold you. Henry told me." She let out a choked noise, then her eyes went to us. "But not to these guys, obviously."

Polly smiled at her friend. "No, not these guys." She

stepped back from Nim, but still kept a tight hold on her arm like she was worried she'd disappear again completely. "Guys, this is Nimah. My sister. Nim, this is my Beta, Max, and my Alpha, Rio—they rescued me from the warehouse. This is August, my Omega," she said, her smile mischievous. Then she looked at me with soft eyes. "And this is my Alpha, Llew."

Nim ran her fingers through Polly's short hair. "He's the reason your hair is growing back? I forgot it was this color. I almost feel like I forgot what your face looks like without the veil."

Polly twined her fingers in Nim's. "No, I abandoned the veil as soon as I knew I'd been lied to, that the world outside the walls wasn't filled with monsters."

That was not technically true. There were plenty of monsters outside the walls too. But I would protect her from those.

Nim smiled. "Good. Because I missed your face." With that, she linked arms with Polly. "Come on, every-one's missed you."

And just like that, all the worry I felt was gone.

There were thirteen kids from the Homestead, aged from three months to seventeen years of age. The older ones looked shell-shocked still, wary of strangers, of other Alphas, of the outside world in general. It was a lot for a kid to take in.

But the younger ones? They were laughing and

playing on playground equipment in the backyard, like they'd just stepped foot into an amusement park. "Higher," one little girl around the age of six screamed from the swing, and I dutifully pushed her slightly harder, though the height she was already going made my Alpha want to catch her and set her down on solid ground.

These little ones were the real lucky ones. They hadn't seen the terrible side of the Homestead yet. Didn't have parents that they missed. But they did know that out here there were foods they'd never tried, animals they'd never seen, television, cartoons, storybooks, clothes that were the color pink. The little girl on the swing told me all about the new things she'd seen and explored.

Every time one of the kids came over and showed Polly something they hadn't ever seen before, with wonder in their eyes, I saw the guilt leave her a little more.

Max was talking to a little boy who was looking up at him with amazed, wide eyes, and August was talking soothingly to some of the older kids. His Omega pheromones would relax them, even if they didn't realize it. The haunted look in the eyes of the older girls was worrying, and I wondered if we could pay someone to end the rest of the Leaders in their jail cells.

It wasn't perfect, but at least now, everyone had a chance to heal. To live.

Henry appeared beside me, a baby attached to his chest in one of those carrier things. I wasn't quite sure how they'd managed to convince Child Services to let them all stay together, but from what Henry told me, the sweet older Beta couple we'd met at the front door had agreed to run this place as a group home until everything got sorted out, including determining everyone's family lines. They seemed happiest together, so I couldn't fault them for their decision.

The baby on Henry's chest was sleeping soundly. "How are you coping?" I asked softly, and the young Alpha shrugged.

"There's good days and bad days. The guilt can be a lot—the guilt we were too slow, that this is all too much..."

I patted his back gently. "Polly feels the same way."

Henry looked down at the baby on his chest. "But this little one will never know living inside those walls, or doing chores so they're allowed to eat when they're four, or being beaten for asking questions. This little one will be happy, as long as they don't send him back to his parents." There was anger there, a trauma that would only heal with time and a lot of therapy.

"You did that," I told him softly. "You gave them freedom." I cleared my throat. "Have you decided what you'd like to do after this is all over?"

His eyes slid to Nim, who was laughing with Polly. Those two had barely been out of touching distance this whole time. "I'm not sure."

"Aren't you?" I asked him lightly. "You're always more than welcome to come and live with us, or we can set you up in your own place nearby. You can bring whoever you like with you too. There's room for all of Polly's family."

Finally, the little girl on the swing sighed. "I'm hungry now. Can we have ice cream?" She directed it at Henry, who raised an eyebrow at her.

"Will you eat all your dinner, Ari?"

Ari contemplated his words, then nodded. "Yep."

"Even the vegetables?"

The girl screwed up her nose. "Are we having sprouts? I hate sprouts."

I lifted her off the swing. "Me too. Don't tell Polly. I think they're gross," I said conspiratorially, and the little girl swung furtive eyes in my Omega's direction.

"They taste like farts."

I nodded solemnly, and Henry rolled his eyes. "There's no brussel sprouts."

Ari grinned widely. "Yay! Then I promise to eat my dinner."

Yeah, I wasn't convinced.

"Go and ask Mrs. Wilson, but if she says no, that's final. All right?"

With a squeal that seemed to rally the other little ones, she torpedoed into the house. Henry shook his head. "Mrs. Wilson won't say no. She looks at them like they're lost little puppies and they've already scented her weakness." He gave a bitter laugh. "We got lucky. The Wilsons are kind and haven't tried to take over the parenting role. I know Nim and the others felt better that they weren't going to be relegated to being children themselves, or shut out of the only life they've ever known." He turned back to the house. "I'll keep your offer in mind. I don't think Arkansas has anything left for any of us."

He disappeared inside the house, and I went to find my Omega. All these kids had made me a little clucky, although we'd never had a conversation about kids. It didn't matter to me if we did or didn't; I was just happy that Polly was ours. She was more than I ever thought we'd have.

THIRTY-FIVE
POLLY

I was cross-examined for three days during the trial of the Leaders and the elders of the Homestead. Apparently, they might have been shut off from the world living the prepper life, but their investments had continued, earning them a healthy amount of money to buy great lawyers. Lawyers who tore holes in my story, even when there weren't any. Lawyers who tried to shift the blame onto everyone but the people who'd created and led the Homestead. Except for Leader Malakai. He was a conveniently dead scapegoat.

They might try and wiggle out of it—especially the trafficking charges, when it came to me—but there was a multitude of evidence about all the terrible stuff they'd done.

By the time we left Arkansas, I never wanted to go back. I never wanted to leave our Packhouse, or my

Alphas, ever again. I felt raw, like every nerve ending had been set on fire.

The guys had closed ranks, and for the week after we returned from the trial, we'd done nothing but just *be*. We slept in the nest, ate in bed, watched movies on a sea of blankets in the media room, and I felt like I surfed from chest to chest. It was what I needed, what my soul needed, and I felt myself unwind.

My old life was officially behind me. There was only happiness in my future, and I was going to grab it with both hands.

"Sweet Thing?" Llew murmured into my hair.

"Yeah?"

"I'd like you to meet my mom." I must have looked terrified, because he chuckled and pulled me closer, until his whole body was wrapped around mine. "Don't look so scared. The worst she will do is hug you until you're sure you'll suffocate." He cleared his throat. "I thought it might be good to have a family thing and invite every-one's folks. With Henry and Nim as your family, so all the pieces of my heart can meet." He looked over at August, then leaned down to wink at me. "I'd like to announce that we are courting August, if it's okay with him."

I crawled over to my sweet Omega, cuddled between Max and Rio. He held out his arms, and I straddled his lap, wanting to crawl inside him so we could be one person. He'd been here this whole time, like a steady calming presence, but something about his scent was clouding my brain today.

"We might need to put a small raincheck on that, because I think I'm about two days from my heat. I have a feeling my heat will trigger Polly's again too, so they'll sync." His cheeks flushed, the color running down his neck and up to the tips of his ears. "And my Omega will probably insist on bonding you all."

I remembered that aching need in my chest to bond the guys, how hard it was to resist. If August asked me to bond him, it would be impossible for me to keep a clear head. If I was in my heat as well? We were definitely coming out of the heat a bonded pair of Omegas.

I pulled back, so I could look down at his warm brown eyes. "Is that something only your Omega wants?"

August held my gaze as he shook his head. "I want it too. So much." His eyes drifted around the room, the sounds of *Easy A* playing in the background. "I already feel like a Pack with you, and I am desperate to make it official."

I chewed my lip, until Rio's fingertip reached over and pulled the flesh from between my teeth gently. "But we haven't courted you properly yet," I told August softly.

He leaned forward and kissed me. "We've done so much together already. More ups and downs than some people have in their entire relationships. We're past silly courting rituals."

I frowned and looked at the guys, an understanding passing between us. I felt it down the bond, the certainty that we were all on the same page. "How many days until your heat again?"

"Two."

I looked at Rio, then Max, then back over my shoulder at Llew, who was smiling widely, because he knew what I was thinking. We'd basically planned this already—the timeline was just getting expedited.

Leaning forward, I brushed my lips over August's one more time. "You should go home and get a good night's sleep. Tomorrow, you're going to be express courted."

August blinked. "Express courted?"

I nodded, climbing off his lap. "Uh-huh. I mean it, go home, August. Pack up your stuff because by tomorrow night, the only place you'll belong is by our side, or in our nest."

Max slumped back against the pillows, his eyes hooded. "Am I the only one turned on by bossy Polly?"

I was tired but excited. I bounced in the front seat of Rio's car, a rumbly old hunk of metal that sat in the garage most days, because he still struggled to be inside a car since his tour and the IED that had exploded his convoy.

But desperate times called for desperate measures.

The rest of the guys were in other places, getting

things organized, and I was absolutely giddy with excitement. It helped that Llew and I had planned this in those early hours while the guys were away.

We pulled into the parking lot of August's apartment. It was a little run-down, I guess, judging by the peeling paint and broken pipes on the side of the building. The other cars in the parking lot didn't look quite as shiny as the guys', so maybe they were older too. I really had no touchstone on why Rio thought this place wasn't safe, but I trusted my Alpha. If he didn't think August was safe here, then I was happy he was coming to live at the Packhouse with us. The sooner, the better.

Bounding out of the car, I bounced on my toes until Rio joined me. I dragged him along as we walked up to the entry door. There were a whole lot of buttons beside the door, and I looked quizzically at him.

"They're buzzers for each apartment. Hit number seventeen."

I pressed the number, and it let out a choked buzz. "Hello?"

I jumped into the air as August's voice came through a tiny speaker. Rio laughed, and I gave him my best death glare. Leaning forward, he held down the button. "It's Rio and Polly."

"Come on up!"

With that, the door popped open like magic. Gripping the edge, Rio pulled it open and ushered me through. Climbing the stairs, we soon stood outside August's door.

When the man himself appeared, all the plans I'd been making all night disappeared from my head. He looked beautiful. His hair was curling softly, still damp from his morning shower. He had a soft, sage-green shirt on and dark blue jeans. He smelled so good that I found myself drifting toward him, climbing into his arms and licking a long stripe up his neck.

Rio groaned. "Fuck," he said beneath his breath. "Cut that out, Polly, or all your plans for today are going to disappear, with us going back into August's apartment and you both letting me fuck you senseless."

I groaned, but wiggled out of August's arms, putting a few inches of space between us. I cleared my throat. "You look wonderful."

Leaning down, he brushed his lips gently across mine. "As do you, Polly. There's something to be said for Rio's plan," he growled low, and I could almost see the Omega surging up into his eyes to take control.

With strength I didn't know I had, I took another step back. Then one more, for good measure. "No way. There's time for that tomorrow, and the next day, and the next day," I purred out in promise. "Today's for showing you how much we want you and love you. How happy we could make you forever."

He gripped my hands. "I already know how happy you make me, baby." Sucking in a few fortifying breaths, he looked up at Rio. "Okay, we better leave my apartment while we still can. I'll just go and grab my wallet."

He disappeared back into his bedroom, while I

looked around the small apartment. It looked exactly like him—masculine but with a few concessions to his Omega nature: soft pillows, throw blankets everywhere, candles that smelled like... jasmine?

He was filling his home with a scent similar to mine? My Omega preened, and I had to hold on tight to stop myself from marching into his bedroom and showing him just how special I thought he was.

When he reemerged, he inhaled deeply. His pupils were wide, his cock now semi-hard behind his jeans. Rio groaned, gripping the back of my dress gently and twirling me out the door. "If someone told me I was going to be the level-headed one between two horny Omegas, I would have laughed them out of the room," he muttered. "Go on now, sweetheart, while we still can."

Then he reached over, gripped August by the front of his shirt and kissed him until he was perfuming. Watching the two of them, my entire body was clenching with need. Pulling back from the dazed-looking Omega, Rio tugged him out the door too, making sure the apartment was locked.

"If this isn't proof of my dedication to you, I don't know what would be," he grumbled, and I wasn't sure if he was talking to me, or August, or us both. I reached back and held both their hands.

"Thank you, Alpha," I purred, and Rio's eyes closed slowly, like he was trying to find strength behind his eyelids.

Laughing, I looked over at the amused face of

August. His cheeks were pink, and his scent was thick, and I knew his heat was almost here. I was so fucking excited.

This was the start of a perfect day. No, this was the start of a perfect *life*.

Thirty-Six

August

The plan started at a diner. Not just any diner, though—the one I'd told Llew about in passing one night while we were sitting around watching movies. Rio had dropped us off, telling me he'd wait outside.

Polly looked beautiful, her sundress so soft that it fluttered around her thighs as she walked. I wanted to put her on my lap and kiss her until she was as breathless as I was. We ordered and cuddled on the same side of the booth while we waited for the food.

"How are you feeling?" I asked softly into her hair. I could see the long glances of the Alphas in the diner around us; our combined Omega scent was a delicious mix. But no one made any move to come closer, and I knew that Rio would be watching the room like a hawk from wherever he was. I trusted that Alpha implicitly with our safety, even if I couldn't see him right now.

Polly shrugged. "Like this is the rightest thing I've ever done? And that you smell so good. And that I'm kind of glad we're in public, because I want to climb beneath this table and—" I placed a finger over her lips, because if she finished that sentence, I was going to drag her to what was definitely a gross public bathroom and fuck her on the sink. My Omega panted at the idea, but I'd seen how excited Polly had been for today's events, and I didn't want to disappoint her.

They didn't need to do this. I didn't need to be courted, because I'd committed to them a long time ago. I never went on dates, convincing myself I was just too busy, when in reality no one had ever measured up to Rio and Max, and the way they made me feel.

Polly and Llew were just the icing on the cake. A fate-given reason to have waited.

I removed my finger from her lips. "If you finish that sentence, this day is going to end really quickly. I'm way too close to my heat to resist you, pretty girl."

The harried Unshown waitress appeared with armfuls of plates and two large mugs of hot cocoa. "I hope you two are hungry," she chirped, and I snorted a laugh. I was starving, but it wasn't for the stack of pancakes in front of me.

Polly smiled at her happily. "Thank you!" She looked at the meals in front of us. "I saw a man on television who tours around the country trying food, and I wanted to try this one when I saw it." She pointed to the sausage gravy and biscuits. "I'm so glad it's on the menu here."

Sometimes I forgot that she was just experiencing the world for the first time, especially now that she'd been with us for a while.

I grabbed my fork and got the perfect mouthful of gravy and biscuit. I fed it to her, trying not to think about her mouth wrapping around other things, and she moaned. My cock immediately hardened in my jeans, and I internally grumbled that I was wearing these torture devices in the first place. Poor planning on my behalf.

"Good?"

She nodded and had another bite. "So good. Maybe I should become a cook?" She took a sip of her cocoa. "Now everything else is... done." She cleared her throat. "I've been thinking about what I actually want to do or be. There's a whole world out there to explore."

She was so fucking beautiful. As we fed each other breakfast and went over different careers and hobbies, I fell more and more in love with the woman in front of me.

I was stuffed full when we left the diner at exactly 10:05. Stumbling into the parking lot, I saw Rio on his phone, a smile on his face. When he saw us, he hung up and climbed from the car. "How was breakfast?" he asked, leaning down to kiss my cheek, then Polly's.

"So good! Have you ever tried sausage gravy?"

He chuckled. "Yep, sweetheart, I have. Come on, we have fifteen minutes to get to our next spot."

As if summoned, Max rolled up in a Mustang convertible, his smile warm. "Hey, fancy meeting you here." He climbed out and kissed me softly on the lips. "I'll see you soon. I'm here to collect this Omega for phase three of the plan." He scooped Polly up, but not before she snagged my shirt and pulled me in for a messy kiss.

She was definitely picking up on my Omega hormones. There was no chance we wouldn't sync our heats, because she already smelled divine.

Rio cleared his throat. "You better whisk Polly out of here. It's been an exercise in restraint the entire morning, and I'm not sure how much more I can take."

Max slapped Polly's ass cheek, making her squeal as he put her in the passenger seat of the car. Making sure she was buckled in, he climbed into the driver's seat, threw me a wink, and pulled out of the parking lot.

We watched them go, then Rio threaded his fingers between mine, pulling me toward the car. "Come on. I want to show you something."

We stood beneath a large Ferris wheel. Rio was talking to an elderly man, who was looking between us with a goofy expression on his face. Finally, he nodded, and they shook hands.

Smirking as he came back over to me, Rio grabbed my hand and pulled me toward one of the little gondolas.

"The old guy was a romantic, but he made me swear no dirty business on his ride." I snorted.

A bored teenager hit a button and held open the gondola door for us. "Don't climb out of the cage. Don't spit over the side..." He gave a monotone spiel, and I tried not to roll my eyes. Rio led us onto the ride, then pulled me close.

This was almost adorably cheesy. "This is nice. Not what I expected from you, though, I'm not going to lie."

Rio shook his head. "Polly's been watching a lot of rom-coms to catch up on the world outside, and she has in her head that a Ferris wheel is the most romantic thing an Alpha can do to show someone he's serious. I didn't have the heart to tell her otherwise. It was either this or me rowing you into the middle of the lake. You can blame Llew for the regency romance ideas, though. He showed her *Pride and Prejudice,* and she's watched it seven times in a month." I laughed at the idea of that giant Alpha being a Jane Austin fan.

As the Ferris wheel reached the pinnacle, I could see all over the nature preserve that doubled as an adventure park. There was a lake, and trails that had people horseback riding, and a hedge maze. It was truly beautiful out here.

"We should bring Polly out here one day too. That lake looks nice for her Mr. Darcy moment."

"We will."

The ride shuddered to a stop when we were at the

very highest point. It was like we were on top of the world.

"August?"

I turned to Rio, and in his hand was a small velvet box. I sucked in a breath. "Yes?" My voice sounded rough, and he chuckled.

"This might feel fast from the outside, but to me, it's felt like the slow culmination of something that was almost inevitable. The second time I met you—once I was over my pricked pride and stupid belief that I couldn't be a man *and* go to therapy—I knew you were special. I didn't think I deserved you then, and even now, I'm not sure I do. You're kind, and so smart, and so fucking handsome that you make my balls ache." I snorted a laugh, because that was so charming. "I dreamed about making you my Omega back then, though I could never have guessed how truly lucky I would end up being."

He gripped my hand. "August O'Hare, I swear on my very life that I will love and care for you until the end of my days. I will treat you with the respect you deserve, the challenge you crave, and shower you with all the love I have to give. Will you accept my courting gift?"

Apparently, it wasn't just Polly who was pulling out the old-style romance. I swallowed the large lump in my throat. "Absolutely."

I took the velvet box and opened it. Inside was a set of dog tags. The top one said *Pack Barrie* and on the flip side, everyone's name was inscribed, including mine. The tag underneath had a quote:

There's nothing as strong as gentleness.

"It's part of a longer quote that wouldn't fit. 'There's nothing as strong as gentleness, nothing so gentle as real strength'. I thought it would fit our little Pack well."

I swallowed hard, feeling seen by these men, these Alphas, in a way not even my family truly saw me. At home, with my family Pack, I was their coddled Omega in a family of mostly Alphas. They loved me, but treated me like I was breakable.

These guys *saw* me, saw what it took to shoulder the burdens of veterans every day.

"I love it. Thank you."

He leaned forward and kissed me once more. It was a promise, just as much as the dog tags were. The promise of something long-lasting and special. His lips were smooth and firm, and his tongue dipped out to taste mine as we deepened the kiss. I groaned, my heat surging up, demanding we fuck this Alpha *now*. We needed to bite him, bond him, make him mine.

I pushed the urge down, drawing away, panting. His eyes were wide, lips parted, and I knew he was as affected as I was. I could smell his desire on his skin. I could taste it on my tongue.

He groaned, looking up at the sky and huffing in deep breaths. "I swear, this day might be a divine punishment."

Finally, the ride continued, and I held out the necklace. "Help me put it on?"

His fingers were deft as he placed the tags around my neck, his fingers brushing over my nape. I snuggled close to his side, and we sat silently, bodies pressed together. I rubbed the tags on my neck, resting my head on his shoulder.

Polly was right. Ferris wheels really were peak romantic gestures.

THIRTY-SEVEN
MAX

I thought, of all the parts of "The Plan," this was the phase that Polly was most excited for. You could tell, because she hadn't sat still since we'd arrived at the nature reserve that was currently housing the Ferris wheel. When we'd done some research last night, I'd been kind of disappointed that Rio wouldn't have to row to the middle of the lake. This was fortunate, though, and while I needed Polly for my part, I'd be able to bring her back to go on the Ferris wheel. Maybe we could pretend to be teenagers and get to second base right at the very top.

"There they are!"

She climbed out of the car and ran toward them. I grinned, her joy infectious. When she ran into August's arms, he caught her easily, spinning her around. Her dress climbed up her thighs a little, and my breath froze in my lungs. Fuck, they were so beautiful together.

I dragged my phone out of my pocket and took a photo for Llew, then set it as my wallpaper. My two Omegas, bracketed by a Ferris wheel, my Alpha watching over them with so much love in his eyes, it made me feel emotional. It was perfect.

I didn't think she realized it yet, but we were courting Polly too. Even though she was completely enamoured with us, and was already irreversibly part of our Pack, she deserved this. I'd just taken her to buy the bonding ring for August that we'd give him this afternoon, but while she was busy, I'd gotten her a necklace with a large drop emerald that was cut to look like a star had exploded inside it. It was beautiful, just like our Omega.

"Come on, you two. They're waiting for us," I called over to them.

Polly wiggled to her feet and dragged August along behind her. Rio shook his head. "Are they all ready?"

I nodded. We'd called ahead to Otillie-James and Lance, and we'd meet them at their rescue. I'd actually asked Otillie-James for more than that, but I had to keep that bit a secret until we got there.

My Omegas crawled into the back of the car, Polly scooting almost all the way onto August's lap. Rio slapped the back of my head. "Concentrate on the road, and don't get distracted. Because they will be *so* fucking distracting," he groaned. "Thank god the top comes down on this; I can't even imagine being trapped in all those heat pheromones."

He wasn't wrong. "Llew is waiting for you."

Rio nodded and leaned into the back of the car, kissing August and then Polly. "Be good. Don't distract the driver."

"Yes, sir," Polly quipped, making Rio groan again.

I took that as our cue to leave. I pulled back out onto the freeway, glancing briefly into the rearview mirror. The wind whipped away their scents and words, for which I was incredibly thankful, because they were kissing like they couldn't get enough of each other.

Maybe doing this so close to August's heat was a mistake, but so much of our courtship had been focused on Polly. Not that I felt bad about that—she deserved the attention. But I wanted August to know that we wanted *him*, not just what he could do for us.

After the longest twenty-minute drive of my life, I pulled off into the driveway of Lance's house, and the dirt road left a cloud of dust behind us. OJ and Lance were on the front porch of their impressive-as-fuck house, two baskets at their feet as well as Doodles.

When we rolled to a stop, I adjusted my cock in my jeans before climbing out. Fuck, this was painful. Smiling at the Omegas in the back seat, I reached in to lift Polly out.

August jumped out of the convertible easily, giving me a cheeky smirk. "I've always wanted to do that."

I wrapped my arm around his shoulders, and he smiled widely up at Lance. "You're a sight for sore eyes. I was worried about you, until Rio and Max told me that you were in love. Congrats are in order, I hear?" He gripped Lance's hand, shaking it heartily.

"The healing power of love, am I right?" Lance said lightly. "This is Otillie-James, my Omega."

The Omega in question looked like a riot. That was the best way I could describe her, really. Her hair was crazy, and she had mud on her overalls and a smile on her face.

"Lance says I have you to thank for him still being here today," she whispered to August, and then hugged him. She pulled back quickly, her nose twitching. "Woah, they weren't kidding about you being close to heat. I wouldn't fuck around, if I were you." She looked at Polly and hugged her too, her face softening. "It's good to see you, Polly."

Polly threw herself into the hug, and I smiled. She'd come so far.

OJ looked misty-eyed as she pulled back. "Okay, here are your sweet treats. Let's go, before your boy goes into heat on my front porch," she joked, directing us to a path that ran down the side of the house. "They came in earlier in the week, and I thought they'd be perfect for you guys."

August narrowed his eyes at me. We hadn't told him a lot about Lance's new Packmate, but maybe he was making some connections. I just grinned and held him tight to my body as Polly ran ahead.

Lance walked beside us. "She looks good. Happy."

I smiled, because she was better than good. She was

great. "My mission in life now is just to make her as happy as possible until the end of my days." I looked at August. "Both of you."

August reached down and laced his fingers with mine. "You already do."

Lance made a gagging noise. "God, was I this disgustingly sweet?"

I gave him the finger. "Worse."

We reached a large barn, where the noise was insane, an absolute cacophony. Polly looked so excited, I suspected she'd forgotten all about the impending heat, and the fact we were meant to be courting an Omega. It didn't matter, though, because August watched her with such obvious heart eyes that I almost laughed.

"You're already all in, aren't you?"

He leaned over and kissed me. "From the very first day I stepped into your living room and saw her. I knew then that this was it for me. Nothing else would do."

I buried my fingers in his hair and kissed him, with all the feelings in my soul. Someone cleared their throat, and I pulled away, flushed. "Then enjoy the day, and know I'm going to spoil you like this every day for the rest of our lives."

"Here we are," OJ said loudly, a grin on her face. "Polly, if you ever want a job, you're more than welcome to come and help me out here. I can't pay you a lot, but the work is rewarding."

My Omega's eyes got so wide, I thought they'd pop out of her head. "Seriously?"

OJ grinned. "Absolutely. Your Pack isn't the only one with two Omegas getting taken out of action for a couple of days, every two or so months. If I had someone I knew who could take care of the animals while we're, uh, otherwise indisposed, it would be a weight off my mind. Besides, the guys are sick of being unpaid labor, so I could use some help."

Polly jumped into her arms once more. "Yes! Thank you!" She looked at me, her excitement dimming slightly. "I'll have to ask the Pack first..."

I waved a hand. "Sweetheart, whatever you want is yours. We'll make it work."

She let out a hushed squeal and nodded. "Then I accept, thank you!"

August gave me a look, and I was beginning to think he was onto us making this a double courting. I hadn't forgotten him, though.

"In here," OJ told us. "I'll leave you to it. This is the most we've ever had, and honestly, it's nearly impossible to be down here giving them all the attention and handling they need. You're doing me a solid favor."

When we went in, there were fifteen kittens in a straw-filled horse stall. Some were curled up under a heating lamp, while others were wrestling around or climbing.

Polly melted into a puddle. Grabbing August's hand, she pulled him down to his knees. Noticing their captive audience, the kittens bounded over, meowing loudly.

"There are cat treats in there too," OJ called from

outside the gate, indicating the picnic basket. "Have fun, kids. Just so you know, they're all adoptable." She cackled evilly as she left.

Kitten Picnic had been my idea, because August had told me that he'd had a cat growing up, and he missed him a lot. The idea was to show him that we were committed to being a Pack by adding another member to the family, a shared pet. But looking at Polly's face, I was beginning to think maybe it wouldn't be just a single member being added.

As August lay down in the straw, he was immediately attacked by tiny little floofballs. I lay down beside him, and a sleepy little white kitten with a gray nose crawled onto my lap and went to sleep.

God. I was in love.

I looked down at August, whose eyes were laughing at me. "I think this might have been an error in judgement," I said resignedly. Polly was giggling as one of the kittens tried to attack her fingers like a fierce predator.

"You think?" August said lightly, a kitten was making biscuits on his chest. "Best bad idea ever."

Yeah, there'd been a few of those in my life. Raiding that warehouse was undeniably a terrible idea, with the best outcome I could have ever hoped for.

"My favorite kind," I murmured, leaning in to kiss him. I hoped it was one of many wonderfully terrible ideas we'd make together for the rest of our lives.

THIRTY-EIGHT
POLLY

Max had turned down my request to keep all fifteen kittens. No matter how much I pouted, he'd warned me that we couldn't spend enough time with that many cats, so it would be irresponsible.

I saw his point, but I didn't like it.

However, when August had said that black cats were less likely to be adopted, I saw Max making a mental tally of how many black kittens were in the batch. Spoiler alert, there were two black ones and one tuxedo—which I argued was almost all black—who had fallen asleep around August's neck and basically cinched the deal.

So now we were the proud owners of three kittens. They were staying with OJ, who'd take them to get their shots and chips, and hold them until after August's heat. Every part of my body was buzzing with elated happiness.

"This has been the best day ever," I murmured into August's ear as we sped away from OJ's house, and back to our own. The last phase of the day was the one I was most nervous about. It had taken both Llew and Rio most of the day to do, but it would be amazing.

August's face was flushed, and I remembered the feeling. "Are you ready to go home, Omega?" I whispered in his ear sultrily, despite being an Omega too, and when his eyes widened and then darkened, I knew I'd do it again. This feeling of being desired was heady.

"Yes." His scent swirled around me, making my libido do the macarena. I'd recently learned about the macarena and had mastered the dance in record time with the help of Llew.

Max was grumbling in the driver's seat, making me chuckle. August was achingly hard in his jeans, and honestly, it looked kind of painful. Sliding my hand down his chest, I ran my fingertips across the bulge there. I could feel the dampness of his slick already soaking the denim, and I wanted to taste it.

Maybe I could give us both a little relief. Unzipping his pants, I held in my yelp as his cock sprung free, hard and ready. "Polly," he breathed, and I couldn't tell if he was begging or issuing a warning. Maybe both.

"August," I whined back. "I think you need a hand. Or maybe my mouth?"

Llew had recently introduced me to the sheer thrill of fucking him with my face, and I might be a little addicted to the way he moaned and grunted as he was completely at my mercy. I wanted to know if that applied to my Omega too. Given the way his breath hitched as I wrapped my fingers around his cock, I was pretty sure it would.

I stroked up and down slowly at first, watching his responses. Did he like it when I stroked my fingers over the head? Did he buck his hips up when I squeezed? He was so responsive that I was fairly sure I could just look at his dick intently, and he'd come.

I was going to do way more than look, though; I wanted to taste. Pulling my seatbelt down to my waist, I leaned over and kissed August. He kissed me back messily, filled with frantic need and tasting more than a little wild. Relishing the feel of his lips on mine, I captured his Omega whine in my mouth and swallowed it down. I wanted more. More of his need.

Bending myself in half, I gripped him in my fist as I licked across the head of his cock. "Jesus fucking Christ," he grunted, his hand cupping my head. My hair was almost an inch and a half now, long enough that it sat up at odd angles, allowing the guys to run their fingertips through it, which I loved.

I tongued the little slit on the underside of the head, and his muscles quivered. Lapping it furiously, I discovered his slick tasted amazing. Like chocolate and coffee and sex. I sucked the head into my mouth, desperate to taste more. His other hand came up until he was cradling my head and panting my name.

"Fuck, Polly. *Fuck*."

I did this thing that Llew always enjoyed—I took him in as far as he could go, then I swallowed him down more. His shout was whipped away by the wind, and the car swerved a little, but soon righted.

One of August's hands left my head, and when I looked up, he had it slapped over his mouth to muffle his shouts. I went back to what I was doing, with slow, languid, teasing strokes until he was vibrating beneath my hands.

"Please... Polly, please," he groaned, and I sucked harder. I lifted one of my hands, first gently cupping his balls, which still felt freaking weird. I didn't care what anyone said about testicles being an integral part of the male anatomy—they looked so weird and felt even weirder, and they moved like they were little aliens. And did I mention they were weird?

But when I cupped them, tugging them softly, August slammed his head back against the headrest of the seat. Yeah, they might be weird, but apparently, they felt good.

Moving on from his balls, I wrapped my hand tightly around the base of his cock, where his lock was already swelling, trying to lodge him inside the warmth of my mouth. That was a little adventurous for right now, so I fisted his lock in my hand and let him thrust up through it.

"Holy hell, little Omega, where the hell did you learn to do this?" he groaned, but I didn't answer, because my tongue was otherwise occupied.

Soon, he was wildly thrusting into my mouth, controlling the pace and depth, but never going too far. My eyes were watering, but he tasted so good. I was an addict. I wanted to swallow down every drop of slick he would give me.

"Polly, baby, I'm going to blow and... it's a lot." He pulled off his shirt and held it over his cock, and my Omega was outraged. He was going to waste his precious release on a shirt instead of inside me?

I pushed the shirt to the side, as well as his hands, and I took his cock in as far as I could. His cum was mine. He shouted, and gush after gush of cum exploded inside my mouth faster than I could swallow, making my cheeks swell. It leaked out the corners and dribbled down on his shirt anyway.

I mourned the lost drop, but I was content. I'd made my Omega happy, and when he pulled me into his side, his skin warm, I pushed the feelings of contentment down my bond.

"You're something amazing—you know that, right? You're the best thing that's ever happened to me, Polly Barrie." August kissed the top of my head, then my lips, tasting himself on my tongue. Did he taste as good to himself as he did to me? "I can't wait to slide inside you."

"We're nearly there," came the strangled sound of Max's voice in the front seat. He looked strung out and desperate. "Thank fuck," he continued under his breath. I could smell his arousal, and I felt a little guilty.

"You know, there's always the option of pulling over

and fucking us both on the hood of the car," August teased, and Max gave him a stern look.

"Don't tempt me." We pulled into a familiar driveway. "We're here."

Rio was waiting on the porch, looking pleased with himself. That was good—it meant phase four was on track. Or maybe he could just feel the pleasure I was experiencing down the bond.

He bounded down the stairs and opened the car door. "Looks like I missed all the fun," he teased, wiping the corner of my lip. "Come on, Omegas. From the scent of this back seat, August's heat is going to start sooner rather than later, and we have one more gift."

THIRTY-NINE
LLEW

I heard the crunch of gravel, and nerves fluttered in my stomach as I went through the final preparations. It was rushed, but I was proud of it. We could tweak things later, however August wanted it.

Wiping my hands on my pants, I dusted plaster from my shirt and set the robotic vacuum to go and hopefully collect the last of the dirt and dust I'd missed. While the last details had been a flurry of activity, this had been something I'd been working on slowly, in the hope that August would join us.

I smelled the heady combination of my Omegas' scents before I even heard their voices. It wafted down the hall like the most delicious perfume. I doubted I'd scent anything this amazing ever again.

Except maybe the combined scents of us all during the heat. That had been... really something.

"We got three. How were we meant to say no?" Polly

asked indignantly, and given where they'd just come from, I noted that I should probably build a catio in the backyard too.

Max met my eyes and shrugged. Yeah, I wouldn't have been able to tell her no either. Following his gaze, Polly saw me, and her face lit up like she couldn't imagine anything better than ending the day in my arms.

That look healed something inside me. *She* healed something inside me.

"Llew," she breathed, moving toward me, dragging August along with her. He was flushed, and when I pulled him tightly into my arms, he felt hot.

I tilted his head up to look at me. His eyes were glassy, and his scent was so strong, my cock was like stone. "My perfect Omega, has your heat arrived?"

He groaned even as he tried to swallow it down. "Definitely a heat spike. Not long now," he whispered, and I purred, rubbing my face over his. Marking him as mine. My Omega. Then I rubbed my cheek over Polly's too.

How did I get this lucky?

She reached up and kissed my cheek. "Take care of our Omega, Llew. He needs his Alpha," she whispered. I wasn't sure if it was August or myself who made a pained noise, but she skipped away with a grin on her face.

My Sweet Thing was learning her true power, and I was here for it. She had us all wrapped around her dainty little finger. But she was right; August needed me. His skin was so hot, I knew he'd need relief soon.

"May I kiss you, Omega?" I murmured, and his wide eyes, so filled with trust, healed another wound.

I kissed him softly at first, a promise.

I stroked my tongue over his full bottom lip, a taste.

I pulled him tight against my body and plundered his mouth with mine, a pleasure.

I lifted him into my arms, and he let out a blissful little sigh. Yeah, August was strong. He could shoulder anything life threw at him. But he didn't have to anymore.

"We will love you so fiercely, August O'Hare. The sun will rise and set with your happiness. We will be your lovers, partners, a place to hone your strengths, and a place to protect your weaknesses. Do you believe me?" I whispered against his lips, moving him further into the house. He was heavy; he wasn't a small Omega. But I was big. I could carry both him and Polly in my arms, right where they belonged.

The guest room had once sat beside the office that none of us ever used. We hadn't had guests in a year or more, and while that might change, our Omega needed his own space more. His own nest.

I stepped into the refurbished second Omega suite and held my breath. What if he hated it? I shook away the doubt. If he hated it, we'd change it. We'd keep changing it, until he was so in love with the space, he'd never think of leaving.

I could feel the rest of my Pack behind me. "It's just a start," I whispered in August's ear before lowering him to the ground and spinning him. "You can change whatever you want."

The main bedroom was recreated as close to his apartment as we could, with a similar color palette, including the lush greenery that he seemed to enjoy. Muted, relaxing tones and clean furniture lines. I'd relied on Rio's memory of the apartment to have something to work from. There were bookshelves running around the top of the walls on all four sides, because Rio had said that he had stacks of books everywhere in his apartment.

"Wow," August breathed, moving further into the room. "I love it. When did you *do* all this?"

I beamed at him. "Last night and most of today. We didn't have time to paint, but if you want to change anything, we absolutely can. This is your space now, if you want it to be," I hedged. I didn't want him to feel pressured. "But that's not all."

The guest room had an ensuite, but we hadn't really styled that, so I left it out of the tour. No, the next part was the important part.

Stepping up to the normal-looking bookcase, I slid it across recessed tracks to reveal the nest. I heard his gasp of wonder, and I grinned over my shoulder at him. Who didn't love a hidden door?

But beyond the door was what really made me nervous. I held my breath as he stepped forward into his nest. It wasn't incredibly fancy; we'd done what we could, but from what I'd read, a nest was an intensely personal thing. I didn't want to assume what he'd like.

However, I'd added things with our scents in here, as well as generic Omega bedding. Soft mattresses and furnishings. Dimmable light sconces. So many pillows. There was a little fridge to the side for snacks and hydration, in case we struggled to get out of the nest for sustenance.

"It's not much, but it's yours. Anything you need, we can get for you." It wasn't soft and girly like Polly's, because although August was an Omega, he wasn't feminine in any way.

He turned, his eyes glassy with tears. "You guys did all this for me in one night?"

I stroked my fingers over his sharp jaw. "More or less. Polly and I had been discussing making this a second Omega suite for a while, and we'd cleared out most of the furniture, but with all hands on deck, it went pretty quickly." I kissed his cheek. "You're worth every ounce of effort."

He launched himself forward and kissed me. Wrapping his strong arms around my neck, he held me tightly as his teeth scraped against my lip. My arm around his waist, I walked him backwards, before halting. We had to do this right.

"Omega, can I enter your nest?"

"Fuck yes," he breathed, pulling me down onto the soft mattress with him. I chased his lips with mine, kneeling between his thighs. His strong hands held me tightly, and I groaned into his mouth. He was addictive, and I was losing myself to the haze of the rut. It was only the sweet scent of jasmine and vanilla that reminded me we weren't alone.

My Pack stood at the door. Kissing my way from the corner of August's mouth and down his jaw, I used these few seconds to regain control of my Alpha. "Omega, are you in heat?"

"No," he groaned, though his temperature wanted to tell me otherwise.

"You need to eat, and maybe have a nice cool bath before your heat hits. There is an eternity to kiss you senseless in your nest, but I would be a bad Alpha if I didn't take care of you in your preheat." Sitting back onto my knees, I looked down at him, all flushed pink with hooded eyes, begging me to fuck him. I sent a prayer up to the Patron Saint of Sexual Restraint for a little control.

Max, bless him, took pity on me. Appearing beside us, he gripped August's hand. "Come on, let's go and carb load, because I intend to fuck you every which way, until you'll feel like you've run an ultra-marathon."

August laughed softly, but let himself be pulled to his feet. I watched them go, sucking oxygen in through my nose. Fucking mistake, because all I got was a lungful of Omega pheromones. My knot was throbbing.

Rio, the fucker, laughed at the expression on my face as he came over and helped me to my feet. "I hope to god their heats sync, because I'm not sure I could do this alternate months without my dick falling off and dying of dehydration." He grinned. "But what a way to go."

FORTY

AUGUST

This had been the most perfect day of my life, but I swore on my collection of original Tolkiens that if I didn't get one of their knots soon, I was going to fucking lose it. My body throbbed, and I whined, even as Max hand-fed me my favorite dumplings from the dumpling house near my apartment.

He leaned closer. "Are you full, Omega? Or just anxious to be full of something else?"

I moaned, and the noise set off Polly, because she abandoned her own food and climbed onto my lap. Her skin felt normal to me, which was definitely a sign that she was feverish, because I was burning up.

"Does she feel hot to you?" I breathed, even as she nipped her way down my throat, her teeth pressing hard into the pulse point on my neck. "Fuck." I gripped her hips, grinding up into her soft warmth. I needed to be inside her.

Max's hand reached between us, and he grunted. "Yep. You've definitely knocked her into heat with you." He grinned. "I don't know if I should be excited or terrified."

Both was the intelligent response.

But I couldn't tell him that, because the Omega in my arms was kissing me. She tasted like heaven, and I found myself climbing to my feet and carrying her down the hall to my nest. I was on the same side of the house as Rio, and his scent was stronger in this hall. I didn't like that all their scents weren't there equally, but there was time to fix that. What I didn't have time for was delayed satisfaction.

I wanted, and I wanted *now*.

I stepped into my nest with its perfect hidden door, and smiled. Llew might've been the Alpha who'd known me the shortest amount of time, but somehow, he understood me. The rest would come. I was as enamored by the big, damaged Alpha as I was with the sweet little Omega in my arms.

I laid her down in the middle of my nest, then sat back on my knees. She looked perfect here. I wanted her to stay, become part of my nest forever. I wanted to fall asleep and wake up beside her.

I felt Max's hand roam down my spine. Beside *them*.

Rio and Llew had gone to prep for the heat, taking the pets to OJ's sanctuary and grabbing food from the Omega supply place. It was just me, my Beta, and my Omega, and I was going to taste them both.

"In the nest, Max," I rumbled, like I was a damn Alpha. He grinned and crawled into the nest, naked like this was some full-moon ritual. Maybe it was. It was an act as old as civilization itself. He leaned over my Omega and kissed her, and I caught my breath at how fucking hot they looked.

I wanted to be in the middle of them. "Can you satisfy two Omegas all by yourself, Maxie?" I purred, and his eyes sparkled with the challenge.

"I'm going to try," he said cockily.

I knew what I wanted, but I wondered if he'd submit to it. "What if I told you what I wanted you to do?" I asked, raising an eyebrow. Rolling onto his back, he pillowed his head on his crossed arms, making all the beautiful skin stretch, and his muscles flex. *So beautiful.*

"Are you trying to top me, Omega?"

The long lines of his body were too much for Polly, who was running her tongue down between his pecs and the lines of his abs.

"Not today, Beta, but one day," I groaned, my cock weeping at the sight they made. "Today, I'm a needy Omega, and I need you to *fuck me already.*" The last words were a needy whine, quickly echoed by Polly.

Max half laughed, half moaned. "I look forward to it."

Yeah, I knew he was perfect for me. It wasn't lost on me that we hadn't had sex outside a heat yet, but one day, we'd have sex where neither of us was driven by insane biological need, and instead just ordinary lust.

Rolling Polly onto her back in the pillows, Max gave me a filthy look. "You ever heard of a Lucky Pierre, Omega?" He gripped my hips and pulled me closer, kissing my skin as he peeled off my clothes.

"Can't say I have," I murmured, kissing him in between items of clothing being removed.

"Well, I guess you're going to experience it first-hand." I was finally stripped bare, and he sucked in a breath. "So fucking hot. You should come with a warning label," he growled, pulling me in for another kiss. "Now, fuck your Omega, and when you're locked tight in her pretty body, I'm going to fuck you. How do you feel about that?"

My only answer was a grunt as I dived on top of the naked body of Polly. Her cheeks were flushed; actually, maybe her whole body was flushed. She cradled me between her soft thighs, running her hands all over my exposed flesh. She smelled amazing, and I wanted to taste her, but not as badly as I wanted to be inside her.

"August," she whined, and that was all the encouragement I needed. I slid into her tight little cunt like I was made to live there. There was nowhere else I wanted to be. Clutching her thighs, I pulled them wide so I could fuck her harder. Deeper. More.

The madness of the heat ebbed a small amount, so I could appreciate the love in her expression. The way she chased my touch as much as I chased hers. The way her tits bounced.

My heat ebbed, not broke. I couldn't ignore bouncing tits, even if I wanted to.

When Max knelt behind me, his hands running up over my back and down to squeeze the cheeks of my ass, I realized why Pierre was so lucky.

I pressed my body to Polly's and kissed her, buried so deep in her body that one strong sneeze might turn us into a single person. But when Max slid his way inside me, I realized I'd found the place I wanted to be for the rest of my life. Between these two people that I loved? This was my home.

Max's long arms draped over me, pressing me flat into Polly, and he gripped her hips, fucking us both. *Oh god.* The sensations washing over me were beyond mind-blowing. Fucking. Being fucked. It was something else.

No. I was loving and being loved. That was the difference.

"I swear on my life, this is the greatest moment ever," he breathed above me. "I love you both so damn much."

I wanted to answer, but he shifted positions and hit all the happy places inside me, causing me to come and lock all three of us together as I released burst after burst inside Polly. Her fib locked around me, holding my seed inside her, and for a brief moment, I imagined her round with my child, riding me like an Omega goddess.

Max's teeth pressed against the hard muscles of my shoulder, but didn't break the skin, and I whined. I wanted him to bond me. Wanted it more than *anything*. I wasn't above begging. "Please, Max," I panted, and he gripped Polly's hips tightly, wedging us together as we rolled to the side. I didn't want to crush the small Omega.

"Soon, August. Soon, you'll be ours forever. But we should all be here when we consolidate our Pack. Then I promise to bite you over and over, until all you can feel is me."

That wasn't really how it worked, but I smiled softly as I drifted off into the preheat sleep.

I came to with my skin on fire and a cock in my mouth. Rio was feeding me his dick, and when I slipped off, he sighed with relief. "Holy shit, you're back. Thank god. For such a gentle man, your Omega is a beast," he teased, tucking his cock back in his boxer shorts.

I looked around and saw Llew with an extremely messy Polly draped across his chest, sound asleep. "How long was I out for?"

Rio pulled me up so he was spooned around me. "You were in full-blown heat by the time Llew and I returned. Max said it hit you like a freight train. One minute, you were asleep, the next, you and Polly were going at it like feral monkeys. He thinks your heats fed off each other, and you also went into some kind of rut. It was why you were so frenzied."

I looked over at Max, who was passed out and almost gaunt. Rio stroked my back. "It's all good, my Omega.

Don't stress. Everything is okay." He paused. "It's been two days."

Two days! I'd been a sex-mad Omega monster for two days?

On the tail of that thought were images—memories, probably—of me stretched into positions with all of them. Pressed between Max and Rio. Being pounded by Llew. Slow, dirty fucking with Polly. But only flashes, like I'd swum up from the insanity.

"Oh," I choked out. "I'm sorry."

"Me too. Not that it happened, but that you don't really remember it, because I'm putting the last two days in my spank bank forever. The full forty-eight-hour, unedited Director's Cut."

I laughed and snuggled into his chest, subtly searching him for bite marks, but there weren't any.

Nothing got past Rio, though. "There are no bonding marks, but not from lack of trying on your Omega's behalf. He's as persistent as he is horny." He laughed and brushed my lips with his, a reminder he was joking. "But we wanted you to be clear-headed when you bonded into our Pack. When we make you ours, and you make us yours. If that's still what you want."

I pushed up and kissed him, the heat still riding me, but I was beginning to feel the ache of my muscles. "I want to. I want to right now."

I felt him shift, and Max's body jiggled as Rio kicked him gently. "Max, wake up. It's time."

Max bolted upright. "No, I'm fine. I can definitely go

again," he said with slurred words that directly contradicted him. He needed electrolytes, and apparently, Rio agreed.

"Grab an electrolyte drink, Beta, then it's time to bite your Omega and tie him to us forever."

Finally.

EPILOGUE
POLLY

I rubbed my bond marks absently. The action was a source of reassurance, and I'd swear the guys could feel it when I did. A pulse almost always came down the bond. It was nice, a comfort that I'd never thought I would get.

Llew had tried to re-bond with the guys during August's heat, and while the connection wasn't as strong as it had once been—or even as strong as mine was with any of them—there was a fine thread of bond there that I hoped would grow and strengthen over the years. It was a start, anyway.

Nim sat to my left. "It really doesn't matter what the report says. Family are the people you commit yourself to, and Henry and I are your family, regardless of what a silly DNA test says."

We'd all gotten DNA tests to help narrow down who belonged to whom at the Homestead. It really only mattered for the younger kids, because most of the teens had applied for parental emancipation, and given the court case, it had been granted. They all lived together in a house with Jewel now, who was slowly helping them reintegrate into society.

Only one mother had come forward to claim her babies without having to rely on DNA tests, though due diligence had to be done. Sister Eloise was young, barely more than thirty, but she'd been only seventeen when she'd run away and joined the cult with her boyfriend, Brother Frederick. He'd been ten years older than her, a Beta to her Unshown, and life hadn't been easy for her.

Although she'd lived in a different house, she'd always been kind to me, despite the fact I was an Omega. She'd looked so sad for the last few years, and now I knew why. She'd wanted her babies. The two youngest children were hers, and I was happy they were going into a home with their mom and not into the system.

Sucking in a deep breath, I pulled the papers out of the envelope. But still, I couldn't look. Henry took them gently from my hands. "Do you want me to get your Alphas?"

I shook my head. I needed to do this alone. Well, not alone, but with people who understood what this moment would be like. The guys had given me the space I'd asked for, but I knew they were probably hovering somewhere close by, in case I needed them.

My Pack. My safety net.

Handing the papers to Henry, I sighed. "You read it."

He hesitated too, and Nim made an annoyed squeak. "Honestly, you two *have* to be related with the amount of angst-ridden dithering. Let me do it." She flipped the pages over, her eyes skimming the words and graphs that made no sense to me. "Congrats, guys. You're twins."

I blinked at Henry, who blinked back at me. *Twins?* I looked at the boy across from me with wide eyes, like I was seeing him for the first time. We didn't look identical; we had different hair colors, different noses. But maybe there was something in the shape of our brow, in our lips.

I had a twin.

"That's, wow... Thank god I didn't have a crush on you, like Nim did. That would have made this really weird."

Nim gasped, slapping my arm, her cheeks flushed. "Traitor. For that, I should make you both read the rest." But she kept the papers and continued reading silently. She frowned, and my heart stuttered in my chest. Her face was solemn when she looked up again. "Your mother is Sister Roberta. Your father is Leader Victor."

I blinked. I didn't know how I was supposed to feel.

Throwing the papers on the table, Nim gripped my hand, and Henry's too. "You are wonderful people—the best people I know. Your parents mean less than nothing. Neither do mine. We are who we are *despite* the hell they put us through, do you both hear me?"

I nodded, swallowing hard. We'd been instrumental

in putting both of our parents in prison. That was a lot to come to terms with. Just because they were biologically related to us, didn't make them any less awful. Sister Roberta must have known she was my mother as she'd branded me and sold me to some Alpha she'd never met.

She wasn't worth the guilt I felt right now. I'd gained a brother, a twin, and that was far more important.

I hugged Nim close. "I hear you."

Today was sentencing for the Ozark Homestead cult leaders, and I'd purposefully decided to check the DNA today rather than earlier. I didn't want to know the outcome of the sentencing either. As long as they weren't a threat to me or any of the people who'd once lived behind their walls, I hoped they all rotted in their misery, whether that be in a jail cell or in a society that was disgusted with them.

Instead of focusing on the negative, my Pack had decided today was the day for a bonding party. Normally, we would've had a ceremony, but that seemed a little redundant, given we'd quite thoroughly bonded already. A party was better.

"Polly?" August called from the living room. "Is everything okay?"

My Omega. I smiled softly and stood.

Nim gagged. "I swear, if you could see your face right now... It's so damn sweet, I'm going to get a stomach ache."

Henry cackled, and I flipped them both the bird. I

loved giving things the finger. It was so satisfying. I could convey so much meaning with that one little gesture.

I skipped out to meet my lover, my bondmate, my Omega. I ran into his arms, because the way he picked me up and spun me made my heart race every single time.

Rufio was in timeout in the mudroom after screaming out, "Feathery Fuck Face," so loud, the neighbors had probably heard it. "GIVE ME MY FUCKING CHEERIOS! RUFIOOOO... WHERE'S MY MONEY? HERE BIRDY BIRDY." He was on a tirade, so everyone in a one-mile radius knew he was mad about being stuck inside while there was a party going on.

August shook his head at the bird, then gave me a soft smile. "My family's here. Are you ready to meet them?"

I nodded, even though I was nervous as hell. It was reassuring that my Alphas were just as nervous, like this feeling was... normal.

I was normal.

The squeeze of August's hand in mine chased away the last of the nerves, and I drew strength from him. August's family were in the backyard, along with OJ and her Pack. Max's parents too, who were just as sweet and wholesome as he was. They'd accepted me so easily that I'd cornered Max to ask him if they even knew my history, and didn't want some normal Omega for him. Someone like August.

He'd kissed me and told me of course they knew. Everyone knew. It was still a hot topic, even after all these months, but my history wasn't who I was, and they knew that. Rio's foster parents were both deceased, but Max's parents loved him as much as they did Max.

August's family were turned away from me, and I took a quick moment to appraise them before they appraised me too. His dad and two older sisters were all tall, definitely Alphas from their scents. But his mom and youngest sister were both Unshown, which was a surprise. He'd never said anything, and I'd never thought to ask. Actually, I'd never asked about any of their families' designations, because it didn't matter to me.

August smiled at them with so much love pouring down our bond, I was shored up by his belief that they'd adore me. He led me over, and his dad turned first. "There's my boy."

August grinned at the man, who was an exact replica of August in thirty years' time. "Polly, this is my dad Paul, my mom Delilah, and my sisters Shell, Autumn, and Lisa. Family, this is my Omega, Polly."

His dad was a big, brawny guy with a kind face and lines around his eyes. His mom was shorter, with a full colorful skirt, and wild, dark curls like August's.

But it was the youngest, Lisa, who stepped forward and hugged me. "There's a sentence I never thought my brother would say. Welcome to the family, Polly. Though you could probably do better than this bonehead. Do you know I once caught him drinking toilet water?"

August gasped. "I was *two!*" He looked at me with wide eyes. "Jesus, Lisa, could you at least wait five minutes before you pull out the embarrassing stories?" They bickered like siblings, and I found myself grinning so wide that my cheeks hurt.

Later, as Max's dad operated the grill, and August dragged his folks around, introducing them to everyone, I watched the backyard filled with people who just loved. Without guilt. Without rules. With kindness and empathy.

The doorbell rang again, and by the process of elimination, I knew it had to be Llew's mom. He came over and gripped my hand, pulling me along gently to the front door, and Doodles scrambled toward it first. Somehow, even with three legs and zero coordination, he managed to beat us there.

Llew kissed my temple. "Be prepared. I think she's been cooking for a month for this occasion." I didn't even have time to be nervous, because he was throwing the door open to a huge stack of Tupperware containers.

"Llew, is that you? Take some of this Tupperware, son, before it all ends on the floor for the ants."

Dutifully, Llew took the containers and revealed a tiny woman. Honestly, it was difficult to imagine someone as big as Llew could have come out of someone as tiny as his mom.

"Oh gosh, look at you. You're a beautiful little thing." Before I could blink, she had her arms around me in a hug, her cheek to mine. "Thank you for saving my boy." She held me tightly, a wealth of feeling in her shaky breath and the slow drip of tears onto my collarbone.

I stood frozen, but eventually, I lifted my arms and wrapped them around her, rubbing her back in slow circles, in what I hoped was a soothing manner. "He saved me too," I whispered back.

Pulling back, she sniffed a little, wiping her forearm across her damp cheeks. "That's good. That's how it's supposed to be." She cleared her throat, smiling at me brightly. "Now come, I've made you some tiddly oggies, and if you don't try one now, they'll be gone as soon as those boys smell them." She held my hand, squeezing it reassuringly as I followed along behind her like a little puddle duck.

This must be what family really felt like. What happiness was. Because I couldn't imagine any moment that could be better than this one.

About the Author

Grace McGinty is eclectic. She has worked as a chocolatier, a librarian, a forensic accountant, and finally, a writer. Like her professional career, the genres she writes are chaotic and out of control. From contemporary new adult to smutty reverse harem novels of every sub-genre, if you like it, she's probably written it.

Except dark romance. She's a marshmallow, and somehow the mean guys always end up cinnamon rolls.

Grace lives in rural Australia with her crazy family, an entire menagerie of pets, and will one day be crushed by the giant piles of books that litter every room.

Head over to www.gracemcginty.com and join the mailing list for sneak previews into what she is working on and to stay up-to-date with new releases and giveaways!

Looking for more Grace? Check out the first chapter of MAKE MY HEART RACE over the page!

MAKE MY HEART RACE
PROLOGUE - TALLY

There were only three things in life that gave me the same risk-to-reward thrill as motor racing.

Discounted end-of-day sushi.

Petting an orange cat.

Sleeping with another driver on the grid.

So far, only one of those things had blown up in my face, as evidenced by the sports commentators talking way too loudly outside my garage.

"After crashing out in last week's race, Ryclo Racing must be wondering if Tally Palmer's head is in the game at all. I'm not sure she has the stamina to make it out here, racing with the big boys. She's the third driver for the team, but I don't think her position over there is quite as solid as she'd like, and there's still some who say she stole the position from a more deserving driver."

The other commentator made a disgusted noise. "More like she stole the heart of the right man, wouldn't you say, Dan? The Romeo and Juliet of NASCAR—that's what they call Tally Palmer and Buck Willtot of Willtot Racing. Of course, Buck's father, Brick, is the owner of Willtot Racing, and it can't hurt having someone as powerful as Brick in your corner when you're trying to find a team, even if it is with your most fierce competitor."

I knew that voice. Rupert Ballantyne was commentating royalty, but he was also an epic dick weasel. Not just your average douchebag either; he believed he was God's gift to motor racing, even though he'd never been behind the wheel of any vehicle professionally.

I snorted as I secured myself into my suit. You'd think they'd have the decency to loudly question my talent and integrity somewhere other than in front of the very garage where I was getting ready to race.

Besides, they were so fucking wrong. Brick hadn't helped me get onto Ryclo at all, not even a little. In fact, he was one of the loudest naysayers about women in NASCAR.

No, my hard work had gotten me here, from racing three-quarter midget cars in the rain when I was six and could barely reach the gas pedal, to fighting my way onto podiums and proving my worth every weekend for as long as I could remember.

It had also been my dad's hard work, driving cabs on nights and weekends to pay for the thousand things that needed to be bought as I progressed through my career, while legacy kids like Buck Willtot got it all handed to them, as if it was their birthright.

Not that I begrudged Buck his place on the track. He was so talented—and fucking hot, I might add—that it was hard to begrudge him anything, including my body.

Rolling my shoulders back, I pushed down the swelling emotions in my chest. Thoughts of my father made my heart squeeze painfully. He was the reason I was here, driving in the Cup series for the first time, but he wasn't here. He would never see this moment. It had been five years since he died, and the best way I could make him proud was by going out there and driving like the skilled driver I knew I was.

I repeated the words my therapist had told me for years in my head. *My dreams are worthy. I'm making my family proud.*

"Tally, let's go!" one of the mechanics yelled.

I sucked in a deep breath, told myself I was a badass bitch once more, and walked through the garage. Some of the guys slapped me on the back, while Hayes handed me my helmet and the rest of the gear I'd need.

"You got this. Leave everything out on that track and prove to everyone you deserve to be here." Hayes wasn't chief mechanic, or anything like that. He was almost as far down the totem pole as I was, but he'd been one of the few who'd gotten friendly enough to give a shit if I won or lost.

I gave him a tight smile, pushing my sunglasses up the bridge of my nose. "Thanks, Hayes."

They'd already moved the car out onto the track, and I sucked in a deep, fortifying breath. This was it. Either I won this one from the back of the field and got into the playoffs, or I went home.

I smiled and waved at the crowd, though it was more jeers than cheers. Ignoring the negativity, I thought about the fact that out there in that crowd was probably another little Tally Palmer who wanted to drive stock cars, or ride bikes or bulls, or fly fighter jets. I could be someone they looked up to, and I would race for them today.

The team went over all the last-minute details, but my head was already in the race. I was playing scenarios over and over in my mind, and even if they never happened, I had a backup for that backup. I was ready.

We stood for the anthem, and as I watched the fighter jets fly over, I tried to talk myself out of puking. I was shaking so hard that I'd curled my fingers up into my fists and held them tight to my thighs. I couldn't let anyone see I was rattled, because the other drivers on this track were like sharks; they'd smell my fear, the blood in the water, and it would be all over for me.

Pulling on the head sock that went under my helmet, I looked down the row of cars and drivers, searching for one pair of sparkling blue eyes.

Buck met my gaze and winked at me, and my heart fluttered in my chest. The press called us the Romeo and Juliet of NASCAR, but it wasn't that serious yet. Maybe one day it could be, though. Buck was everything an All-American NASCAR driver should be—handsome enough to tempt a nun, with that Southern, good ol' boy charm and a smile that could drop panties. And he fucked like he drove; like getting you to the line first was the only thing that mattered on God's green earth.

I blew him a kiss, even knowing the cameras would pick it up and probably play it on the late-night recaps of the race. He grabbed it, mimed slapping it onto his cheek, then shoved on his own helmet.

Chuckling softly, I got my head in the game. I could put kisses on those high cheekbones myself later. Dragging myself up and through the window of my car in a maneuver I'd done hundreds of times before, I put on my helmet. The team continued to give me instructions while strapping me in, and I just nodded along. I knew my job. I trusted that they knew theirs too.

"Drivers! Start. Your. Engines."

Giving my team one last smile, I pulled down the visor on my helmet and started the car. The feel of the engine vibrating below me mellowed out the nerves that were threatening to make me throw up what little food I'd had earlier.

I'd made it here. That was something my dad would have been proud of.

The fact that Rupert Ballantyne and Dan Baker thought I'd slept my way onto a team was beside the point. I hadn't. I'd done the time on the tracks. I'd clocked up more hours iRacing at home than was probably healthy. I'd sweated my way into this spot, and I was going to enjoy being here.

We rolled out onto the track, and all too soon, came the words over the radio. "*RACE. RACE. RACE.*"

Time to go to work.

It was a fucking mess. A win here could send any of us into the playoffs,and we were all driving like we knew it. I'd barely missed a huge wipeout earlier, when #34 went into the wall and got himself all the way around. I was twelfth back in the pack, all but landlocked in place, but there were still ninety-six laps to go. Anyone could get it.

Both of my teammates were ahead of me, running fifth and sixth, according to the team radio. My job was to be the little yappy dog snapping at the heels of the people who wanted to take them out.

No one wanted me to win. I couldn't win, not really. But I'd be fucked if I wasn't going to try.

The thing I loved most about the sport was the unpredictability of it, and when another huge smash had smoke flying into my windshield, electricity raced through my veins. I dodged the cars ping-ponging around the track, just in time to see a car bounce off the outside wall, flipping end over end as it rolled into the infield. Just a flash of color, but it made my heart pound.

"Whose car was that?" I demanded over the radio.

"Just checking," came the voice of Tyler, a gruff older man in his fifties. "It was Willtot."

My heart thundered. It was bad. I knew it was bad.

We saw crashes every single fucking race, but some just made your blood freeze. "Is it rough?"

"Yellow flag, Tally. I'll let you know when I know."

As the cars slowed, I couldn't help but look over. The car was on fire, but that was okay. We wore fire suits for a reason. He could still be okay.

"Get out. Get out. Get out." I chanted the words under my breath as the safety cars raced in, fire extinguishers already out as they landed on their feet to extinguish the blaze.

"Red flag."

Almost out of muscle memory, I stopped my car, angling it infield. "Ty. Is he out?"

"Not yet." Something in Ty's voice had me on edge.

Why the fuck wasn't he out yet? "Come on, Buck. Come on."

I kept half an eye on the track, enough to see the paramedics fly to the infield. I could hear my blood whooshing in my ears.

No, no, no. "Ty, tell me what's going on!"

"They're choppering him out. It seems serious."

Fuck.

"Hold your position and then come in."

I watched helplessly as two medics loaded Buck onto a stretcher and tore out of the infield, even as the track maintenance team cleaned up the debris from the crash. The amount of cars remaining in the race had nearly halved, with eleven cars knocked out by that crash. I couldn't care less. Not when I knew deep down that something was really wrong with Buck.

"Yellow flag. Maintain position, Tally."

Distracted, I didn't even remember replying to Ty's directions. Instead, I lost myself in the pattern of the drive.

The second I climbed out of the car at the end of the race, I ripped my helmet off my head. "Is there any news?"

No one would meet my eyes. Every single person in the pit had something they needed to do right then, and dread washed over me.

"Someone fucking *tell* me!"

Hayes gave me a look filled with sympathy, and I was already shaking my head when Ty appeared beside me. "He didn't make it out of the infield, Tally. They worked on him all the way to the hospital, but he was pronounced dead on arrival."

I shook my head furiously. Ty was wrong. He was *wrong.* "No."

"I'm sorry, sweetheart. It was a freak accident. They think a piece of debris came through the window at a high enough speed and hit between his Hutchins and his helmet, getting the jugular. He lost a lot of blood before they could get the fire under control." He swallowed hard. "I'm so sorry."

My knees gave way, shock sending me to the ground. My head battled with my heart, like that traitorous bitch wanted to scream *I told you so* to the aggressively beating organ in my chest. This sport had fatalities. We knew every time we drove out onto the track that we might not come back.

I'd known that Buck was a driver—a wild and aggressive one at that—before I started dating him. I should have been at least a little bit prepared for this.

But my heart screamed and screamed at the loss of what could have been, even if I did just sob silently with my head hanging, defeated. Arms picked me up, shuffling me out of view of the crowd and the garage crew.

I looked up at Hayes, and something about the concern on his face made me pull myself together. I cloaked myself in numbness. Shook away the pain in my chest, and replaced it with a black abyss of nothingness.

Wiggling out of his arms, I stood on my feet. "I'm okay," I said weakly.

Hayes shook his head. "No, you're not."

I swallowed hard as the tears threatened to well in my eyes once more. He was right; I wasn't. "I'm okay enough to get out of here."

Sam Ryker appeared in the doorway of the garage we were standing in. His face was a mask of neutrality, though I could see regret in his eyes. "Tally, can we talk?"

I knew, deep down in my bones, I wasn't going to like what he had to say.